A Heart Unclaimed

Nancy Richmond

Contents

Prologue

Ayezah's POV:

I never took anything seriously, not even life. I treated my life like a non-stop party.

Love was just a meaningless & stupid word to me until I unexpectedly crossed paths withHim, five years ago at my cousin Addin Shah's birthday party.

Rahil Ahmed Khan, Addin's best friend.

Calling him handsome would be an understatement. He is just beyond gorgeous. The moment my eyes met with his pretty brown orbs, I felt ticklish.

He was exactly my type - a perfect blend of sweetness and hotness. His presence was like eye candy, and I was instantly drawn to him the moment my eyes fell on him.

I'm a very straightforward person & I love to talk what's on my mind, so I couldn't help but blurt out : ' Are you single? Would you like to date me?' The way he choked on his drink and the way nervousness displayed on his face, only made me want him more.

He looked so adorable.

I'm a straight-up flirt, and he was undeniably shy. I asked him to dance, and although he was hesitant, I wasn't about to let him off the hook. With a mischievous smirk, I took matters into my own hands and playfully dragged him onto the dance floor.

His hesitation and nervousness were written all over his face. Beads of sweat formed on his forehead as he barely touched me, his finger lightly brushing against my waist. A clear sign of his inexperience and unfamiliarity with being this close to a girl.

I let out a sigh internally and decided to take the charge. I grabbed his hand, pulling him closer and boldly placing it on my waist. The shock in his gorgeous brown eyes was evident as they widened in surprise. I smirk enjoying his state.

Oh god why is he so cute?

But my smirk vanished when I felt something indescribable. I couldn't quite put my finger on it, but as he stared into my eyes and I gazed back at him, it felt like an electric current was passing between us. The way his arm wrapped around my waist and our fingers interlaced sent my heartbeat into a frenzy state for reasons I couldn't explain. It was a strange feeling, unlike anything I had ever felt before.

It's not like I haven't danced with anyone before. I have. I Even dated many but none of them were serious. It was just teasing and for fun. I only dated when I knew that the other person also knows the rule : no strings attach.

But right now being in Rahil's arms, makes me feel something. I just met him today but I feel like we are connected.

What bullshit are you even thinking ayezah?

I groaned internally, shrugging all unnecessary & idiotic thoughts crossing my brain.

After that party, I was determined to date Rahil because I was really attracted to him. Also my dad had some business in London so I was here for few months.

I was the Ayezah shah. Gorgeous & hot was my middle names. Boys drool over me & I can get anyone on their knees for me. I fucking knew it because I had boys chasing after me.

But here I was, chasing after Rahil Ahmed khan. As much as I was determined to date him, he was beyond determined not to date anyone.

He then offered to be friends with him. Like fucking friends?

I liked him way too much that I couldn't refuse him. I was desperate to spend time with him. Like I don't fucking know what's gotten into me. The last time I checked, guys were desperate to spend time with me.

ugh whatever.

And I later realised that I ended up doing a great mistake by accepting to be friends with him.

I let myself feel for him when I fucking knew that he don't feel anything for me nor wants to date me.

The way he treated me with such kindness and care, it was very hard not to be drawn to him. He was the most purest and sweetest soul I have ever came across.

We used to hangout like normal friends, and just a mere brush of his finger on my skin though even when he didn't intend to touch me, like it's just happened bymistake, would still sent electric jolts all over my body. The way his pretty brown orbs would gaze into mine & he would offer me his cutest smile, displaying his dimples.

I knew i fucked up big time.

I wasn't a fool, I knew I was falling in love.

As the days passed, with our growing friendship, my feelings intensified. I couldn't hold back anymore. And I confessed to him.

somewhere I was prepared for the heartbreak because I knew I was walking on broken-glass filled path and it would hurt.

But I didn't knew that it would hurt like a bitch. He politely rejected me. He wasn't harsh at all. He tried his best not to make me feel bad, he was very careful and gentle and that pained more, realising that I can never get him. He also told me that he liked someone which ached my heart in worst way possible.

Lucky girl she is, afterall the most incredible person likes her.

I knew I can't blame him in all this because it was always me. He was never interested in me.

I was not a fucking weak woman, I knew how to fix myself! So I returned to Australia and tried distracting myself with anything. I eventually joined my dad's company and engrossed myself totally into work.

Destiny can be such a bitch sometimes. After four long years, it brings me face to face with him again. My dad opened few branches in London and wanted me to handle it and shift to London permanently.

To make it worst guess who is my business partner? None other than Rahil Ahmed khan himself.

I couldn't say no to my dad, so I had to work with Rahil again. And being around him, the feelings which I buried resurfaced, pulling me to him again, infact even more. I couldn't help but notice how more gorgeous and handsome he has gotten.

It's like I was swept away by my emotions once again, as if my feelings for him never left in the first place.

I loved him & I still love him fiercely.

Destiny has always being a bitch to me, it plays games with me every single fucking time, and this time too was no different.

I am married to Rahil Ahmed Khan. Yess married to the man I love so deeply, but who doesn't feel the same for me.

It was actually my cousin, Addin Shah, and his wife who suggested that we get married.

I don't know why would he suddenly agree to marry me.

Did he fell for me as well? did he start having feelings for me? What about the person whom he liked?

I couldn't help but wonder.

Later I came to know that, the person he liked wasn't alive anymore.

I did ask him about why was he marrying me & he told me that because he just wanted to.

And me being a desperate bitch, I agreed marrying him in an instant.

Had I known his actual reason before, i would have never married him.

I'm fucking idoit! I'm fucking fool! Knowing very well how he rejected me twice. I still crushed my self respect under my heel and I married him only to make a fool of myself.

When i unintentionally eavesdropped his conversation with his bestfriend on our marriage night, my already wounded heart broke into millions of pieces.

One thing was now very clear to me that Rahil Ahmed khan would never love me.

Chapter 1

Ayezah's POV:

I discarded my white, long, warm, fluffy overcoat, revealing my all-black attire.

I was dressed in sleek black tight leggings that hugged my legs perfectly, paired with a black full-sleeved, tight, warm turtle neck top. My hair neatly tied into a high ponytail.

I placed my coat to the side and stood at the edge of the ice skating rink, taking in the sight before me. It was my own private ice skating rink.

A place where i glide whenever things get too much for me to handle.

I clutched onto my snowflake pendant with my palm, which delicately hung on my turtle neck top.

The pendant was very dear to me.

My mother made me wear it when i was young, saying that I should never take it off. Unfortunately my mom wasn't alive.

It was plain shiny chain with a medium sized delicate snowflake hanging through it. The snowflake was very beautiful with its bluish intricate details which made it look like almost real snowflake.

I curled my bottom lip between my teeth, Holding the pendant tightly, I took deep breaths.

"Addin, I could never hurt her. I married her because I didn't want to hurt her more. I have hurt her enough by rejecting her twice. And who could better know how badly it hurts to be in one-sided love than me?"

I gracefully glide across the ice rink, Rahil's words from earlier when he was talking with his bestfriend, who is also my cousin, on the call, echoing in my mind. The weight of his words hit me like a ton of bricks.

I couldn't believe what i unintentionally heard from his conversation with Addin.

The pain in my heart was unbearable and without any single thoughts I left his house.

Now, here I am, all alone at the ice rink on the very first night of our marriage.

He married me just because he didn't wanted to hurt me? Does that mean he married me out of pity? to spare me from the heartbreak of further rejection? Because he understood the pain of unrequited love?

I hoped and thought that the time we spend 4 years back as friends, also the time we spend as business partners recently because of the collaboration of our companies, had made him develop feelings for me. I thought he too had started to feel something for me.

But it turns out that it was never the case. It has always been only me.

He never fell for me nor he will ever fall for me. This was crystal clear to me now.

He only married me because he felt guilty about rejecting me twice. He's just too good-hearted to intentionally hurt me any further.

I didn't know what to do? What was i going to do Now? Should i just pretend I didn't hear anything but how?? How could i live with him knowing this? Knowing he just pities me. I couldn't do that.

With each sleek glide, the pain in my heart intensifies. I push myself to glide faster, raising my back foot smoothly.

The emotions overwhelmed me. A tear rolled off from the corner of my eyes. I felt myself loosing balance and almost falling.

You are not gonna cry Ayezah! You are strong. Stronger than you think.

No tears Ayezah! Hold yourself together.

Get a grip of yourself.

My mom's word ranged in my head and i immediately balanced myself and wiped off the tears which slowly started cascading down my cheeks with the backside of my palm.

I was standing straight when i suddenly felt a sharp pain in my chest. I lightly tapped my chest and then sat down on my legs, well, not completely, because I had my skates on.

I took deep breaths, calming myself down, gulping and rubbing my face with my palms.

I arrived at Rahil's mansion, and it was almost past midnight now.

As Rahil had previously told me the password to his door, I unlocked it and entered his absolutely stunning cozy mansion with two floors, which was made mostly of glass.

My coat was hanging on my hand as I made my way to the living room. There, I saw Rahil sleeping on the couch. I reached into the pocket of my coat and took out my phone, noticing numerous missed calls and texts from him.

Did I make him worry by disappearing just like that?

Clutching onto my snowflake pendant, I bit my lower lip.

Slowly, I made my way towards Rahil and kneeled in front of him. He was sleeping with a frown on his face, as if he had been exhausted but resisted sleep. However, he had eventually fallen asleep.

I couldn't help but gaze at his gorgeous face. His long, beautiful curly lashes rested on his cheekbones, complementing with his perfect eyebrows. His full, dark pink lips made me gulp, and my heart raced. I lost track of time as I just gazed at him with my heart thumping loudly.

It was hard to look away, and suddenly, he opened his eyes, catching me off guard.

" Ayezah!! where the heck were you?? I called you so many times and even texted you! Do you realize what time it is? What were you thinking before vanishing just like that? Do you have any idea how worried I was? I couldn't even reach your dad because it's freaking midnight! " He yelled slightly, jumping up from his seat.

" I had no clue where you were, and I couldn't just wander the streets like a maniac. Well, actually, I was about to do just that, but I thought you were a responsible woman who would come back soon or atleast call me or text me back, so I waited. But how could you be so irresponsible? " I slowly stood up too.

"Answer me! Where were you?" he demanded. I found myself staring into his warm brown eyes, feeling a huge lump forming in my throat.

I gulped, feeling my vision blurring and things infront of me rotating slightly. I shut my eyes, and opened it again to clear my vision.

"I'm exhausted. I'm just gonna go get some sleep," I managed to say, gesturing towards the room behind with my hand.

"But-" he began, but I quickly interrupted him.

"please."

He let out a heavy sigh, nodding his head, and ran his hand through his already tousled hair, making it even messier.

I turned around and hurriedly walked towards the room upstairs without looking back.

As soon as I reached the room, I unzipped my suitcase and pulled out my pastel blue pajamas. The full-sleeved shirt matched perfectly with the pants, adorned with delicate white mini flower prints.

I sensed his presence entering the room. I licked my dry lips and made my way towards the washroom, but suddenly, everything around me blurred again, and my head spun as if the world was spinning too.

I almost lost my balance, falling backwards, when a strong arm swiftly got wrapped around my waist, preventing me from hitting the ground. His other hand held my shoulder blade, keeping me in place.

"Ayezah!" He called out, his voice filled with concern. My vision cleared slightly, and I found myself locking eyes with his warm brown gaze, brimming with worry.

I straightened up immediately, my hand pressed against my forehead. He was still holding my waist firmly.

"I'm okay," I muttered.

"No, you're not! Come here." He gently held my shoulders and guided me towards the bed.

He made me sit on the bed and hurried over to the bedside table. He poured a glass of water from the jug and rushed back to me, kneeling down.

He held the backside of my head, Bringing the glass close to my lips, he carefully made me drink the water with his hand. I sipped the water, gazing at him.

"Are you okay?" he asked, his eyes filled with concern as he looked at me. I nodded, letting out a huff. "It's probably because I haven't eaten anything since morning."

"What? WHY?" he suddenly exclaimed loudly, making me flinch slightly since he was sitting close to me.

"I'm sorry," he quickly apologized.

"I was so busy getting ready for Nikkah that I didn't have any time at all." I said.

"But still, Ayezah! You need to take care of yourself first! Skipping meals and that too all your meals is not acceptable at all, so next time you better don't repeat this." He spoke out sternly.

My heart thundered at his words and I found myself nodding absentmindedly.

His soft caring side is my weakness. Whenever he shows his caring side for me, I couldn't help but fall more for him.

" you really okay right? " He asked and i mumbled a small 'yes' nodding my head.

He smiled slightly, saying " Okay, Now you go and freshen up! I'll quickly cook for you."

"That's really not necessary-" I tried to say, but he didn't let me finish. "I'll freshen up in the front room! You quickly come downstairs, okay?"

With that, he immediately left. I watched his retreating figure moving outside.

I was sitting on the long stool near the kitchen slab, holding a hot coffee mug with both of my palms which was placed on the table.

Mindlessly caressing the warm mug, I couldn't help but gaze at the gorgeous man standing before me. He was wearing an apron, his t-shirt sleeves rolled up, revealing his attractive veiny hands. His wet hair was messy, falling on his forehead, indicating that he had just taken a shower.

After taking a relaxing bath and putting on my pajamas, I sat with my damp hair flowing freely.

He tossed the spaghetti noodles into the pan of water, spreading them out, and suddenly looked up at me.

Caught off guard, I immediately looked away, focusing on my coffee mug.

I heard him chuckle, and when I looked up, I saw him smiling widely, while shaking his head and looking down at the pan.

My cheeks turned red with embarrassment, realizing that he had caught me gawking at him without even realizing it.

To hide the embarrassment I suddenly took a sip of the hot coffee without thinking and let out a little hiss as it burned my tongue.

"Hey, be careful!" he exclaimed. "You should focus on one hot thing at a time!" He smirked at me playfully.

Oh!

Placing the mug on the table, I pressed my lips together.

"But you know, I'm Ayezah Shah! I have experience of handling a lot of hot things together." I smirked back at him, and he raised his eyebrows as if to say, 'Oh really?' Then he chuckled shaking his head, making me smile widely.

He served me the spaghetti and sat down beside me on the long stool. I muttered a quick 'thank you', Grabbing the fork and immediately started to gobble down the spaghetti.

I stuffed my mouth full and had to bend down a little because the spaghetti noodles were so long. My damp hair fell over my face, but I remained unbothered as I continued stuffing my mouth.

Suddenly, I felt his fingers brush against the side of my forehead, sending electric jolts through my body.

I stopped midway, the fork remained in the air. He gently tucked my hair back, looking at me with a soft gaze. I gazed back at him.

"I never thought Ayezah Shah could eat like this too," he chuckled. "I thought you always ate very slowly and neatly, like you usually eat in business meetings and such."

"Ah, well, I'm just really hungry right now. When I'm starving, I tend to eat like this, you know." I hesitantly replied, holding my one palm to my mouth, covering it.

"It's cute," he said with a smile.

"What's cute?" I asked, confused as i again turned towards the plate and stuffed my mouth full.

" You are cute." He said while smiling widely, and i snapped my head towards him immediately with a stuffed mouth.

My stupid heart thundered very loudly and i felt like it was beating in my ears.

What's wrong with him today? He never said such things to me ever! Not Even when we were friends 4 years back, not even when we were business partners since almost one month now.

We just gazed at each other for few seconds, before i forcefully looked away.

It was kinda hard to tear your gaze off his warm brown eyes.

"Umm, you aren't eating?" I asked chewing slowly and he shook his head.

"Well, I thought that only I could impress myself with my cooking skills, but you too cook damn good! Spaghetti is so yumm!" I exclaimed.

"Oh, gurl, you have no idea how great of a cook I am! You'll doubt your own skills if you try my cooking," he confidently replied.

"Huh! No chance," I retorted.

"Well then, let's do a cooking competition someday, appoint a judge, and see who comes out on top. What do you say?" he asked, extending his hand for a shake. I looked at him, then at his hand, and smirked. "Ayezah loves challenges," I said as I shook his hand.

" By the way, can I ask where you were earlier?" He asked, my smile faded a bit. I slowly freed my hand from his hand

"I just sort of went to my regular place to clear my mind," I replied, looking at spaghetti and tucking few hair strands behind my ear.

" Is something bothering you?" he asked and I immediately looked at him, concern evident in his warm eyes.

"Addin, I could never hurt her. I married her because I didn't want to hurt her more. I have hurt her enough by rejecting her twice. And who could better know how badly it hurts to be in one-sided love than me?"

I gazed into his eyes, his words from earlier echoing in my head.

"Umm, Rahil! I'm really, really drained, Can I just go to sleep?" I pleaded.

He looked at me for few seconds as if trying to read me. He then nodded slightly, sighing.

"By the way, can I stay in the front room of yours just for few days? Like, you know I'm not used to sharing one room with someone so it will take a little time for me." I said.

I need to clear the mess in my mind and it's not possible if I stay with him in the same room.

Chapter 2

- -

Ayezah's POV:

The sharp yet warm rays of the sun caressed my face, causing me to groan and hide my face into the cozy embrace of my blanket.

Just as I hoped to catch some more sleep, my alarm rang, making me groan some more.

With difficulty, I reluctantly pulled my one hand out from under the warm blanket and reached for my phone on the bedside table, as my phone alarm was ringing.

As I grabbed it, I came out from the comforting cocoon, sitting straight, i glanced at the flurry of missed calls and texts.

Just as I was about to look further into my phone, a familiar name flashed on the screen: Laila, my personal secretary and best friend.

Last night Rahil told me that he understands my need for space, and graciously allowed me to sleep in a different room. He said that I can take my time to get completely comfortable here.

His kindness and understanding always tug at my heart.

It pained to know how nice of a person he is.

The phone rang again, and with a grunt, I answered it.

As I placed the phone against my ear, I had to quickly move it away as my dear best friend-cum- personal secretary let out a piercing scream.

I cautiously returned the phone to my ear, " Could you please not speak so loudly in the early morning? " I lazily mumbled.

" Loud voice huh? I'm gonna turn you into minced meat! " she yelled.

" Where on earth did you go last night? Rahil called me, asking about you! I didn't had any clue but eventually I guessed it. Yet I couldn't say anything to Rahil. Tell me, did you go ice skating again? " she continued. I nonchalantly hummed in response

"Ayezah? is something wrong? What happened? Tell me every-thing. I know you wouldn't go ice skating for no reason. What happened? You were so damn happy just yesterday! Finally, you married the man you love so dearly! Everything was perfect! Then what happened suddenly? " she asked calmly through the phone. I stayed silent for a few seconds, clutching my delicate snowflake pendant and chewing on my bottom lip.

"Are you going to say something or you'll just keep fiddling with your pendant, more like suffocating your pendant and nibbling on your lower lip? Ye tumahari jhalli wali harkat kab chootay gi pata nahi! " she said, making me chuckle. I could actually imagine her palming her face and shaking her head.

" I wonder when you will stop with that silly habit of yours."

She knew me very well. Even though we've only been friends for three years.

" Have a little bit of manners, my dear! I happen to be your boss." I playfully remarked.

" Oh really? Meet up with me, and I'll show you who the real boss is." She said.

" Okay, my dear mother, you're the boss" I said, chuckling.

Laila has been my personal secretary since I started working at my dad's company three years ago. She's been the only one with me throughout this time.

Just in few months, I became really close and completely comfortable with her. While I had a few friends here and there in college and universities, no one ever compared to Laila. She was different. No one understood me like she did. She felt like home. A home where I feel safe.

Laila was actually a few months younger than me, and we are both from Pakistan. Although I was young when my family moved to Australia, I still knew Urdu very well.

It was surprising to Laila that I spoke Urdu fluently, because I was brought up completely in different surroundings, I was brought up in Australia. While she had lived in Pakistan her whole life before moving to Australia for work. She was impressed by my fluency in Urdu.

Now that I shifted to London for business, she didn't have any other option rather than moving to London with me. Not that I gave her any choice either.

"Ayezi? Are you there?" I heard her say on the call. "Umm, yes! By the way, you coming with the stylist in the evening to get me ready for the reception, right? I'll tell you everything at that time! Now I gotta go and do some important work!" I said.

"What important work? There are no meetings scheduled? Today is your day off!" she exclaimed.

"Did you get my lengha? Is the alteration done properly?" I immediately changed the topic.

"Yes, I got your lengha and it's perfect. Now, don't take me for a fool who wouldn't notice how you changed the topic! Please tell me what that important work is," she replied.

I sighed, knowing how she wouldn't let me hide anything from her. She knew everything, literally everything.

"Okay fine! I'm going to Addin's Company. You should come there too, and then we can ride back home together. I'll tell you everything," I replied.

"Okay, done!" she said before hanging up.

I immediately got up from the bed to get ready.

I quickly took a refreshing shower and then got dressed in my white t-shirt, which I tucked into a mini grey skirt. The skirt had a thin belt that added a touch of elegance.

To accessorize, I wore my lovely golden round small top earrings and golden wristwatch. Sprinkling some perfume around me, I let my waist length hair flow freely while curling my brown highlights at bottom. For makeup I did my regular ones. Mascara, a dust of blush on cheeks, skin colour eyeshades and nude lipstick.

Lastly, I completed my look with two things. First, I put on my medium-sized light brown coat, which was more like a blazer and Second, I slipped into knee-length black boots.

After getting ready, I let Rahil know that I had some important work to do and that I would meet him directly in the evening.

He insisted me not to leave empty stomach but I assured him that I would grab something to eat on the way and not skip my breakfast.

I made my way to my car and headed towards Addin's company.

I banged my palm on the desk, and Addin let out a grunt from his chair.

I was standing in front of his chair in his cabin since 15 minutes now. "What the fuck do you want to know?" he groaned.

"The truth!" I replied. "Tell me why Rahil agreed to marry me? " I completed.

"How many fucking times do I have to tell you?He married you because He just wanted to" he grumbled.

"Oh really? That's it? Just because he wanted to? Last time I checked he had no interest in me. Then what on earth magic happened that he suddenly wanted to marry me? tell me, how much did it take for you to convince Rahil to marry me?" I asked firmly, again banging my palm on his desk.

" Fuck! crazy woman c'mon! I've already told you so many fucking times that he genuinely wanted to marry you. I didn't force or convince him. What the fuck has gotten into you so early in the morning?" he groaned, holding his head.

"You better not lie to me, Addin! I overheard your conversation with Rahil on the call last night. I know everything," I said, pointing my finger at him while he shut his eyes in frustration, leaning back in his chair.

"I don't know what you actually heard, but let me make one thing clear: Rahil married you because he genuinely wanted to. That's it. And maybe he actually have started liking you? You fucking never know Ayezah! "

As soon as he finished speaking, my heart started racing like crazy! It was like a battle between my heart and mind had begun.

My heart desperately wanted to believe every word Addin said, but how could I just ignore the things I heard last night? It sounded like he married me out of pity, and my mind couldn't shake that thought.

I felt so torn, not knowing what was right or wrong. The battle between my heart and brain was giving me a terrible headache.

"The conversation between us stays between us only. You better not spill any of this shit to Rahil!" I warned, glaring hard at him.

" okay fine! " he groaned.

" Now, leave me fucking alone for fuck sake!" he grumbled, and I ran my fingers through my hair, sighing heavily.

"Just go with the flow," Laila said as she helped me fix the crop top of my lengha, holding me close. It was almost evening and I was getting ready for the reception now.

I had already shared everything with Laila on our way back from Addin's office, including what happened in his cabin. She was furious at first, but when I told her about Addin's words, she became just as confused as I was.

"What do you mean?" I asked, as she sat me in front of the dressing table's mirror on a stool and the stylists began working on my hair and makeup.

"I mean, leave everything in Allah's hands and try to make this marriage work! Be happy! Enjoy your married life! You're married to him now, Ayezah! Make him fall for you! Believe me, you don't know the power of Nikkah! Even if he didn't like you at first, he'll definitely fall for you now!" she said with a smile, playfully brushing my cheeks with a huge blush brush.

Her words increased the pace of my heartbeat.

How am I supposed to make him fall for me?

But nonetheless I nodded, smiling.

I'll just go with the flow, yeah!

" you look so pyaariii, Ayeziii! Masha Allah!" Laila exclaimed, giving me a kiss on the cheek. I stood in front of the mirror, gazing at myself.

I wore a stunning silver shimmery and glittery full-length lengha with voluminous layers, paired with a shimmery crop top that revealed a hint of skin on my stomach and waist. The crop top had full shiny sleeves and it was covered completely from backside as i avoid wearing backless.

my hair was styled into beautiful tiny braids at the front, carefully weaving each strand to perfection. The back cascaded down in loose waves. The hairstyle was adorned with delicate white flower pins, It felt like I was wearing a half crown of flowers at the backside of my head.

A silver shiny manga teeka adorned the center of my hair. My makeup was bold yet minimal, with foundation, mascara, eyeliner, a coat of pastel pink blush, silver glitter eyeshadow, and a matte rose shade lipstick.

For jewelry, I wore a mix of silver and green. A stunning silver necklace with green coloured diamonds on it adorned my neck, with my snowflake pendant hanging down.

I also wore long silver earrings which again had green coloured diamonds on it.

The dupatta was pinned to the side of my shoulder blade. I completed the look with a silver clutch in my hand and silver Heels.

"Okay, I gotta go and get ready as well. Catch ya at the reception venue!" Saying this, Laila hugged me and hurried outside. I smiled at her retreating figure and looked at the mirror, muttering to myself with a smirk.

"You slay in everything, Ayezah! "

Rahil's POV:

I straightened my white sherwani, staring at my reflection. I fixed my hair and sprayed some perfume on my wrist and neck. My hair was neatly gelled.

The sherwani had a beautiful combination of white and golden colors, adorned with golden buttons. A glimpse of a silk plain golden cloth peeked out from one of the pockets of the kurta.

As I looked at myself in the mirror one last time, I couldn't help but feel a mix of emotions.

I was now a married man! married to her. A smile formed on my lips as I thought about her.

I knew I couldn't stay single forever. I had to marry one day.

I had to move on.

And when Addin proposed the idea of me marrying Ayezah, I couldn't refuse him.

How much more can I run? I knew that one day I would need to stop.

And it took me two whole days to realise that Ayezah was the one for me.

Ayezah was the most incredible, understanding and strong woman I have met in my life. She never made me feel guilty about me rejecting her twice.

I had rejected her twice, 4 years back. Four years ago, she had asked me to date her, I refused because i was really not interested in dating and all. I asked her to be friends with me, and she agreed.

Her friendship meant the world to me, as I never had a proper female friend before. She was really an amazing friend one could ever have, i found her really cool. I truly enjoyed her company. She was flirty, silly and funny.

Everything was going great between us. But Later on She confessed that she had started growing feelings for me, and it broke my heart the most to reject such a wonderful person like her.

Because i wasn't ready at the time. I was afraid of another heartbreak, fearing that I wouldn't be able to pick up the pieces.

Amal Shah, Addin's sister, was my first love. She was the sweetest person I had ever met, and I fell for her instantly. However, destiny had different plans. She loved someone else, who betrayed her in the worst possible way, leading to her tragic end. She died.

It was too much for me to take in. I couldn't get over the pain that time.

I knew i left Ayezah heartbroken and it somehow pained me too. But i couldn't help it. I was miserably and somewhere i feared i would make her miserable as well.

Ayezah left for Australia and i knew our friendship ended there. I couldn't be more selfish by asking her to still be friends with me.

I don't know i blamed myself for breaking her heart badly, because i very well knew the pain of unrequited love and it pained me so much knowing that I have hurt her, but i couldn't help myself.

After that she didn't contact me at all and Honestly i missed her a lot.

After 4 years she was back to London and we met again. I thought she wouldn't be happy seeing me but i was wrong. She greeted me with a huge smile, and gladly accepted the collaboration of our companies knowing very well that she had to face me everyday. This only showed how strong of a women she was.

Also she is very kind hearted.

We then become business partners and our friendship kinda started again. I felt so happy that she was back again.

Ayezah shah made me the happiest and this confirmed it that I wanted to spend the rest of my life with her.

I stepped outside my room to check if she was ready. I had agreed to give her the space she needed, so she stayed in the room just in front of mine. Our rooms were separated by a huge round staircase railing.

I looked ahead just to froze in my tracks. Ayezah was also coming out of her room, holding her voluminous lengha and trying to manage it as she walked out.

Her gaze was fixed on her lengha, while my gaze was fixed on her. I gulped hard, feeling my heart race suddenly. It was the same feeling I had when I saw her yesterday during our nikkah, wearing a golden sharara.

She looked unreal, probably the most beautiful bride I had ever seen.

Undoubtedly, she was the most finest and gorgeous woman I had ever encountered, but right now she looked absolutely breathtaking in that silver lengha.

The lengha hugged her slender waist perfectly, and her makeup was on point. Words couldn't describe the beauty I was witnessing in that moment. I couldn't understand why my heart was racing so damn fast.

I had always found her gorgeous, ever since the first time i met her. But right now, she looked something beyond words.

I swallowed the lump in my throat and placed my hand over my chest, near my heart. What's happening? Calm down Rahil!

She adjusted her lengha and looked up, meeting my gaze.

As her eyes met mine, I could literally feel my heart beat fastening more beneath my palm. We stood there, staring at each other in front of our respective room doors, for what felt like an eternity.

I maintained eye contact as I crossed the railing and approached her. I noticed her eyes scanning over my body before she blinked and looked away.

" You look so pretty." the words slipped out before I even realized it, and she looked at me.

"And so do you." she replied immediately, her bottom lip curling in as if realising that she had said something silly.

' Pretty ?' I chuckled. She seemed a bit embarrassed as her cheeks turned a slight shade of pink.

I smirked and said, " But you called me something else when we first met! Remember?" The flashback of when we first met four years ago at Addin's birthday party instantly flashed in my mind.

" Hi, I'm Ayezah shah, and you are ? " she said forwarding her hand for handshake and smirking at me.

I nervously smiled and accepted her handshake muttering a 'Rahil Ahmed khan'

" Damn your name is hot and so are you ! "My eyes slightly widen. I could feel her gaze roaming over my body, checking me out.

"Oh yes, I remember very well!" Her voice brought me out of the flashback, and I saw her smirking at me.

"Oh, you do?" I asked, smirking back. She nodded, raising her one eyebrow and tilting her head sideways a little.

"Yes, let me correct myself then." She suddenly leaned near my face, making me blink and wiping off my smirk instantly.

She whispered near my ear, and I held my breath. Her warm breath fanned my ear, making my heart race.

" You always look damn hot! Rahil Ahmed Khan, just like your name! And right now, you look incredibly appealing, like a hot sizzling barbecue and I'm badly craving some." Goosebumps erupted on my nape. Her voice sounded seductive and hot.

I felt myself growing hard. What the actual hell on earth I'm feeling right now?

She slightly moved back from my ear and suddenly pressed her soft lips on one of my cheeks.

The moment her lips came in contact with the skin of my cheek, i felt like an electric current surged through my whole body. She pecked my cheek and moved back slightly.

I tilted my neck to look at her, and our eyes met. Her smirk was gone, replaced by a gaze filled with different emotions swirling in herBeautiful Amber eyes.

Words cannot fully capture the mesmerizing beauty of her eyes. They were simply captivating.

Captivating amber eyes.

Our gaze locked, and our noses were almost touching. Our audible breaths mingled together.

I had never been this close to any girl before, and the proximity made me gulp.

Her features looked even more stunning from this close. My eyes roamed all over her face, and she mirrored my actions.

My gaze fell upon her smooth lips, which appeared even softer from this close. I had this sudden urge to feel their softness.

Her scent filled my lungs, she smelled so nice and soothing, like a fresh bouquet of flowers and I wanted to just nuzzle my nose and keep inhaling the scent.

What's exactly happening to me?

Do we feel like this when we are falling for someone?

Am I falling for her?

Chapter 3

Ayezah's POV:

Dad kissed my forehead, hugging and smilingly muttering ," Masha Allah, My lovely princess! May Allah bless you with all the happiness in the world."

I smiled at him widely. He then gave Rahil a slight hug, showering us both with blessings.

Right now, we were seated on the velvety white huge couch on the stage of the grand wedding hall! It was a magnificent mansion, with rooms upstairs and a massive hall downstairs.

The hall was adorned in a beautiful white theme, with delicate white flowers and shimmering silver lights.

As the guests arrived, they showered us with their blessings and good wishes. I glanced at Rahil to see him looking straight ahead. As if he sensed my gaze, he turned towards me, and our eyes met.

In that moment, memories of our previous encounter at his mansion flashed through my mind, causing my heart to race isanely.

Earlier the tension between us was palpable, thick in the air. Even now, I could feel it as Rahil nervously looked away, his palm flew on the back of his neck, cupping his nape. I blinked my eyes and looked ahead.

Our lips were so close! I could literally smell his musky woody cologne, which almost made me moan.

AYEZAH STOP RYT THERE!

My lips on his cheek felt so right! I felt bundle of things in the pit of my stomach, and not to forget the way he was gazing at me Oh god!

He never ever looked at me like that! There was something else in his eyes! Something like desire? Something very different which I never witnessed before.

The way he was continuously staring at my lips. DAMN! it fucking gave me wild thoughts.

I was this close to losing my sanity and kissing him breathless right there! I almost leaned in too but-

Before I could do anything Rahil's phone rang interrupting us.

It was his personal secretary Adam, He informed us that we were getting late and that a car was ready for us.

The car ride from home to the wedding hall was filled with nothing but pure awkwardness. I stole a few glances at Rahil in the car and saw him gulping and wiping the sweat beads from his forehead with his handkerchief.

" BHABHII!! you look so gorgeous as always, Masha Allah!!!" My trance broke, when I saw Najma and her husband Irfan making their way up to the stage. Najma was Rahil's younger sibling.

Najma gave me a tight hug while squealing with excitement! And Irfan hugged Rahil congratulating him.

" Thanks Najma! You look so pretty as well! " I smiled at her, pulling away.

"So! You finally made it, huh! I mean, you literally saved my brother's single ass from staying single forever. And you know what? I knew this would happen one day! I knew from the moment you told me you were going to pursue my brother. I just had this feeling that you two were meant to be together." She teased me with a smirk.

I chuckled, remembering the first time I met Najma. I had told her that I found her brother very attractive, and she responded by saying that he was too much of a goody-good boy and would love to stay single forever, so she offered to help me pursue him.

" BHAI !!! You look so handsome! " Najma chirped moving towards Rahil and hugging him as well And Irfan greeted me with a smile and I smiled back.

We chatted with Najma and her husband for a few seconds before Rahil's entire family arrived. His mom and dad are the sweetest people I've ever met. Nafisa aunty and Rashid uncle, who now demanded I call them ammi and abbu, and I gladly obeyed. They were so warmly welcoming and kind.

We all talked and laughed for few minutes, before they all went to attend guests.

Noor and Addin then arrived, looking stunning as always. Noor is Addin's wife. Noor hugged me, and Addin hugged Rahil.

" You both look so damn good together! Masha Allah! " Noor exclaimed.

" Right, Addin? " Noor nudged Addin, who replied with a boring .'Yeah'

Noor gave Addin a sharp, deadly glare.

" It's your bestfriend and cousin's reception! Atleast pretend like you are excited." Noor whispered to him, which was audible to me.

" It's okay, Noor! I don't expect anything from that cranky and cantankerous guy! Like, this creature didn't even call me for his waalima! So, what can i even expect from him? " I said, and Noor laughed out loud, throwing her head back, and Addin grumbled out a 'whatever fuck.'

Just when we were chit-chatting with Noor and Addin, Najma climbed the stage with her and Noor's best friend, Sammy, who congratulated us and brought a gift too.

Sammy and Najma greeted Noor happily.

Then suddenly, Najma exclaimed, " Bhai! You gotta do something! Look, bhabi isn't wearing the most important thing!"

She said to Rahil, standing near him. Rahil frowned and looked at me, saying, " What? She's wearing everything! And she just looks so pretty and perfect."

He said, still looking at me from head to toe.

" Ooooohoooo prettyy??" Najma teased.

" and perfect?? " Noor joined in near Najma, smirking and teasing Rahil!

I looked at Rahil, and our gaze met. We stood there gazing at each other until Najma cleared her throat and giggled along with her best friend, Noor.

" You both can continue the staring contest later, right now we were discussing something else? " Noor said.

" Ohhhhfooo bhai! bhabhi isn't wearing gajre! look at her wrists." Najma said, grabbing Rahil's attention.

Rahil looked at my wrists and muttered an 'Ooh,' and I too glanced at my wrists.

"Here, make her wear it." Najma forward the fresh white gajre, which were clad with delicate fresh roses on it.

" Me? " Rahil blinked.

" Again who? Me? " Noor asked sarcastically, chuckling. " You only, bhai! " Najma sighed and handed him the gajre, which Rahil hesitantly took.

Rahil extended his palm towards me, telling me to place my hand on his.

"Ya Allah! Najma! How can your brother be so clueless? I mean, I never thought I would say this, but you really need to take some lessons from Addin on how to be romantic," Noor huffed.

"Get on your knees, bhai!" Najma exclaimed, covering her face with her palm. Rahil's eyes widened slightly. "What?" he asked.

"Knees! She said, get on your knees!" I said, smirking.

I was enjoying this a little too much. Rahil looked so adorable when he was nervous.

He gulped and nodded, slowly lowering himself onto his on knee.

I couldn't help but suppress a wide grin as I pressed my lips together. He gently took one of my hands in his and delicately made me wear the gajre. He repeated the same for my other hand as well.

Everyone clapped as soon as he finished placing the gajre, and I passed him my widest grin.

He still held both of my palms in his, gazing up at me. His eyes were filled with a different kind of emotion, his expression was soft.

Again he is looking at me so differently.

Then, his gaze shifted to the gajre. He looked at my gajre clad hands for few seconds and what he did next left me completely stunned, along with everyone else.

He bent his head and kissed my knuckles, one by one, sending a burst of electric jolts through my entire being. My eyes slightly widen. I felt butterflies in the pit of my stomach.

The room erupted with cheers, bringing him back to reality as he immediately stood up and nervously looked away.

I could feel my cheeks warming up, and a silly grin spread across my face.

Oh my god! What's with him? why would he do that?

Even His simple gesture make me all giddy.

Ayezah you are so deep into this shit! FOR REAL.

"Bhai! I guess now that you made her wear the gajre so you can let go of her hands," Najma teased, and everyone burst into fits of laughter. I looked down and realized that he was still holding my hands in his.

He immediately released them, cupping the back of his neck and looking away, a slight smile playing on his lips.

Did I just see him blushing? Oh my god!! I'll die.

They all left us alone, saying they'll attend to the guests, and we sat back in our previous positions.

"Sorry, sorry, sorry! I'm so sorry I'm late," Laila hurriedly climbed up, managing her huge shimmery maroon gown which had a silt on one side.

Her luscious, dark auburn locks were elegantly styled into a sleek and polished bun and she had done bold make up with her lips painted in deep red colour.

"But you know what Rahil jij! Your secretary Mr Adam THARKI Hussain is to be blamed as well!!! He stopped me at the entrance and flirted with me for a straight 15 minutes! I'm telling you, I'll murder him or, worse, I'll kick him in the balls so he better not mess with me. Tell him!" she said to Rahil, who looked at her nervously.

I gave Rahil a hesitant smile and pulled Laila towards me. she bent down since I was sitting.

"Are you stupid? Or are you the stupidest?" I whispered in her ears.

"What? His secretary is damn annoying, I told you!" she replied.

"If his secretary is troubling you, then why are YOU troubling my husband? I mean why are you saying all that to him? Just handle him your way! And please, he's not tharki, he's kinda cute! He likes you! " I said.

"Well, let me tell you that i wasn't trouble your precious husband, I was just letting him know that how shithead of a secretary he has appointed and secondly I'm your best friend first, so you must agree to whatever I say or else you know very well I can chop you off! And about that douchebag! I would puke, please. He is everything but cute, and you know I'm into hot guys. Cute ones are not my type!" she exclaimed. I rolled my eyes at her saying a 'yeah whatever.'

" Oh anyways! Congratulations to you both." She straightened herself and smiled widely while congratulating us both.

Rahil smiled at her back and politely thanked her.

" Anyways guys! Where is the nach gana?? Why is the reception so dull?? " She exclaimed.

" Look Laila Nooo ! " I warned her.

" Hell yess!!! Now that Laila is here, I'll make this boring reception exciting! I'm going to be the DJ and play all desi wedding songs!!! Let's make your reception rock!!! " Saying this excitedly she went away. I sighed heavily, shaking my head and chuckling a little at the thought of how now my bestfriend would turn my reception into whole vibe.

The desi wedding songs started blasting through the entire wedding hall, filling it with energetic beats.

The infectious rhythm brought everyone together, and the dance floor quickly became the center of all the action.

I couldn't help but chuckle as I spotted Najma, Sammy, and Noor tearing up the dance floor, their moves wild and carefree. The sight of them was pure chaos.

As the music continued to play, even the elders couldn't resist the temptation to join in on the fun.

They gracefully made their way to the dance floor, their smiles radiating pure joy.

The song ' Nachde Ne saare ' filled the air, and it seemed like everyone's hearts were pouring out onto the dance floor.

In the midst of all the excitement, I couldn't help but steal glances at Rahil. His eyes were fixed on his family, a wide smile adorning his face.

Seeing him so happy made my own smile widen, and I found myself staring at him, grinning like a fool.

But then, he suddenly turned his gaze towards me, and I quickly averted my eyes, feeling a rush of embarrassment wash over me.

I looked away, closing my eyes tightly, wishing I could disappear in that moment. His chuckle broke the silence.

and even though I was embarrassed, All I could think was that his laughter had a certain charm to it.

It was downright hot!!

"Alright, alright, it's time for the star couple of the day to hit the dance floor for the couple's dance! " Noor climbed up on the stage, declaring it with excitement, and pulled me and Rahil into the center of the dance floor.

We stood there hesitantly, looking around at all the other couples who were also paired up.

Noor made her way to Addin and wrapped her arms around his neck, while he immediately pulled her closer by the waist, almost lifting her up. Najma and Irfan were also dancing with each other lovingly.

Suddenly, the music changed.

Wait I know this beats!

Rahil slowly took my hand and placed it on his shoulder blade, all the while I gazed at him.

" Ishq mein dil bana hai, Ishq mein dil fanaa hai, OOO "

As the lyrics played, I realized it was the song'Chaleya' by Arijit Singh.

Laila, being the Bollywood fan she is, would always play Bollywood songs, so I knew this song as well.

I looked up at Rahil, and our eyes met, a spark of current running between us.

" Mita de ya bana de, Maine tujhko chuna Hai, OOO "

In that very moment, he snaked his whole arm around my bare waist, and swiftly pulled me in causing my breath to hitch.

" Tere saare Rang odh ke dhandh odh ke "

Our faces were just inches apart.

" Tera hua mein sabko chhod ke, OOO "

He was gazing into my eyes deeply with a very different kind of emotion twirling in his warm brown orbs. Our noses almost touching.

He held my other hand with his, and we started moving together, slowly and gracefully.

" Oh main taan chaleya teri or tera chaleya hai zorr "

He twirled me around, making my lengha flare around me.

He then hugged me from behind. My arms neatly folded around my stomach, and his hand rested on mine.

" Tera hoya main yaar ve buleya ae sansaar ve "

I could feel his hot breath fanning near my ear, his breathing charged and hard. I literally felt him inhaling my hair, as he pressed his nose on the side of my head. I gulped, feeling something indescribable.

Suddenly, I noticed something that made me frown, and it had been catching my attention for the past few days now.

The red hoodie!!

It was a person wearing a red hoodie, talking to a waiter. I had been noticing this same red hoodie-wearing person following me for few days now.

Their back was facing us as Rahil twirled me around, but when I swiftly turned to look back, the person had disappeared, deepening my frown.

"What happened?" Rahil's voice made me turn towards him, and I smiled slightly, shaking my head.

The music was fading into the background, and I found myself dancing mindlessly, my mind preoccupied with trying to spot that one person in the red hoodie.

I wondered if I was hallucinating or if there was something more to it.

However, these situations were not new to me. Growing up, I had business rivals who would send people to investigate or even harm me.

My dad, being wealthy, attracted such rivals, and as a result, I had a bodyguard assigned to me during my childhood.

But now, I knew I could handle it myself. I took few self defence classes and I was also taught how to keep my senses alert.

My gaze caught that same person in the red hoodie climbing up the stairs.

This was very suspicious and my first instinct was to call the cops! but before that, I needed to confirm if he was really tailing me or if there was some other reason for his presence.

I quickly came up with an excuse, telling Rahil that I needed to use the restroom. He suggested that I take Najma with me, but I assured him that I'd be fine on my own.

With a sense of urgency, I rushed upstairs, carefully holding onto my voluminous lengha with both of my palms, so that I don't trip and fall.

The upstairs area was vast, with a lot of rooms and only a handful of people around.

I meticulously searched each room, struggling with my lengha badly.

Just as I was about to enter another room, my gaze noticed- the person in the red hoodie.

I instinctively halted in my tracks, hiding behind a massive pillar as I discreetly observed the person in red.

That person was again engrossed in conversation with another waiter,their back was turned towards me.

I stood there for a few seconds, keenly observing them. The person in the red hoodie reached into their pocket, and before I could get a proper look at what they pulled out, someone called out my name.

"Ayezah?" My heart skipped a beat as a hand landed on my shoulder. My eyes widen.

Shit it's Rahil!

Panic surged through me as I saw the red hoodie person turning towards us.

Without hesitation, I swiftly spun around and grabbed Rahil, pressing him against the massive pillar. I hovered over him completely, to hide myself behind the pillar as well,

I pinned my one palm near his head to steady myself against the pillar and gripped his wrist with my other hand.

Rahil's eyes widened in utter shock.

Chapter 4

Rahil's POV:

Ayezah took a lot of time to come back from the washroom, and with everyone downstairs, it made me worry that she was all alone upstairs.

Without a second thought, I went up to search for her.

As I approached the upstairs, my brow furrowed when I saw Ayezah hiding behind the pillar, her gaze fixed on something.

I called out her name, but before I could finish, my eyes widened as she swiftly pinned me against the pillar, completely trapping me. Her one hand held my wrist firmly, while her other palm rested near my head against the pillar.

"Ayezah, what-" I started to say, but she immediately silenced me by pressing her forefinger gently against my lips, uttering a soft 'shhhhh'

I obediently pressed my lips together, captivated by her presence. She hovered over me, her eyes focused elsewhere, while mine were locked intently on her.

I felt my heart race insanely as she leaned even closer, her body pressing against mine.

I couldn't help but notice her exquisite features. Her face had a beautiful shape, with a defined jawline and perfect cheekbones that accentuated her captivating eyes. And her lips,

Oh her lips, they looked incredible smooth. The urge to feel their softness was getting too real in me.

Rahil get back in your senses!

I gulped hard, looking away.

"Ayezah? What's wrong?" I whispered,"Why are you behaving this way?"

"I'll tell you everything, just give me a minute, please," she whispered-yelled back. I nodded slowly.

she leaned more closer, causing her hair to cascade down over my face, as she stood on her tiptoes, looking ahead and placing her palms on my shoulder blades for support.

I could smell her hair. They smelled heavenly. I couldn't help but shut my eyes, inhaling deeply, savoring the intoxicating fragrance of her hair.

What the actual hell on earth?

Why am i behaving like some creepy pervert?

I scolded myself silently. Slowly, I turned my face away.

She pressed her body even closer, if it was even possible, and brought her face dangerously close to mine, making me instinctively shrunk back against the pillar.

My heartbeat raised to the maximum level as if my heart would jump out of my chest right away.

Her eyes were shut, and her forehead lightly touching mine.

From this incredibly close distance, I couldn't help but again get lost and admire her beauty. Every detail of her face, every curve and contour, seemed more mesmerizing than ever before.

She is so ethereal.

Time seemed to stand still as I found myself lost in the captivating allure of her features.

Her lips were so close to mine that the slightest movement would cause them to touch my lips.

I feel like my heart would burst out any moment.

Her eyes remained shut, and I sensed movement from the corner of my vision. Glancing ahead, I spotted a person in a red hoodie making their way downstairs, who seemed to not notice us as we were completely hidden behind the grand pillar.

As soon as the person left, I noticed her exhaling a huff of breath. Our eyes met, and it seemed like she suddenly realized our position, causing her eyes to widen slightly.

She nervously chewed on her lower lip before swiftly moving back, only to let out a hiss of pain as one of her earrings got tangled in the lace of my kurta.

"Ouch," she whispered, trying to free herself.

"Wait, wait, Ayezah! You'll hurt yourself even more. Let me help you," I said, gently removing the long silver earring from her ear.

The earring got stuck on the kurta and the backside of the earring fell somewhere.

She held her earlobe, wincing slightly, and I immediately removed her hand, saying " Let me see." Her earlobe had turned dark pinkish color.

"It'll be fine if we apply some cool ice on it," I suggested, gently caressing her soft earlobe between my thumb and forefinger.

I looked at her and she simply gazed back at me, our eyes locked. I quickly pulled my hand away from her earlobe.

"Okay, now tell me, what was all that fuss about?" I asked, attempting to move forward from behind the pillar.

Suddenly my leg got entangled in the voluminous folds of her lengha, causing me to almost lose my balance and stumble to the ground. Thankfully, she held my hand and pulled me back up, but I still lost my balance and ended up falling to the floor, with her on top of me. As she was holding my hand.

I couldn't help but let out a pained 'Ouch'.

I looked at her hissing while holding my hip, and she was already staring back at me with eyes wide open.

We stared at each other for few seconds before bursting into fits of laughter together.

"Oh god!" she said, laughing loudly and suddenly adjusting herself properly on top of me, causing me to freeze.

She placed her palms on either side of my chest, trying to get up.

As she leaned down her head a little, our cheeks brushed against each other, and I swallowed hard.

Her cheek felt soft against mine.

She slowly turned and looked at me, and I blinked nervously.

Oh god, why does her closeness make me so damn nervous?

"Can you get up, please?" I asked, feeling my heart race increasing at an abnormal level.

But instead of moving, she smirked at me, making me blink even more.

She adjusted her palms on my chest and said, "Why? Are you getting nervous now? I mean, you were too bold today during the dance. That's was unexpected actually. But what now? Are you nervous? "

She is such a tease. Always.

"I'm not nervo-" I tried to say, but she didn't let me finish. She causally leaned even more closer to my face, making my breath hitch.

" Yeah? You were saying something." She whispered, right on my lips.

"I'm not nervous, it's just that we are in the corridor, and anyone can come," I said, my voice trembling because of the close proximity.

she suddenly blew over my head, making me shut my eyes.

"Oh, there was something on your hair," she smirked.

I knew she was doing it on purpose, teasing me more, making me more nervous, and I know she enjoys my nervous state. I knew her so well!

So I thought why not play along?

I snaked my whole arm around her slender, smooth, bare waist. Her expression said that she was caught off guard as her eyes slightly widen.

I brushed my fingers on the side of her forehead, gently pushing back her few locks of hair, all the while i felt her gaze on me.

My one whole arm was securely wrapped around her bare slender waist.

" No doubt that You're absolutely breathtaking! But you look way too gorgeous from this close." I playfully teased, gazing at her whole face. she blinked at me nervously and it was my time to smirk.

Our eyes got connected, and I found myself captivated by her enchanting amber orbs.

Her eyes. They were so alluring and mesmerizing, they had the power to hypnotize anyone who looked into them.

And once you look into them, you feel like you don't wanna look away. Ever.

My heart raced madly. We gazed at each other for a few precious seconds, before she suddenly started to struggle and got up from above me.

I closed my eyes, trying to calm the rapid beating of my heart, and stood up straight as well.

We stood there in an awkward silence, and I noticed her adjusting her lengha, jewelry, and hair.

Meanwhile, I nervously cupped the back of my neck, avoiding eye contact

" Um, yeah, I totally forgot to ask, but what was going on here? Who were you hiding from?" I inquired.

" Oh, that! Actually, I have this suspicion that someone has been following me for the past few days. Ever since our marriage was arranged, I have noticed a person in a red hoodie trailing behind me everywhere. Even during our nikkah ceremony yesterday, I caught a glimpse of that person and even today he was here. I'm not entirely sure... " She tilted her face and narrowed her eyes, lost in deep thought.

" Did you inform the cops? " I asked.

" No, not yet."she replied.

" what? WHY? " I suddenly yelled, causing her to flinch slightly.

" I'm sorry" I immediately apologized. " I mean, what are you waiting for? That person could be dangerous, Ayezah! " I exclaimed.

" Don't worry, I know how to deal with these fucking morons very well! They're probably just some business rivals trying to keep an eye on me." she said confidently.

" If they are indeed business rivals, then it could be even more dangerous! What if they're after your life? " I asked, suddenly feeling my chest tighten at the thought of something happening to her.

" 'It's a possibility." she shrugged casually, as if it wasn't a big deal, leaving me staring at her.

" Ayezah, how can you say that so casually? We're talking about your life being in danger!" I said, gently holding her shoulder blades.

" Relax, Rahil! nothing will happen to me." she chuckled.

"And nothing should ever happen to you." I said, sliding my hands from her shoulder blade down to her palms, gripping them firmly.

She looked at me and I gazed back into her eyes. Her gaze had turned soft and warm.

She smiled at me and held my palms back by entwining her fingers with mine.

" You know, you shouldn't really worry about me. Instead, you should be concerned about those who are trailing behind me. Once I catch them, you won't believe what I'll do with them. After all, I'm Ayezah Shah," she smirked, and I couldn't help but chuckle, shaking my head.

"Oh, yes, the great Ayezah Shah. But still, you should consider hiring some protection, like a bodyguard or something!" I suggested.

"Nope! I don't do bodyguard shit. I'm more than capable of protecting myself," she confidently declared.

"Okay, then how about you hire me? I'll be your bodyguard! I know martial arts too." I offered and She laughed out loudly.

" I just said I don't do bodyguards, and if it's about martial arts, I know it better than you!" she continued to giggle.

I frowned "Are you challenging me?" I asked.

She smirked, mischief dancing in her eyes. "Oh, Mr. Rahil Ahmed Khan, no one can beat Ayezah in martial arts," she confidently declared.

"We'll see about that," I replied firmly.

"One more challenge?" She asked raising her one eyebrow.

"Yes," I replied.

" Oh, you love challenging me, don't you?" she asked, smirking.

"Hey, you challenged me first this time, claiming you're better than me! I've been learning martial arts since I was young, so I really want to see how good you are," I explained.

" okay then we'll see." she smirked, and I smirked back, determined to prove my skills.

There was no way she knew martial arts better than me.

Ayezah's POV :

I tightened my neat high ponytail, feeling the strands of hair pulled back tightly.

I stretched my arms and cracked my neck. my gaze fixated on the man in front of me, diligently doing his warm-up.

The early morning sun cast a soft glow on Rahil's private gym, illuminating the space.

He wore a casual grey t-shirt paired with black pants, looking tempting as ever.

I was dressed in a white crop top with full sleeves, revealing a hint of skin at my waist and stomach, perfectly complemented by my black tight leggings.

After the reception, we returned exhausted and quickly found the way to our respective beds.

However, Rahil made sure I ate something during the event. Ever since our first night of marriage, where I nearly fainted due to not eating, he has been vigilant about my meals, always checking on me if I have eaten properly or not.

It warms my heart to see how much he cares for me.

"So, you know self-defense?" Rahil's voice snapped me back to the present moment. I nodded confidently, a smirk playing on my lips.

"Yes, I do! I'm well-versed in self-defense techniques, and my senses are always on high alert. Plus, I hit the gym every day, so I'm stronger than you might think!" I folded my arms neatly against my chest. He raised his eyebrows at me indicating he is impressed.

Suddenly he walked behind me, a mischievous smirk playing on his lips, and I couldn't help but furrow my brows in response.

He positioned himself right behind me, his presence felt electric, and I could feel his warm breath close to my ear. In that instant, my heart began to race insanely.

"So, you know self defence very well?" he whispered, his husky voice sending a shiver down my spine.

Oh lord! Why is he sounding so sexy?

I mustered all my strength to reply, trying my best not to get affected by the proximity.

"Yes!" I managed to say, my voice tinged with both determination and a hint of vulnerability.

Then, he leaned in even more closer, his nose gently grazing the side of my head, and I could feel the soft brush of his breath against my hair as he smelled my hair. My heart pounded in my chest.

Suddenly, his one whole arm encircled my shoulders from behind, creating a sensation that was both comforting and slightly suffocating. His grip was firm, yet very careful, as if he was trying his best not to hurt me at all.

"What would you do if someone grabbed you like this from behind?" he whispered, his lips almost brushing against my ear.

As his warm breath caressed my neck and his hand remained securely wrapped around my shoulders, my breathing quickened.

Focus Ayezah FOCUS!

Summoning every ounce of strength, I seized his arm that rested on my shoulders and attempted to twist it.

Fuck! He is stronger than I thought he is.

I exerted all my might, managing to release his arm, and swiftly spun around, twisting his arm behind his back.

"So, what do you think?" I smirked, holding his twisted hand. He smirked right back at me, swiftly pulling his hand out of my grip. Before I could even process what was happening, he pinned me against the mirrored wall of the gym.

My breath caught in my throat as his arm rested on my neck, his face mere inches from mine. We locked eyes, both of us breathing heavily, our foreheads and noses almost touching.

In a swift motion, I managed to reverse our positions, pinning him against the mirror.

He smirked at me and uttered, "Not bad, my tigress!" The rush of adrenaline coursed through my veins and I stared at him.

Did i hear it right? My tigress?

I felt ticklish in the pit of my stomach.

He leaned his forehead against mine, closing his eyes, and I couldn't help but lean in too, surrendering to his warmth.

We stood there with our foreheads connected and noses touching.

Slowly, I pulled my arm away from his neck.

Taking the opportunity, he swiftly tried turning me around, but my reflexes worked on time.

with a controlled force, I banged him against the mirror hard and a pained hiss escaped his lips.

My eyes widened, and I panicked, asking, "Oh, I'm so sorry! Did I hurt you?"

He took advantage of my distraction and pinned me back against the mirror. "You cheat!" I screamed, and he chuckled.

Early morning went quite fun with Rahil.

I just finished taking a shower and was strolling through the walk-in closet in the room. Rahil's house wasn't bad at all, but I couldn't help but miss my own walk-in wardrobe and cozy penthouse.

I tousled my wet hair, contemplating what to wear as I gazed at the hangers hanging in the open cupboard.

Finally, I decided on a pure white silk shirt, which I neatly tucked into a pair of white pants with a golden thin belt on it.

I parted my hair in the middle, leaving it flowing freely behind with my brown bouncy curls and for accessories, I adorned myself with dainty golden earrings and a golden necklace with round loops.

I also wore a few delicate golden rings and a golden wristwatch. Oh, and let's not forget the perfume! I sprayed some perfume around me, inhaling the sweet soothing scent while closing my eyes in satisfaction.

I love perfumes.

I went with my daily makeup routine : mascara, skin colour eye-shades, a dust of pale pink blush, and nude lipstick.

For my bag, I chose a trusty brown Gucci pouch-like bag that I could carry in my hand.With my heels on, I confidently stepped outside.

Oh how much i love to get dressed.

I was actually heading to the office! Even though Rahil and I had taken holidays due to the wedding, I needed to confirm my suspicions about that red hoodie.

As I stepped outside, I saw Rahil walking out of his room, which was right in front of mine, wearing casual clothes. He frowned when he looked at me and asked, " Where are you going? "

"Oh, I really have some important work to do, so I need to go to the office-" I replied. But he interrupted me, saying, " But we're off, right? "

" yeah but you know, i have to look into this mysterious red hoodie person! So for that i need to go." I said.

" Then I'll come too." He replied immediately.

" No no Rahil! I'll be fine and I'll be back soon, don't worry! " I assured him.

" Are you sure? " he asked, and I could see concern in his eyes. I smiled at him and nodded.

" Be safe okay? " he said making my smile widen more.

It feels good to have someone who genuinely cares about you.

" Okay i will." I replied, the smile not leaving my lips.

Rahil forcefully made me have breakfast with him, even though I had told him I would grab something on my way. Reluctantly, I joined him and we sat down to eat together.

After finishing breakfast, I made my way towards my sleek black car. I prefer driving myself and enjoy the freedom of being behind the wheel.

As I accelerated, the wind brushed against my face through the open window, I turned on some music, letting the melodies fill the car.

I really enjoyed the combo of fresh cool air and music.

However, my enjoyment was interrupted when I noticed a red car persistently following me in the rearview mirror.

My confusion turned into concern as the car suddenly sped up, closing the distance between us.

My frown deepened as I wondered what was going on. Before I could react, the red car forcefully collided with the back of my car, jolting me forward with a powerful impact.

What the actual fuck?

The relentless jerking motion continued, as the red car kept purposely colliding with the backside of my car, making me jolt forward every now and then.

I couldn't help but scream in frustration. " WHAT THE FUCK??? "

In that moment, I had to think quickly. I gripped the steering wheel tightly, making a split-second decision to turn sharply to the side of the road and slam on the brakes, bringing my car to a screeching halt.

The sudden stop caused my forehead to collide harshly with the steering wheel, sending a sharp pain through my head and momentarily blurring my vision.

Chapter 5

Rahil's POV:

I mindlessly scrolled through Netflix on the sleek LCD in-front of me, growing more and more frustrated by the lack of suitable options to watch.

I was sitting on the couch in my living room, constantly stealing glances between the clock and the main door.

The digital numbers on the clock displayed 8:oo in the evening.

Why wasn't she back yet? She told me that she would return soon! And To make matters worse, she hadn't even answered any of my calls.

The entire day had felt excruciatingly dull, especially since it was my day off from work, so I didn't really had anything to do the whole day and it went so damn boring.

I really wished she had stayed home too, so like that we could have spent some time together.

Sinking deeper into the plush cushions of the couch, my fingers absentmindedly worked the remote, endlessly scrolling through the Netflix library, while my eyes remained fixated on the main door.

I sighed heavily, sulking internally.

What on earth was keeping her so long?

My phone suddenly rang, and I immediately snatched it up, hoping it was her calling.

But to my disappointment, it was Najma. Letting out a frustrated huff, I reluctantly answered the call.

"Yeah, okay!" I replied, cutting the conversation short.

After talking with Najma, she informed me that she was coming over to my place with dinner.

I engaged in a dull conversation with her, as my mind was constantly wandering back to where Ayezah could be and my eyes fixated on the main door.

I scrolled through my phone mindlessly and my fingers, almost as if they had a mind of their own, dialed her number.

why is her phone off? Is she okay?

This girl makes me worry so much, i tell you.

Wait! I should call her secretary, Laila. She would probably know where Ayezah is, yeah!

I immediately dialed Laila's number, and after a few rings, she answered the call.

"Hello, Laila! Is Ayezah with you?" I asked anxiously as soon as she picked up.

" Nope, jij! She left for home," Laila replied from the call.

"Why is it taking her so long to come back home? She said she'd be back home soon, and it's already so late! She didn't even bother calling me once the whole day," I complained, frustration evident in my voice.

" Woah jij, calm down!!! I didn't know you missed her so much, I mean you can't stay without her even for a day now, huh?" Laila teased from the call.

My heart did a somersault all of sudden hearing her words.

I used to live all alone in my mansion and I was used to it. I never got bored or felt this lonely before. But today, it was different. I felt so damn bored, lonely and empty.

I guess i really missed her.

What's happening to me? can't i really even go a single day without her?

She doing something to me! I was never like this. It's not even been properly a week that i married her and I already feel like I can't stay away her.

I'm going nuts. She driving me crazy.

" Rahil jij? Are you there? " Laila's voice from the phone broke my trance.

" Yeah... I'm sorry." I mumbled.

"Actually, today was really hectic you know," Laila began.

"We were tirelessly tracking down a red car that nearly caused Ayezah to have an accident-"

The word 'accident' hit me like a jolt of electricity.

Interrupting her mid-sentence, I immediately shot up from the couch, my heart racing.

I let out a panicked yell, "WHAT? Ayezah had an accident?"

The mere thought of something happening to her sent a wave of suffocation through me, tightening my chest.

"No, relax, it's nothing serious," Laila reassured me, her voice coming through the phone. "I mean, she's fine-"

Before she could finish her sentence, I heard the distinct sound of the main door clicking shut, signaling someone's arrival.

"Laila, I'll end the call now. I think she's back! Thank you so much!" I hastily ended the call and hurried towards the main door, my heart pounding hard in my chest and breathing turning heavy.

I saw her walking in, and her eyes blinked with surprise as she noticed me standing there. "Hey?" she said, a slight smile forming on her lips.

Without hesitation, I moved towards her, gently gripping her both the elbows, I pulled her closer, her eyes widened slightly at my sudden action, and I could feel her gaze fixed on me, filled with surprise.

Frantically, I scanned her body, searching for any signs of injury, but thankfully, there were none. As I did so, a wave of relief washed over me, causing my breathing to become normal.

"Rahil, what are you-" she began to ask, but before she could finish, I instinctively held her head in my hand and pressed it against my chest, holding her close to my heart, trying to calm my racing heartbeats.

She's fine.

The moment Laila mentioned the word 'accident', at that very second, flood of terrifying thoughts overwhelmed my mind.

I don't know, It's just so suffocating to even imagine anything happening to her. I just can't bear it.

I held her close to me tightly for a few seconds, My palm remained on her head, while my other arm encircled around her shoulders firmly and I could sense her stillness and frozen state.

I pulled back immediately, realizing what I was doing. My heart raced as she blinked at me, and I looked anywhere but her, avoiding eye contact.

she straightened herself, fixing her hair and I stammered, "Ah, umm, that... Laila told me about your accident! I really got worrie d...Are you okay? Are you hurt anywhere?"

She looked directly into my eyes, her captivating amber orbs drawing me in. We stood there, motionless, for a few seconds, lost in each other's gaze.

Finally, she spoke, her voice soft yet reassuring, "I'm fine, Rahil! It was nothing-"

But before she could finish her sentence, my eyes caught sight of a purple bruise right in the middle of her forehead, accompanied by a small bump.

I gently brushed my fingers on her front hair locks, tugging them behind and taking in the clear view of her forehead.

" Oh lord! You have a bump on your head! " I said.

She touched her forehead slightly saying, " Ah that! It's not a big deal-"

Interrupting her, I immediately took a hold of her palm in mine and guided her to the living room.

I made her sit on the couch, her eyes fixed on me all the while.

" We need to apply ice on it! Otherwise, it might swell. Wait here for a minute." With those words said, I hurried to the kitchen to fetch an ice pack.

I brought the ice pack and kneeled in front of her. Slowly, I moved closer to her face, carefully and gently pressing the cool ice pack on her forehead bump.

she hissed slightly, shutting her eyes.

"You didn't even bother calling me and letting me know what happened to you?" I blurted out, my words overflowing with worry.

" I was sick worried, you know! Why weren't you picking up my calls? You even came back so late, and I was literally waiting. You could've at least informed me, and you didn't even let me come-"

Before I could finish my worried rant, she called out my name, interrupting me.

"Rahil!"

Her softened eyes locked with mine, our faces just inches apart.

In that moment, her palm reached out, gently touching my cheek. She placed her whole palm on my cheek, and softly caressed it with her thumb pad.

I couldn't help but feel a wave of comfort wash over me.

Her touch felt so good and so soothing.

I unknowingly leaned closer to her palm and her face. The proximity made her blink. Our faces were so close, her palm still resting on my cheek.

"You worry too much!" she said, a slight smile gracing her lips. Her voice was filled with warmth.

"Then don't make me worry!" I responded immediately.

Her gaze locked with mine, and I could sense a different emotion swirling in her amber orbs.

We found ourselves lost in each other's gaze, our faces were so close that it felt like the world around us had faded away.

with a hint of mischief in her voice, she spoke those words that made my heart skip a beat.

"If you keep caring for me so deeply and keep leaning this close, I might just end up kissing you breathless."

Her eyes never left mine as she uttered those words, her lips tempting me to no extend.

Unable to resist the magnetic pull between us, I pressed my forehead and nose against hers, our breaths mingling in the space between us.

Desperation filled my voice as I whispered, "What's stopping you then?" Every fiber of my being yearned to feel her lips against mine.

She looked at me with slight surprise as if she wasn't expecting me saying that at all.

My gaze dropped at her smooth lips. My breathing turning uneven and heart racing madly.

I couldn't hold back any longer. The desperation consumed me entirely.

I wanted to taste her lips in that very moment, like nothing else mattered.

It was a feeling I had never experienced before.

she gazed at my lips, mirroring my own actions. And in the very next second, she smashed her lips on mine.

Our lips collided with a force that made me stumble back a little, but she immediately fisted her palm onto the collar of my t-shirt, pulling me closer.

Her lips were as smooth as finely melted chocolate, tempting me with their irresistible softness.

As I finally experienced the sensation of her lips against mine, a rush of giddiness washed over me.

They not only looked smooth, but they felt even smoother, like a velvety caress.

she parted her lips and took my lower lip between hers, gently sucking on it, causing me to drop the ice pack I had been holding onto the carpet.

Her palm remained tenderly pressed against my cheek, while her other palm firmly held onto my collar, keeping me close to her.

In that moment, all my self-imposed limits crumbled away, and I instinctively wrapped my arms around her waist, drawing our bodies even closer.

The kiss grew intense, as we kept kissing each other like there's no tomorrow.

I found myself lost in the sensation of sucking on her smoothest lips.

She dominated the kiss and I gladly let her.

The intensity of the kiss continued to escalate, with neither of us willing to pull back. I leaned in more, making our bodies to completely press against each other.

Eventually, we had to break the kiss, our foreheads connecting and our eyes closed, catching our breath.

" Fuck! I feel like I could do this all day! " she exclaimed. Her voice, raspy and heavy with each breath she takes.

" Me too." I replied and without hesitation, I smashed my lips back onto hers, pushing her gently onto the couch as I hovered over her.

The desire between us was palpable.

I savored the taste of her soft, velvety lips, but again she didn't allow me to take control as she more passionately sucked on my lips in return.

I found myself hovering over her, her back pressed firmly against the headrest of the couch. One of my palms sank into the plushness of the sofa near her head, while the other cupped her cheek, feeling the warmth of her skin against my fingertips.

The kiss deepened, I couldn't help but be captivated by her irresistible flavor.

She tasted like the most scrumptious chocolate, leaving me craving for more.

she abruptly broke the kiss and hurriedly removed my t-shirt, her gaze roaming hungrily over my exposed body.

A 'woah' escaped her lips, igniting a rush of desire within me.

unable to resist, I immediately closed the distance between our lips once again.

My addiction for her smooth lips already growing stronger with each passing moment.

I kissed her desperately and she kissed me back with same desperation.

Her warm hands explored every inch of my upper body, sending electric shocks coursing through me.

I felt myself growing hard down there.

She broke the kiss once more, teasing me with a mischievous smirk.

" So you too go to the gym every day, huh? " she playfully remarked, her eyes roaming over my sculpted physique.

My heart pounded wildly in my chest.

I was really a sporty person! I loved playing outdoor tennis and I would do gym frequently so I was sure that I had a good well-built physique.

" Assalam walikum bhai! We are here!!! " Suddenly, Najma's chirping voice was heard from the main door, making my eyes widen.

How could I forget that she was coming over with dinner?

And she knew the door password, so she could enter the living room at any moment.

I saw Ayezah's eyes widen too. I was hovering over her, shirtless.

In a rush, I immediately got up and stood straight, while she quickly straightened up and grabbed the ice pack, abruptly slamming it on her forehead in panic and hurry, she let out a slight hiss.

"careful," I said, as I attempted to pick up my t-shirt from the carpet.

But before I could put it on, Najma and her husband entered the hall.

"Bhai-" she stopped dead in her tracks, her eyes widening as she looked at me. Ayezah nervously got up from the couch and greeted Najma with a hesitant. "Oh hi, Najma!"

Najma blinked in surprise.

"It's so hot, I tell you!" I blurted out pretending, rolling up the t-shirt and trying to blow air from it, as if it were a fan.

"I know right! It's so damn hot" Ayezah joined in the act, tapping the ice pack all over her face.

Najma and Irfan looked at us blankly and then looked at each other.

suddenly, they burst into fits of laughter together loudly.

I looked at Ayezah, and she gazed back at me with the same nervousness.

" you guys are seriously so adorable! " Najma said between her nonstop laughter, she was holding her stomach with one hand while her other palm rested on her husband's shoulder for support.

" C'mon! We all are standing in the air-conditioned room! even a fool could find out easily." Irfan said laughing along with Najma.

I felt a bit embarrassed. I immediately put on my t-shirt.

" Oh god! look at their faces! Chill, you guys are husband wife! " Najma continued giggling.

I couldn't help but look away, cupping my nape, and from the corner of my eye, I noticed Ayezah's cheeks turning a shade of pastel pink probably due to embarrassment.

Chapter 6

Ayezah's POV:

" You could have just hit the bitch back, right on his head-lights, completely shattering his headlights! i mean how dare he ruin your favourite Range Rover? " Laila said throwing her fist in air, fuming in pure anger.

I was sitting inside my cabin now, with my legs neatly crossed and my arms crossed too, spinning on my rotating chair, lost in deep thoughts.

Who could it be? Could it be possibly the same red hoodie person?

" Ayeziii are you even listening? " Laila asked and i nodded absentmindedly.

" Thank god that you are fine! I swear Ayezii, if you would even get a single scratch, i would have haunt that bitch down and killed him brutally." She said while gritting her teeth.

" chill babe! I'm totally fine." I winked smilingly, assuring her.

"By the way did you notice anything except for the colour of car? like number plate or something." She asked squinting her eyes at me, as if she investigating.

" The whole thing happened so suddenly that I didn't even have time to process it. Before I could even think, the car zoomed away like a flash of lightning! I could hardly catch a glimpse of the number plate." I replied.

" I guess it's the same person in the red hoodie! I mean, red hoodie and then the same red-colored car, so maybe..." I trailed off, holding my jaw between my forefinger and thumb.

"Ugh, I have no idea who's behind all this! But as you said it might be the same person in the red hoodie. But I don't understand why red? are they trying to show that red means danger or something? It's just so ewwww! I mean, hello why do you want to associate such a hot color like red with negativity? It's supposed to represent love and passion! They've turned it into something dangerous." I shook my head in agreement with Laila's frustration.

" That's because red is also the colour of blood." I said.

" Oh! " she raised an eyebrow at me.

" okay then, if I were to get my hands on those bastards someday, I'd make sure to show them their favorite color, red, in the form of blood! " she smirked and I let out a chuckle.

My bestfriend can be quite violent sometimes.

"Anyways, don't worry! I'll get the CCTV footage of that road and track the car down soon!" she said confidently, and I nodded in agreement.

Hours passed as we tirelessly tried to track down the car, but the CCTV footage wasn't very clear, and it didn't provide much help.

We could only catch a glimpse of a few numbers from the license plate. Frustrated, we decided it was time to involve the cops.

Just as we were about to make the call, the receptionist call buzzed on my intercom. she announced to me that : ' Mr jones is here to see you ma'am'. I groaned and shut my eyes.

Alexander! I should have known!

Alexander Jones, the CEO of the Jones company, was not only the most annoying person I knew but also someone I despised to core.

We had been rivals since our university days, competing against each other in academics sports, and literally everything. And now, he had become my business rival as well.

He never missed an opportunity to mess with me, and I couldn't stand him at all.

Rubbing my temples, I reluctantly instructed the receptionist to let him in. I knew he would waste my time, but I also knew why he was here.

The morning incident was undoubtedly caused by him.

"Alexander!" I huffed, slumping into my seat and muttering to Laila after hanging up the intercom.

"What the fuck? Seriously! How could we miss him? He's surely that person in the red hoodie as well! I mean, the tacky red idea could only come from him!" Laila muttered.

"I know, right! And here I thought there's something serious happening. God, this man! I swear, I'll kill him someday!" I exclaimed, frustration evident in my voice.

Although Alexander was my rival, he posed no real danger. He simply enjoyed messing with me, and I had come to understand that his sole purpose was just to irritate the hell out of me.

So, if he turned out to be the person in the red hoodie, I knew I had to take a chill pill because he was just trying to scare me.

"I'm going back to my seat! I can't even stand that jerk's mere presence!" Laila muttered, clearly sharing my hatred for Alexander.

Her desk was conveniently located just outside my cabin, almost adjacent to it. I watched her figure retreat, sighing.

After a few long seconds, the insufferable Alexander himself sauntered into my cabin, wearing a sleek black suit, hands in pants pocket and the same annoyingly smug smirk.

I squeezed my eyes shut, reminding myself to stay calm, even though he had a talent for testing my patience to its limits.

"Heyyy sweetie!" He said.

"How was your wedding present this morning? Did you enjoy it?" I clenched my fist, knowing that he was here solely to provoke a reaction out of me.

"Hey Alexandar," I forced out through gritted teeth.

"It's Alex for you, babe!" he retorted, plopping down in front of me and casually crossing his legs. I couldn't help but roll my eyes, my annoyance clear as day.

"So, you finally got married, huh? I'm sad that you didn't even bother inviting your dear friend? " He pouted sadly and I held back the urge to throw up right there.

CRINGE ASF!

" I wonder who the idiot was that actually agreed to marry you. But when I saw the pictures in the media, I realized it was that dull, naive and dimwitted CEO of Khan Groups, Rahil Ahmed Khan!" he sneered.

"Okay, but what did you really see in him? I mean, he's not even hot and attractive like me, and he looks so dumb, lifeless and brainless—" Before he could finish his sentence, I swiftly grabbed the glass of water which was placed on my table, removed the lid, and splashed it directly onto his face.

What a jerk! How audacious of him to think that he could speak pure shit about my Rahil and i could hear it all calmly.

He immediately jumped up from his seat, soaked from head to upper pants.

"Oh my gosh, I'm so sorry!" I smirked, pretending innocence. "I was just trying offer you some water, but it slipped from my hands, splashing all over you. My apologies."

He wiped his face with his handkerchief, and chuckled looking down.

I couldn't help but press my lips together, a smirk forming on my face.

Slowly he rounded my desk and made his way towards my chair. "Ayezah Shah, you are one hell of a sly woman!" he exclaimed.

With a firm grip on the side of my chair, he turned it towards him, causing my eyes to slightly widen in surprise.

Leaning his face down, he whispered, "If you weren't this gorgeous, I would have killed you for doing that to me." His words were meant to intimidate, but internally, I scoffed.

I knew his threats were nothing but empty bravado. He was nothing more than a scaredy-cat, and I knew it.

"Oh, you wish! " I retorted, a smirk playing on my lips.

Standing up, I purposely stomped on his foot with my heel, the impact harsh and deliberate.

He winced in pain, quickly lifting his leg from the floor.

Well deserved bastard for daring to come so close to me.

I couldn't help but smirk, relishing in his discomfort.

"Oh, God! What's wrong with me?" I exclaimed, feigning innocence again as I apologized. "I just wanted to stand up! Did I hurt you?"

Inside, I couldn't help but smirk even more. He shot me a hard death glare.

"Youu-" he started, ready to charge towards me, his anger visible.

But I calmly interrupted him, my voice firm and determined. "Oh, and yeah, if you don't want me to involve the cops, then you better compensate for the loss you caused to my precious Range Rover. Otherwise, I'll have no choice but to bring the authorities into this, as it was a clear sign of you purposely trying to harm me."

As I spoke, his eyes widened slightly.

"Don't...don't involve the cops!" he stuttered out. "I have already sent you the money to compensate for your car's loss." His words were laced with nervousness, and I couldn't help but smirk at his sudden change in demeanor.

Told ya he was nothing more than a scaredy-cat with no brains. The audacity of him calling my husband brainless!

"That's great," I replied, my tone dripping with sarcasm. "And now, enough with the red hoodie drama of yours. It's so fucking annoying, you know?" I uttered, my irritation evident in my voice.

He furrowed his brows in confusion, pretending innocence as if he didn't understand a thing, as if he was hearing about the red hoodie for the first time.

" Red hoodie? " he mumbled out under his breath, looking at me confusingly.

Rolling my eyes at his feeble attempt, I returned to my seat, dismissing him with a wave of my hand.

"And now, if you're done wasting my time, just get lost! I'm exhausted," I declared. He gave me a mad glare, his anger simmering, before storming out of the cabin.

My exhausted self made its way towards the entrance of the mansion.

I was dead tired, all I wanted was to eat something warm and snuggle under the covers.

I opened the door, only to come face to face with Rahil, which left me startled a bit.

Shit, I totally forgot to inform him.

My phone screen broke earlier in the morning. As It was placed in the passenger seat, and due to that brainless jerk's stunt, my phone jerked forward and fell, shattering the screen. So, I had to give it for fixing.

Rahil scanned my body, his gorgeous brown orbs filled with so much worry and concern. Before I could even understand what was happening, he pulled me into his warm embrace, making me shock and go stiff.

It felt something new.

It felt so cozy and warm.

His care was clearly evident.

He always worries too much. He's just too sweet and nice to be true.

Gosh, I love this man so damn much.

I was admiring his worried self with a loud thumping heart, who was busy placing ice pack on my forehead bump. He was too close to my face, and the proximity made me blink.

"If you keep caring for me so deeply and keep leaning this close, I might just end up kissing you breathless."

I teasingly uttered those words, not at all expecting the response that followed. My breath caught in my throat as he leaned closer, his presence intoxicating.

Unable to resist, I surrendered to the allure of his luscious, tempting lips.

And oh my, the kiss was- Correction, those kisses were pure ecstasy.

They transported me to another realm, leaving me light-headed and washing away all my weariness in an instant.

His lips were addictive, like a delicious treat I couldn't get enough of.

And boy, was he a skilled kisser?

I couldn't help but wonder.

He was too good like way too good!

Our mouths moved in perfect sync, fueled by the same fire and desire reflected in his eyes, mirroring my own.

A gasped escaped my lips as I removed his t-shirt, revealing a body that could rival that of a Greek god. It was absolutely breathtaking, and I shamelessly gawked at his perfect body.

He took my lips in his in utter urgency.

The desperation in his kiss matched my own, and I eagerly returned his passion. My hands shamelessly explored the hard, sculpted muscles of his body, each touch igniting a new wave of desire within me.

Oh, how badly I wanted to replace my hand with my lips.

But before I could act on that impulse, our moment was interrupted by the arrival of his sister najma and her husband, turning the situation into a super awkward encounter.

The dinner too went by awkwardly. Najma kept giving both of us teasing looks, while her husband laughed intermittently between bites.

My cheeks, already red from the kiss, turned even redder with embarrassment.

Somehow, we managed to finish the dinner, and Najma and Irfan suddenly left, not before muttering a 'continue guys' together and laughing while winking at us.

Once they were gone, the air between me and Rahil was filled with an overwhelming sense of awkwardness.

I didn't know what to say. So, I stupidly blurted out a 'good night' and practically sprinted to my room.

Goodness, when did I become so foolish to run like that?

I groaned internally as soon as I entered the room. After showering and changing into my cozy clothes, I immediately crawled into bed.

Sleep was within reach, but all I could think about was the kiss.

Did he enjoy it as much as I did?

Was it going to be awkward with him now?

What was he doing right now? was he asleep already?

I couldn't help but let my mind wander, even though I was exhausted. The whole night, I tossed and turned, unable to sleep, as the kiss kept replaying in my mind every time I closed my eyes.

I hopped onto the treadmill. Increasing the speed a little more, my heart raced along, matching the rhythm of my feet pounding against the belt.

Beads of sweat formed on my forehead, trickling down my face and neck. I grabbed the fluffy white towel, neatly folding it, I gently tapped it against the damp skin of my neck and face, seeking some relief from the heat.

I had been working out at the gym for a hour now. I woke up early because sleep was nowhere in my eyes.

I slipped into my gym clothes and cautiously glanced out of my room, hoping not to catch a glimpse of him. But alas, he was nowhere to be seen.

with a mix of conflicting emotions, I hurriedly made my way to the gym, to do some workout and take my mind off the events of last night.

It felt both awkward and intriguing, this desire to avoid him yet secretly yearn for his presence.

What's really wrong with me? why would I avoid him? IDOIT Ayezah!

Letting out a sigh, I switched off the treadmill and made my way back to my room, craving a long, soothing shower.

Since I had discovered that jerk faced was behind the mysterious red hoodie incidents, I decided to take a day off from the office.

Why waste my precious day offs on such an idiotic good-for-nothing person?

After taking refreshing bath, I sprayed some delightful body mist which made me feel more fresh.

I slipped into a pastel purple crop top, its full sleeves cascading down perfectly fitting my arms, covering half of my palms.

The top accentuated my waist and revealed a hint of skin, paired with fitted white jeans. I left my hair cascading down my back.

For makeup : I applied moisturizer, a coat of mascara, and a nourishing lip oil.

I got ready and stepped outside the room, to have breakfast because I was literally starving now.

Descending the stairs with a casually, my heart skipped a beat as I caught sight of Rahil.

There he was, shirtless, wearing only pants, his upper body glistening with sweat, his front dampened locks falling over his forehead, almost hiding his eyes.

His one hand held the tennis racket and t-shirt which was dampened with sweat.

He had his tennis court at the backyard of the mansion. He loved playing tennis.

He gulped down the water from the bottle which he was holding in his other hand and damn I felt hot just by looking at him.

Why is he looking so incredibly attractive?

God this man blows out my sanity in seconds.

I gasped, my hand instinctively gripping the railing of stairs for support.

As he approached the stairs, he glanced up at me and our eyes locked instantly.

I felt as if an electric jolt passed between us, causing my heart to race uncontrollably.

He gaze into my eyes for few seconds before his eyes suddenly drifted to my lips, intensifying the already rapid pace of my heartbeat.

I swallowed nervously, chewing my lower lip, I clutched my snowflake pendant.

As if he suddenly realized what he was doing, he immediately averted his gaze from my lips.

Blinking nervously, he hurriedly tried to put on the dampened t-shirt, muttering a quick 'sorry sorry.'

I slowly and gracefully descent down the stairs. I couldn't resist teasing him, saying, "Not anything I haven't seen before."

A mischievous smirk formed on my lips as he blinked, still struggling with the t-shirt. I gracefully moved past him, feeling a warm blush rise to my cheeks, and made my way to the kitchen.

I didn't even realize how the whole day flew by, filled with these awkward encounters.

It felt like he was more embarrassed about our morning encounter now, trying to avoid me politely but still I felt him stealing glances in my direction.

As the day went on, I spent my time binge-watching few of my favourite shows inside my room.

Before I knew it, night had fallen. When I entered the living room, there he was, seated on the couch with his laptop on his lap and legs stretched on the floor.

He sensed my presence and looked up at me. Before things could get any more awkward and we turned into complete fools like we did all day, I decided to break the ice.

"Umm, I'm making dinner! What would you like to have?" I asked, nervously fiddling with my snowflake pendant.

Why on earth was I feeling so nervous?

He quickly got up, almost dropping his laptop, his actions screaming with nervousness.

"I... will cook," he stuttered, trying to stand up straight. I pressed my lips together to hold back a smile because he looked absolutely adorable when he was nervous.

"Nope, it's okay, I'll cook," I said firmly.

"No, no, I'll cook for both of us," he insisted. "I'm telling you, I'll cook!" I replied, my voice growing a little louder.

"And I'm also saying that I'll cook," he retorted. "Gosh, what's your problem?" I said, feeling frustrated.

"Okay, okay, fine! How about we cook together?" he suggested. I squinted my eyes at him. "Yeah, sure! " I replied.

" Wait, weren't we going to have a cooking competition? Do you remember your challenge?" I smirked. He raised his eyebrows and smirked back.

"Oh yeah! How about we compete then? You in?" he asked, and I nodded excitedly.

We found ourselves in the kitchen, both wearing the aprons, ready to compete against each other.

The kitchen was quite spacious, enough for both of us to cook on the huge slab.

I observed him expertly cutting the meat, I couldn't help but notice the grace with which his hands moved, veins subtly visible as he rolled up the sleeves of his brown sweatshirt.

So freaking HOT! as ALWAYS.

We had decided to prepare steaks.

I focused on my own cooking, Hardly shifting my gaze away from him.

Suddenly, he leaned towards my side, causing me to go stiff.

In that moment, I caught a whiff of his woody, musky scent making me dizzy, as he reached for something beside me.

He tilted his head, looking at me with a mischievous smirk playing on his lips?

Oh!

I quickly regained my composure and directed my attention to chopping a few cloves of garlic.

But then, something inside me stirred, and I slowly moved towards him, positioning myself between the counter and him. My palms behind, held the counter as I stood before him.

Our faces were mere inches apart, and I could see a flicker of surprise in his widened eyes.

His gaze roamed over my face, as if taking in every detail, and I couldn't help but notice the subtle gulp that escaped him as his eyes lingered on my lips.

A sly smirk danced across my own lips as I playfully made my way to the washbasin, conveniently located beside him.

I could sense his shaky breath behind me.

You can't tease the biggest tease herself and get away with it Rahil Ahmed khan.

Smirkingly I washed my hands in the basin.

we then playfully kept teasing each other, leaning closer to each other time to time.

As I sprinkled salt and pepper on the steak, preparing it for the oven, Rahil surprised me once again by leaning in near my face.

My eyes blinked in response, feeling his heavy breath against my skin. His intense gaze locked onto my eyes, then slowly dropped to my lips.

oh god! why is he staring at my lips so much today? Does he want to kiss me? Then why doesn't he just do it instead of torturing me like this?

I couldn't help but stutter, "What do you want...?"

" Lips." He muttered as if in some daze, his voice filled with desperation and longing that made me feel things.

His gaze remained fixated on my lips, and my eyes widened in surprise.

"What...?" I stammered.

He quickly realized his slip and hurriedly corrected himself, "Sm ooth... no I mean, butter. I want butter." with that, he swiftly moved to grab the butter from my side, breaking the tension that had built between us.

I let out a breath I didn't even realize I was holding as he retreated to his place.

We both grilled our steaks on by one and I platted the steak, with barbecue sauce.

Rahil skillfully added a generous amount of butter, enhancing the juiciness of the steak.

"Woah, it looks so tempting," I exclaimed, giggling and moving closer to him, stealing a glance at his steak.

He smiled warmly at me, saying " your looks more delicious." I shook my head, smiling.

"I'll take a picture of your steak!" I announced, grabbing my recently repaired phone.

Standing in front of him, I positioned myself between him and the counter. I captured a shot of the mouthwatering steak.

I couldn't help but be impressed by Rahil's plating skills. He truly had some talent.

I gazed at the picture I had captured, a smile spreading across my face as I thought of posting it on my instagram.

"Look, it looks absolutely delicious," I exclaimed, turning to Rahil who stood behind me.

My attention was back on my phone screen. Suddenly, I felt the firmness of his chest pressing against my back.

A jolt of electricity ran through my body as he leaned in, his cheek lightly brushing against mine as he peered down at the photo. "Umm, nice shot," he huskily whispered, his hands resting on the counter, trapping me completely between his arms.

His eyes remained fixed on the phone as I tilted my head to look at him, he too turned his eyes towards me as if sensing my gaze on him.

Our gazes locked, and in that moment, our noses collided.

A rush of anticipation coursed through me as our foreheads and noses touched.

"We should take a picture of your steak too," he breathed heavily, his voice laced with desire. I fought the urge to press my lips against his, knowing that once I did, there would be no turning back.

He pulled away, opening his eyes as if trying to regain control.

I swallowed hard, reminding myself that we were here for cooking, and not to give in to our desires. He took out his phone, capturing a shot of my steak, and I couldn't help but smile.

"Not Addin please! You know very well that grumpy guy has something against me," I groaned.

Rahil and I were standing in the living room, deep in discussion about finding a judge for our cooking competition. It had completely slipped our minds that we hadn't arranged for one yet.

I have decided to call Laila and he said he would call Addin to which I immediately refused.

I know that grumpy creature, who unfortunately happens to be my cousin and Rahil's best friend, would, of course, favor Rahil and make him win.

Rahil paused for a moment, contemplating my words. "If it's like that, then Laila too would ofcourse make you win only," he pointed out.

"Well then, call your secretary Adam!" I suggested.

"Since he's your secretary and friend, also he doesn't have anything against me, maybe it will be kind of equal. Laila and Adam can judge together." I completed saying.

Rahil nodded in agreement. We both reached for our phones, dialing the numbers of our respective secretaries to invite them over for dinner and judgment.

Laila arrived first, her laughter filling the room as we explained the whole cooking competition ordeal.

She found our competitiveness amusing, and silly. I shot her a glare, silently dismissing her teasing, while Rahil flashed her a nervous smile like always.

Laila then excused herself to go to the washroom. And just as she left, Adam walked in.

Adam Hussain, the bubbliest and coolest person ever. He had this infectious energy that could light up any room.

Not only was he Rahil's good friend and secretary but he had also become a close friend of mine ever since our companies collaborated.

He was just as sweet as his boss.

As Adam entered, he couldn't contain his excitement. "Woah, hey gorgeous!" he exclaimed, spreading his arms wide open for a hug.

His words made me chuckle, and I was ready to hug him back.

But before I could, Rahil swiftly stepped in between us, wrapping his arms tightly around Adam, and I blinked in surprise.

Rahil hugged him with such intensity, almost squeezing the air out of poor guy. I could see Adam struggling for breath as Rahil patted his back hardly and vigorously, saying, "You greet your boss first!"

I stood there frozen on my spot.

Chapter 7

Rahil's POV:

I was experiencing a surge of emotions all together that were very new to me.

Anger. Frustration. Irritation.

Normally, i was quite distant from these emotions and i rarely got any, as I have always been a calm person.

But today, something has triggered within me making me feel it all together.

As I stood across the kitchen slab, watching Adam and Ayezah happily clicking pictures of steaks, a scowl formed on my face. Laila, standing by my side, shared the same disapproving expression.

Earlier, Ayezah had taken a nice shot of the steak, and she had showed it to Adam saying she would be posting it on instagram but my over smart secretary insisted that he could capture an even better one as if he was a professional photographer.

I rolled my eyes at him internally.

I couldn't help but feel my frustration growing more with each passing second.

Why the hell were they standing so damn close and clicking pictures? I mean there was absolutely no need to stand this close to click pictures, you can click pictures by keeping some safe distance too.

Ayezah threw her head back and laughed out loud when Adam whispered something into her ears, their gazes were fixed on the phone.

Okay WOW now he is whispering into her ears!

What is it that he is trying to keep so confidential?

And what on earth is so funny that Ayezah has been giggling so much?

My fist is suddenly itching to punch something hardly!

when Laila returned from the washroom, she was enlarged seeing Adam.

She threw a fit, refusing to taste and judge the food with the jerk alongside.

And honestly, I can't blame her. Adam was actually acting like a total jerk today. I mean, usually, he's a nice and sweet person, one of the best secretaries one could have. He's smart, talented, and hardworking too. But today, I don't know why he was pushing me beyond the limits of mere annoyance.

I mean, why would you even try to hug Ayezah like that? I get that you're friends with her and all, but seriously, have some boundaries, will you?

I glanced at Laila to see her piercing glare fixed on Adam. Earlier, Ayezah somehow convinced Laila to stay because she was all set to leave when she saw Adam here.

I observed Laila to notice how hardly she was glaring at Adam, It was as if her eyes were shooting daggers, filled with an intense fury.

The sheer intensity of her gaze made it seem like she could unleash her wrath and bring him down in an instant.

Why is she so angry?

I mean today Adam didn't even attempt to flirt with her. Instead, he greeted her with genuine cheerfulness, while she ignored him brutally.i thought she would be pissed off with him because he would flirt with her but today he didn't and yet she seem so freaking mad?

"Whoa, you're really good at taking pictures!" Ayezah exclaimed bringing me out of my trance.

I looked at her to see her smile lighting up her face as she looked at the phone screen.

I quickly pulled out my phone and checked the picture I had taken of Ayezah's steak earlier.

It was a bit blurry, but heyy blurry pictures are trendy these days as they give off those cool, aesthetic vibes everyone is into.

"I know right! I'm totally awesome." Adam chimed in, leaning a little low and jutting out one of his shoulder blade towards Ayezah as if telling her to pat his back.

How childish! I scoff internally.

Ayezah chuckled and shook her head. She then raised her hand and patted his back gently, still giggling.

Ha! she really didn't had to!

I bit my inner cheek, feeling my frustration reach its limit.

Oh god! What's up with me today? Why am i feeling so riled up suddenly?

what's this weird feeling I'm getting?

Laila suddenly banged her palm on the kitchen slab, making their laughter to come at an abrupt halt and capturing both of their attention.

"If you two are done, then let's get to the tasting and judging. I want to go home!" she exclaimed, her tone as cold as ice.

Ayezah seemed taken aback by the sudden change in Laila's demeanor.

" Ah sorry Ayezi.. I mean since when are you into clicking pictures of food and posting on social media? " She completed sounding frustrated and sulky.

"It's just that I wanted a perfect picture because Rahil's plating is so impeccable. I've never seen such a beautifully arranged and delicious-looking steak in my life." Ayezah explained.

" Also about social media, I just want to brag about my perfect husband's cooking skills, so yeaa! " She shrugged and suddenly looked at me smiling widely.

My heart beat raced to an abnormal level as I gazed deeply into her eyes. Her words stir something in me.

"My perfect husband"

She thinks I'm perfect?

She gazed at me with the sweetest smile, and I couldn't help but smile back at her, feeling a rush of warmth spreading at the back of my neck.

"Okay, princess, as you say! Let's head over to taste and judge the steaks! " Adam cheerfully exclaimed, walking towards Laila and extending his hand as if asking her to hold it.

Laila shot him a look that screamed, 'Are you seriously doing this right now?' Sporting a poker face, she glared at him and made her way towards the table. Adam simply shrugged his shoulders and followed behind her.

"Shall we heat up the steaks?" Ayezah asked, and I nodded in agreement.

We popped the steaks in the microwave, heating it up.

We then carried our respective plates and made our way to the dining table. But out of nowhere, Adam appeared and insisted on helping Ayezah.

Ugh, what's his deal? Can't he give her some space for a while?

He's my secretary, Shouldn't he be focused on assisting me? Why is he behaving so clingy towards her?

As soon as I reached the dinning room, My eyes widened as I spotted Adam, ready to sit beside Ayezah's chair.

"ADAM!" I yelled, my voice echoing through the room, causing both Adam and Ayezah to flinch.

"Uh, um, sorry, I mean, you should sit with Laila since she's the judge. One side for judging and one side for contestants, you know," I nervously stammered, flashing a hurried smile as I quickly made my way towards the chair beside Ayezah and sat on it, slightly nudging Adam aside.

Adam gave me a weird look, muttering 'it's not like it's some real contest.' under his breath but nonetheless obeyed saying a small 'okay sir' and settled himself beside Laila.

Adam placed his palm on his cheek, leaning his elbow on the table, and gazed at Laila with a look of pure adoration in his eyes.

she shot him a hard glare and uttered, "Look away, you weirdo creep."

He shook his head, saying " You are so damn pretty! It's difficult for me to look away."

She scoffed, replying. "You make me feel nauseous."

" And you make me feel like love do exist." He replied without missing a beat.

His words hung in the air, leaving everyone momentarily stunned.

Is this the same guy I hired as my secretary? Well, as long as he's not flirting with Ayezah, I suppose it's fine.

Laila looked stunned and flushed as her eyes widen. She blinked her eyes, trying to mask her shock expression immediately.

" Rahil Jij! Do you mind hiring a new secretary? Because I'm about to murder your current one!" Laila exclaimed, her glare fixed firmly on Adam, who simply looked down, shook his head and chuckled in response.

"Nope, I don't mind," I blurted out without thinking, the words slipping from my lips.

Everyone turned to look at me with surprise.

Adam chimed in saying "Sir? Seriously?" with a wince.

"Guys!!! Let's focus on judging, shall we?" Ayezah interjected, capturing everyone's attention.

Laila took the first bite of the sizzling steak, while Ayezah and I eagerly awaited her judgment.

She savored the flavors, chewing thoughtfully before finally looking up at our expectant faces. "Mmm, both of them taste absolutely delicious," she said, her words muffled by the food in her mouth.

Ayezah grew impatient and urged, "Come on, Laila! Which one is better?" Irritated by the time it was taking her to respond.

"I can't really tell, Ayezi. Both steaks are equally mouthwatering." Laila replied.

Ayezah let out a frustrated 'Tch!' saying"Adam, you tell me!" she turned towards Adam, who was busy staring at Laila.

Caught off guard he stammered out "Um, honestly, in terms of presentation, Rahil sir's plating wins."

Laila's eyes widened as she shot back, "Ha! Are you saying my best friend doesn't know how to plate a dish?"

Adam quickly backtracked, "No, no, princess! When did I even say that? That's not what I actually meant. I said that Rahil sir's plating is just exceptional!" Laila threw him a hard deathly glare.

Ayezah interjected, trying to diffuse the tension, "Laila, it's okay. Adam is just saying the truth – Rahil's plating is outstanding."

"Well, yours is equally impressive!" I chimed in.

Ayezah disagreed, insisting, "It's good, but not like yours, Rahil. Your plating is simply perfect."

" Yours is perfect too Ayezah!" I exclaimed.

" You are not getting it Rahil! yours is beyond perfect! " Ayezah said her voice raising a little.

" Nah it's not that great! " I immediately replied.

" Yess it is, I'm telling you! " Ayezah almost yelled.

The argument seemed to escalate without us even realizing it until Laila and Adam called us both over.

"Okay, okay, guys! It's finalised by the judges that you both have done equally fantastic plating and both gets the points," Laila declared, bringing the bickering to a halt.

We paused and looked at them.

Adam took a bite of the steak, savoring the flavors as he chewed.

"Oh man, both of these steaks are absolutely tasty, guys! you both have done a really amazing job. But Ayezah's steak, oh my goodness, it's incredibly delicious," he exclaimed, his words slightly muffled by the food in his mouth.

Laila gave Adam a sharp look and retorted. " Excuse me? Rahil jij has absolutely nailed it too! What do you mean Ayezah's steak is the tastiest? Rahil jij's steak is equally mouthwatering!"

"Oh come on, princess! What's your problem? Are you trying to pick a fight with me?" Adam, responded frustrated a little with Laila's disagreement to his judgement. She was neither letting him decide nor deciding her self.

Laila shot a furious glare at him before replying, "Dream on! Do you really think I'm that jobless to waste my time arguing with you? I don't even want to talk to you, let alone fight!"

"Oh really, and why is it exactly that you don't even want to talk to me?" Adam questioned, his voice tinged frustration and anger.

" We're supposed to be judging the food together, and our goal should be to determine a winner. But your plans don't seem to align with that and I don't know what's gotten you so riled up! " he added.

Laila's fury grew even stronger and her face contorted completely with anger.

" WHAT! Do you think I'm riled up? " Laila yelled.

" Ofcourse you are! Look at your face it's turn whole red with anger." Adam muttered pointing a finger at her.

The tension in the air was palpable.

This exchange of harsh words escalated into an extreme heated argument between Adam and Laila, leaving Ayezah and me exchanging concerned glances.

We silently communicated through our eyes, both thinking : 'This isn't going anywhere.'

With a heavy sigh, we shook our heads in unison, looking at our secretaries bickering with each other like kindergarteners.

After a continuous 10 minutes of their bickering, Ayezah and I somehow managed to calm them down by assuring them that we believe both of our steaks are equally delicious and that we didn't need any judgment anymore.

However, they still threw a fit and continued arguing, but thankfully, it all came to a halt after a long 15 minutes.

we all were now eating the steaks in silence when Adam broke the peace, boasting about his cooking skills.

"I can cook really delicious chateaubriand, it's a French dish which is basically a sizzling hot steak." Adam chirped excitedly.

" Really? I've heard about it but I never had it, Is it tasty? "Ayezah asked with widened eyes.

" ofcourse it's too delicious! You will love it I'm damn sure! " He went on and on, boasting about how good of a cook he is.

Laila was quietly enjoying her steak, least bothered by the person, who was busy boasting about his cooking skills.

It seemed like he was trying to impress Laila by indirectly telling it to Ayezah. Judging by the way he kept glancing at Laila from time to time.

" If you want, I can make it after we finish these. These steaks won't be enough for all of us for the dinner anyway." Adam said and Ayezah nodded enthusiastically, looking clearly impressed by his offer.

HA! I too can make chateaubriand! Why on earth is she looking so impressed? I mean it's not a big deal.

"I can cook chateaubriand too," I blurted out without even realising the my thoughts slipped from my lips, catching everyone's attention. Adam gave me a look meanwhile Laila smirked at me, as if teasing me.

Ayezah looked at me for few seconds and then smiled hesitantly, saying "Wow, that's really cool!"

I looked down at my plate, closed my eyes, and continued chewing.

Ah why would I say? I feel so embarrassed.

" uff, princess, you're quite clumsy eater." I looked up to see Adam saying this to Laila.

He extended his hand towards Laila's corner of lips and what happened next left everyone stunned.

He ran his thumb along the edge of Laila's mouth, delicately wiping off the barbecue sauce. Then, he brought his thumb to his own lips, sucking it with a mischievous smirk.

Laila's eyes widened, as if they were about to fall right onto the floor.

I glanced at Ayezah, only to find her equally shocked.

After a few seconds of utter silence, Laila suddenly yelled, "YOU-UUU! HOW DARE YOU?? DO YOU HAVE DEATH WISH? I WILL CHOP YOUR THUMB OFF! "

Adam quickly got up from his seat, running and hiding behind my chair. " Sir please save me from this wild cat." He muttered.

I blinked my eyes, trying to comprehend the situation.

Laila, fuming in anger, shouted, " HA WILD CAT? WAIT, I'LL SHOW YOU HOW WILD I CAN GET WITH VIOLENCE!"

They then started running through the entire dining room, bickering and fighting.

Adam kept teasing Laila, while Laila kept yelling at him.

Laila then somehow caught him in firm grip, twisting his hand behind his back, making him wince in pain loudly.

"You both can continue your childish antics later, come here and finish the dinner NOW! " Ayezah's voice echoed through the room, her tone stern and commanding. In an instant, both Adam and Laila halted in their tracks.

They returned to their respective seats, silently glaring at each other, and resumed eating.

As we neared the end of our eating, Adam's cheerful voice again reached my ears.

"Ayezah, are you a clumsy eater too?" He chuckled and I looked at Ayezah to see the barbecue sauce smudge over the corner of her lips.

My eyes widened, and in that moment, an inexplicable impulse overcame me.

Without thinking, I immediately extended my hand towards Ayezah's mouth and delicately wiped away the barbecue sauce from the corner of her lips with my thumb.

And then, almost as quickly as I had acted, I brought my thumb to my own lips, sucking off the sauce.

A collective gasp filled the room as everyone's eyes locked onto me.

Laila and Adam were staring at me with their eyes wide open and jaw hung low.

"I was actually going to pass her the tissues." Adam muttered slowly.

I looked at Ayezah, her expression screamed that she was beyond shock.

She blinked her eyes at me.

Oh god what did I just do?

And in that moment, I wished the ground would swallow me whole.

I stood at the corner of the kitchen, folding my arms around my chest, my gaze fixed on my secretary, a mix of annoyance and exhaustion evident in my eyes.

As soon as we finished eating the dinner, Adam insisted on cooking chateaubriand steak. I immediately declined, as the steaks we had prepared earlier were already so fulfilling.

But he was stubborn enough that he kept insisting and Ayezah gave in to his request.

I don't understand what's his problem? Doesn't he have any work to do? Oh yeah, work! I should give him more work from now on, since it's clear that he has way too much free time.

Adam busied himself in the kitchen for the past 20 minutes now and Ayezah stood beside him, lending a helping hand.

Laila, clearly annoyed, stormed out of the house five minutes ago, saying that she is too exhausted and want to get some sleep.

I felt the urge to kick this clingy man out of my house as well, but I restrained myself.

"And now for the final step," Adam chirped, as if he were the expert.

"We need to raise the flame," he continued, his voice filled with enthusiasm. "You know, the high flame cooking where the dish is lit on fire completely, giving it that perfect char texture that's incredibly yummy."

He carefully lifted the pan off the stove, and with a swift and deliberate motion, he added something to the pan, causing an instant burst of flames that danced and flickered in the kitchen.

The whoosh sound of the fire engulfing the pan filled the room, and suddenly in the next moment, I hear is Ayezah's piercing scream.

I immediately rushed to her side.

"No, no, no!" she stumbled back, her voice filled with desperation.

" NOOO, PLEASE!" She yelled, her words echoed in the room as she stumbled once again, falling to the floor. I instinctively reached out, catching her by the waist, trying to comprehend what was happening.

"Hey, what happened?" Adam asked, his voice filled with worry.

" Ayezah? What's wrong? Are you hurt? " I asked.

I noticed her gaze remained fixed on the towering flames, her breathing becoming heavy and audible.

I could see her chest rise and fall rapidly, her body trembling with fear.

"Please, don't!" she cried out suddenly, her voice filled with pain.

"It stings and hurts so much, please! I'm sorry, Mom!" Her words struck me, leaving me frozen in place.

What?

"Ayezah, listen to me," I pleaded, attempting to hold her cheek gently, but she jerked my hand away, her eyes still locked on the raging fire.

"No, no, please! I'll try my best, don't do this!" she yelled again, tears streaming down her cheeks.

My heart race seeing her condition. I have never ever witnessed her like this.

"What's happening to her?" Adam asked worriedly.

"Stop the goddamn fire!" I yelled at Adam, frustration and panic lacing my voice.

He immediately nodded, understanding the urgency in my tone, and swiftly grabbed a jug of water.

He poured the entire jug onto the blazing pan, repeating the action until the fire finally subsided.

The hissing sound of the extinguishing flames filled the room.

Ayezah sat frozen on her spot, her gaze distant and unfocused, as if she was physically present but mentally somewhere else entirely.

"Ayezah," I called out to her, my voice filled with concern, my own breath heavy from the adrenaline coursing through my veins.

She swallowed and looked at me, her teary eyes meeting mine, and in that moment, my heart shattered into a million pieces.

The pain etched on her face was unbearable to witness.

Next moment she sprang to her feet, and rushed upstairs.

I immediately followed her behind, my heart pounding loudly in my chest, echoing the fear and worry that consumed me.

Chapter 8

- -

Ayezah's POV:

Breathe in breathe out, breathe in breathe out.

I kept repeating the mantra in my mind. My chest tightened, constricting like a vice around my heart, as its rhythmic thumping reverberated through my entire being.

I clutched onto my chest trying to inhale and exhale.

My heart was beating with so much urgency, as if it would just burst out right now.

My back is pressed against the closed door of my room, tears were flowing down my cheeks without a break.

" What the fuck? Stop already." I muttered to myself, wiping away the tears harshly and desperately with the back of my palm.

" Ayezah please open the door for once,please." Rahil's voice calls out from outside, pleading me to open the door, followed by Adam's voice echoing the same plea.

It's been I don't know how long since I rushed into my room and locked myself.

Rahil and Adam keep begging me to open the door, their words somewhere sounded distant and I couldn't comprehend anything.

I try to focus on my breathing but all the bad memories come rushing back, flooding my mind, making it difficult for me to breathe.

The click of a lighter going on and off,fills the room as she plays with the lighter turning it off and on.

My mom's piercing gaze fixed on my trembling figure.

" Since my dear daughter feels really cold all the damn time. why not i provide you some heat? " I hear her say and next second lighter's raising flame is right before my eyes.

" NOOO " I yelled loudly, covering my eyes with both of my palms and fell on my knees crying hard, the memory is so vivid that it seems like it's happening right now infront of me.

I shut my eyes, my chest heaving up and down, tears streaming down effortlessly.

" Ayezah!! Ayezah open the door right now, you are scaring me." Rahil's panicked voice reverberated through the air as he pounded on the door with all his might.

In that moment, a lump formed in my throat, I gulped and hastily wiped away the tears that streamed down my face.

Clutching my delicate snowflake pendant tightly in my trembling hand, I anxiously chewed on my bottom lip, my mind racing with thoughts.

" My precious babie girl." Mom's warm smile illuminated the room as she gently placed the pendant around my neck.

" You look so cute." She whispered pecking my small nose, her voice filled with love.

" This is a very special pendant for my little princess from her mom. Never, ever take it off, okay? If you ever feel that something is wrong, and you don't feel at ease, just hold onto this pendant and take a deep breath. It will bring you comfort."

Her tender words were accompanied by sweet kisses on my cheeks and forehead. I couldn't contain my joy as she lifted my six-year-old self off the ground and twirled me around, my and her laughter filling the air.

Now, as I opened my tear-filled eyes, I clutched the pendant even tighter.

" Ayezah please! "

Rahil's vulnerable plea reached my ears, and in an instant, I sprang to my feet.

Swallowing hard, I spoke, my voice cracking and shaky.

"Rahil... I'm sorry, but can you please leave me alone? I'm too exhausted and just want to sleep, please." I completed my sentence, my voice trembling.

"Are you okay, Ayezah?" Rahil hurriedly asked, concern evident in his voice.

I nodded, tears streaming down my face, and managed to say, "Yes, yes, I'm fine."

"Please, let me in," he pleaded. The way he sounded so desperate and vulnerable tugged at my heart, causing an ache to form within me.

"Please, Rahil, I really need to be alone. I just want to sleep," I whispered, fighting back the urge to cry.

"But-" he started, only to be interrupted by my me.

"Please," I mumbled, my chin wobbling.

Silence enveloped us, lingering for a few agonizing seconds, and then I heard the sound of footsteps slowly fading away.

I think he's gone.

I slumped down, and rested my head against the closed door, shutting my eyes.

Turning off the shower, I let out a deep sigh and wrapped my freshly bathed self in white fluffy bathrobe.

The morning had arrived, but I hadn't managed to get a wink of sleep.

The night had been so unsettling that a throbbing pain pulsed through my head.

I change into a full-sleeved white cardigan that felt like a warm, woolen t-shirt against my skin. Pairing it with black fitted jeans, I took a moment to lazily tie my hair into a loose ponytail, allowing a few strands to frame my face.

I slipped on my black, long overcoat and dangled my white sling bag on one of my shoulder blade.

I opened the door to my room only to widen my eyes.

There, right next to the door of my room, Rahil sat down with his back pressed against the wall.

Eyes closed, head resting against the wall, One knee up, another leg spread on the ground, he seemed to have spent the entire night here?

My heart thumped hard and fast at the very thought.

Why would he do that?

Last night, I acted like a complete madwoman, and he must have been shocked by my behavior.

It's so damn embarrassing!! What should I do oh god? I cried internally.

Unable to resist, I knelt in front of his sleeping form. I couldn't help but admire his gorgeous face.

His beautiful, long lashes rested on his perfect cheek bones, his hair falling messily over his forehead, partially concealing his closed eyes.

I held back the urge to trace my fingertips along his perfect features.

I drank in every perfect feature of his face, captivated by his handsomeness.

Can someone look so damn attractive even while sleeping?

Suddenly, a memory flashed in my mind, and a smile spread across my lips as I recalled how Rahil had been jealous of Adam.

You see, Adam and I were actually trying to make Laila jealous. Adam had asked for my help in pursuing Laila, believing that she had feelings for him too.

But Laila, being Laila, would never admit it. Who knows her better than me, right? We devised a plan to make her jealous, but it became crystal clear that Rahil was also affected by it. And that realization filled me with giddiness and happiness.

I glided across the ice once again, but suddenly found myself landing on my butt with a resounding thud. A hiss escaped my lips as I felt the sting of my scraped palms against the icy floor.

I pushed aside the pain and stood up, gliding again. But with each attempt, I couldn't seem to find my balance.

It's been almost 1 hour that i have been trying to skate. I was here because I wanted to clear my mind.

with a deep breath, I rose to my feet once more, controlling the tears of frustration that threatened to escape.

"Come on, Ayezah," I whispered to myself.

I propelled myself forward, the wind caressing my face as I glided effortlessly for a few precious seconds. But alas, I found myself falling once again.

wiping away the frustrated tears that welled up in my eyes, and started rolling down my cheeks, I scolded myself. " what the fuck is wrong with me? why I'm I crying so much? Gosh I'm so sick of this."

I made my way off the ice rank and drink few sips of water. My hands trembled slightly as I reached into my overcoat pocket and retrieved my phone.

I discovered numerous missed calls and text from three people : Rahil, Laila and Adam.

I had sent Rahil a message earlier, informing him that I had some urgent work to take care of and I would be returning late.

His response, consisting of five unread messages, remained untouched for now.

I was embarrassed to face or even talk to him. What do I do with myself?

Adam had sent apologetic texts, and I reassured him, texting back a small ' it's really fine and I'm okay.'

It wasn't his mistake; he had no idea.

Just as I was about to reply to Laila's texts, her call suddenly popped up.

I answered, but before I could utter a word, her voice boomed through the phone, causing me to quickly move it away from my ear to shield myself from her yelling.

" THE HELL IS WRONG WITH YOU? WHY DIDNT YOU BOTHER CALLING ME FOR ONCE? AND WHERE THE FUCK ARE YOU RIGHT NOW? "

I remained silent as she continued, expressing her worry and frustration. Apparently, Adam had spilled the beans earlier in the morning to Laila and she had rushed to Khan Mansion to find me, only to discover my absence.

"Ayeziii, are you okay?" Laila finally asked, her tone softening as she sensed my silence.

I hummed in response, unable to form any words.

"Oh God, I really want to strangle that stupid Adam!" she exclaimed, her frustration palpable.

"No, it's not his fault. He didn't know," I interjected, shaking my head.

"Whatever." Laila sighed out.

" WAIT! you're at the ice rink, aren't you?" she asked, catching me off guard.

"Ummm, I- umm." I fumbled awkwardly, knowing that Laila wasn't a fan of me going ice skating.

"Ya Allah, what do I do with this girl! Why, Ayezah? why do you have to choose that place always whenever you are upset?" she exclaimed.

"You know I love it here! Skating helps me clear my mind-" I began, but she quickly interjected, saying, "But still, you don't have the best memories at the ice rink."

I immediately interrupted her this time, insisting, "It's not like that, okay! I have good memories too."

I could hear her let out a huge sigh.

"Anyways, I'm coming there, so stay put," she declared, and I couldn't help but yell, "NOO!"

"I mean, I just want to be alone for a while, please," I quickly added.

"Not happening. You need someone by your side, and I'm coming, that's it," she stated firmly before abruptly ending the call.

I sighed, contemplating leaving the ice rank immediately because only I knew how stubborn my best friend could be, and right now, I really needed some solitude.

Laila was definitely my person; she had always been there for me. But sometimes, I just craved being alone especially when I felt really upset and drained. I didn't want to face anyone. It's just how I'm.

Rahil's POV:

It's already 11:00 pm and my patience is hanging by a loose thread.

Ayezah still hasn't returned home. I mean, I know she said she would be late, but at least she could send me a text to let me know where she is or reassure me that she is all safe right?

The whole day, she didn't reply to any of my texts or answer any of my calls.

when I woke up earlier outside her room, I found a blanket over me and a pillow supporting my back.

I knew it was Ayezah's doing because I could faintly smell her sweet scent in my sleep. But I was just too exhausted to open my eyes, and now I regret it so much.

I don't understand what's going on with her. I really want to talk to her, but she's avoiding me.

Just then, my phone buzzed, and I quickly answered. It was Adam, my secretary, calling.

As I held the phone, my grip tightened on it, and raw anger surged through me.

I had specifically asked Adam to track Ayezah's phone, and now he's telling me it's showing a '24/7 bar' as her location!

Her entire day of ignoring me was already making me angry, but this news just fueled my anger even more.

I rushed outside, throwing on a brown overcoat quickly.

I hopped into the car and started driving.

What on earth is wrong with her? A bar? Seriously? Don't she realise that it's too late?

How can she be so irresponsible? I know that she is more than capable of protecting herself yet it's dangerous to be out, especially at a darn bar!

The thought of something happening to her made my knuckles tighten. My heartbeat racing with each passing second.

I pressed down on the accelerator, speeding up and kept driving hastily until I reached the bar.

I quickly parked my car and dashed inside, the anticipation pulsing through my veins.

As I stepped into the bar, the overpowering scent of alcohol and smoke assaulted my nostrils, already making me feel queasy.

The dim lights cast an unsettling atmospheric glow, revealing a bustling crowd of people.

My heart raced as I scanned the room, desperately searching for her. And then, there she was, near the bar, but what I witnessed ignited a fire of fury within me.

A man, leaning in, attempting to forcefully kiss her.

Without hesitation, Ayezah retaliated with a swift and powerful punch to his face, her voice echoing through the bar as she screamed out loud. "Stay the fuck away from me bastard! "

The sudden commotion drew the attention of everyone.

I quickly rushed towards them.

The man, seething with anger, spat out, "Bitch! How dare you hit me? I'll show you your place!"

He raised a glass bottle, causing my eyes to widen in alarm.

Instinctively, I positioned myself between them, wrapping my arms tightly around Ayezah in a shielding embrace.

The glass bottle collided with my arm breaking harshly, the shards piercing through my flesh, sending a sharp, searing pain coursing through me.

In that moment, my entire body trembled with anger.

What if I hadn't arrived in time? What if he had managed to harm Ayezah with that glass bottle, inflicting a stinging pain upon her?

My gaze turned towards the man, who appeared beyond drank as he was unsteady on his feet.

with my arms still wrapped around Ayezah's shoulder, a surge of fury consumed me as I glared at him.

" Even if a single piece of glass had pierced my wife's skin, I would have made sure to break every fucking bottle in this bar over your head," I declared, my voice dripping with anger, my pulse quickening with each passing second.

" Who the fuck are you?" the man yelled out with drowsy eyes and charged towards me, I landed a hard punch across his jaw and he knocked out on the floor instantly.

"Rahil?" she called out, her voice slightly slurred.

I turned to look at her, and my heart sank as I saw her half-open eyes and flushed cheeks. It was evident that she was drunk.

"How did you..." she began, her brow furrowing in confusion.

Taking a deep breath, I composed myself and gently guided her outside the noisy bar.

" Let gooooo of meeee!!! I don't wanna talk to youuuu" she slurred, trying to free her hand from my grip. Her words fell on deaf ears as I held onto her palm firmly.

Once we were outside, I released my grip, she immediately stumbled to go inside and I instinctively grasped her wrist, leading her a little further away from the bar.

"What's wrong with you? Leave me!" she yelled in frustration as I continued to drag her away. I stopped, feeling my patience reaching its limits, and turned to face her.

"Seriously, what's wrong with me? What the hell is wrong with you, Ayezah? I never thought you drink?" I exclaimed.

She appeared somewhat sober now, realization dawning upon her as she blinked.

"Leave me alone," she said, her voice filled with a mix of tiredness and vulnerability.

I gave her a look of disbelief.

"You seriously want me to leave you in this condition?" I asked.

"I'm fine..." she replied, but suddenly she stumbled backward, and I instinctively caught her by the waist.

"Oh, surely you are," I taunted feeling furious.

She held her head, wincing slightly still in my arms and my gaze softened.

Guiding her to sit on a nearby bench, I knelt in front of her.

She looked into my eyes, and I returned her gaze, we locked our eyes for few precious seconds.

Suddenly, tears welled up in her eyes, and she burst into loud sobs making my eyes widened.

"Hey, hey, what happened?" I asked, my voice filled with panic, as she cried even louder, burying her face in her palms.

"Please, tell me what's wrong. Why are you crying?" I pleaded, gently trying to remove her palms from her face.

"I was hiding from you," she sniffed, her voice choked with crying.

"I felt so embarrassed, and now I'm even more embarrassed that I can't help but cry." She cried even louder this time, her tears continued to flow, and I looked at her blinking and next second a chuckle escaped my mouth on its own.

She glared at me with her tears filled eyes," What's so funny, huh? Here I am, feeling so embarrassed, and you're laughing," her fists now pounding against my chest as she started hitting me continuously.

I held her fists firmly in my grip, looking into her eyes deeply.

She looked so adorable ryt now that i couldn't help myself. I softly kiss her clenched hands one by one and she froze on her spot instantly.

Perhaps she was still slightly under the influence of alcohol, as Ayezah Shah behaving like this seemed unlikely to me.

A sweet smile played on my lips as I spoke softly, "You're such a babie." I chuckled, shaking my head.

" sweetheart, I'm your husband, and you never have to feel embarrassed around me, okay?" I muttered and noticed her cheeks flush an even deeper shade of pink, and I resisted the urge to kiss them.

Her eyes slightly grew wider making her look more cute.

Pinkish cheeks, reddish nose, her inviting and irresistible smooth lips. Oh god!

I swallowed hard, looking away.

"Why are you such a green flag?" she winced suddenly, catching my attention and amusing me.

"And why are you behaving so adorable?" I blurted out, causing her to blink rapidly.

We exchanged awkward glances, and I decided to break the tension.

"Ummm..Anyway, tell me what happened to you yesterday?" I asked.

"I can't tell you," she sighed, her reply filled with a hint of sadness.

"Why? Don't you trust me enough?" I cupped her cheeks gently, leaning closer to her face, not minding the blood that had stained her one cheek slightly from my injured hand.

She locked her gaze with mine, her delicate palms reached out to my cheeks caressing them, bringing a sense of relief within me.

Our foreheads and noses touched, and she grazed her nose against mine, causing my breath to hitch and my heartbeat raced.

In the next moment, her smooth lips pressed against mine in a quick peck, catching me by surprise.

"I trust you with all my being, Rahil," she mumbled against my lips.

"Then, tell me," I exhaled, my breathing charged and heavy because of the close proximity.

"It's just that I don't want you to pity me more than you already do." Her words caught me off guard, and I blinked in confusion.

Pity her? When did that even happen?

Chapter 9

Rahil's POV:

I slightly moved back, my brows furrowing in confusion as I looked at her.

" Pity you? When did I? " I asked, my voice filled with genuine bewilderment.

She let out another sigh, and said, "I overheard you talking to Addin on our wedding night,"her words sounded heavy with sadness.

My frown deepened, struggling to comprehend what she was saying.

"You said you married me because you didn't want to hurt me, which means you pity me, don't you?" she questioned, her voice tinged with vulnerability.

Memories of my conversation with Addin flooded my mind.

"Addin, I could never hurt her. I married her because I didn't want to hurt her more. I have hurt her enough by rejecting her twice. And who could better know how badly it hurts to be in one-sided love than me?"

As I recalled my words, my eyes widening in shock.

She has got it all wrong.

"No, no, no! That's not what I meant... I..." I trailed off, still trying to get over the shock that she had misunderstood it completely.

I let out a heavy sigh and asked, "What did you hear, to be precise?" She shared the exact words she had heard.

Well, I guessed it right! I couldn't believe that she could overthink so much?

And out of all things, she thought I pitied her? Seriously? Pity was the last thing on my mind. I was taken aback by her assumption.

"You only heard that much?" I asked, seeking confirmation, and she nodded.

I looked into her eyes, shook my head, and mumbled with a sigh, "I wish you could have eavesdropped and heard our whole conversation."

Her expression shifted, and a frown formed on her face.

Now, she appeared more sober and curious, as she listened intently to my words.

"Well, that night, when Addin called me, he was warning me that if I ever hurt you in any way, he wouldn't hesitate to break my neck!" I explained, watching as her eyes widened in surprise.

I knew she didn't expect this because she had believed that Addin didn't really care about her. But in reality, he cared deeply.

The man doesn't shows it, but I knew he secretly cared for her like his own sister though they weren't much close and I knew it because I know my bestfriend very well.

"Why do you look so shocked? " I chuckled.

" Addin doesn't have anything against you! Sure, he may have a grumpy and sour nature, but his heart is very soft, and he genuinely cares for you." I said, smiling softly.

She continued to gaze at me, clearly taken aback by this revelation.

"He told me that because he thought I married you out of his and Noor's influence or something. He knew that I had rejected you twice..." I trailed off, feeling a lump forming in my throat. I swallowed hard, trying to compose myself.

"I made it clear to him that I married you because I didn't want to hurt you anymore. And that doesn't mean I pity you," I let out a sigh, my words filled with sincerity. "I meant that I regretted rejecting and hurting you in the past, and I couldn't bear to hurt you any further," I explained, hoping she would understand.

She looked at me as if she couldn't believe what she was hearing.

" Yesss, I deeply regret rejecting you and causing you pain in the past, not just once, but twice. Looking back, I realize how foolish and pathetic I was..I was scared, terrified even, of falling for you."

As soon as I completed saying this, I could see shock evident in her eyes, as if that she never expected it at all.

" when I first fell in love with a girl who didn't feel the same way. It shattered me completely, leaving me broken and shaken. To protect myself from further heartache, I closed myself off from any romantic feelings. I didn't want to experience that foolishness again." I continued to pour my heart out infront of her.

" But then you entered my life, and everything changed. I couldn't help but feel drawn to you, despite my best efforts to resist. Even when we were just friends, there was an undeniable connection between us. It was something indescribable, a pull that I couldn't ignore. You were simply captivating, and I cherished our friendship more than anything, you literally made me so happy." I smiled at her widely and her gaze soften immediately.

" However, when you confessed your feelings to me, I panicked. I was so afraid of falling for you that I rejected you." My voice trembles as I gaze into her eyes, baring my soul.

" And when you left me, I realized just how much lost and empty it feels without you by my side. Those four years without you were somewhere frustrating because hanging out with you had become my favorite thing to do and I can't help but feel angry on my past self, for being so lost and not knowing what I truly wanted." As I spoke, her gaze remained fixed on me.

" You have no idea how much I admire you, Ayezah. You are the strongest woman I have ever known. The way you never made me feel bad for rejecting you tugged at my heart. When you returned after those four years, I couldn't have been more happier, why wouldn't I be afterall I got my most incredible friend back."

" But when Addin proposed the idea of marrying you, it caught me off guard. Yet, as I thought it through, I realized that you were the one, you always have been. I couldn't protect my heart from you because I didn't wanted to. I didn't want to settle for just being friends anymore." I added.

I took a deep breath, my hands trembling as I held hers in mine.

"And now, I want to fall in love with you," I confessed, feeling my heart racing insanely.

The weight of my words hung in the air for few seconds before I continued.

" I truly want to experience that foolish feeling again, and I feel like im already experiencing it, but this time, it feels even stronger and deeper than before."

As I finished speaking, I saw tears glistening in her eyes.

She let out a soft sob, "I can't believe this is real," she cried out, her voice trembling with emotion.

Her hands quivered in my hold, mirroring my own nervousness, and I couldn't help but chuckle softly at her words.

"Oh God," she choked out with her tear-filled eyes.

"Why didn't you confront me if you felt that way? And how could you let your thoughts wander so far? Do you really think I could pity you? " I asked, a tinge of offense lacing my words. It hurt that she had jumped to conclusions based on just a few words.

Shaking her head, she whispered, "I'm foolish, very stupid, and an absolute idiot." Tears welled up in her eyes, cascading down her cheeks.

I gently cupped her face, brushing away the tears with my fingertips. Leaning closer, our foreheads touched.

Her eyes closed, allowing her tears to fall freely, before opening again.

Our noses brushed against each other, and in that moment, I couldn't resist any longer. I pressed my lips against hers, and she responded instantly, her lips meeting mine in a passionate kiss.

I savored the softness of her lips, savoring the taste of her.

But suddenly, she pulled back, placing her palm over her mouth.

"I.. I reek of alcohol," she said, her embarrassment evident.

without hesitation, I gently held the nape of her neck, pulling her closer to me and lowering her palm from her mouth.

" i don't care." I whispered desperately, our lips almost touching.

And with that, I kissed her once again, with a sense of urgency and need.

I pulled her closer by waist, attaching her body completely to mine, my heart racing as our lips moved effortlessly against each other.

She cupped one of my cheek, her touch sending shivers down my spine, intensifying the kiss.

I let out a groan in her mouth, unable to contain the desire that consumed me.

But then, her hand found its way to my injured arm, and a sharp hiss escaped my lips.

Instantly, she pulled away, her expression shifted immediately, she looked at me, horrified, her eyes filled with concern.

"Shit, shit! You're hurt, Rahil," she exclaimed standing up, making me raise to my feet as well, her voice laced with panic.

" It's okay-" I tried to reassure her, but she wouldn't let me finish.

Her worry took over, her face skating with panic as if she couldn't even bear the thought of me being in pain.

"No, it's absolutely not okay," she insisted, her voice trembling. "I'm so sorry, it's all because of me. Come on, we're going to the hospital right now."

she grabbed my palm and led me towards the parking lot, before even I could protest further.

She said she would drive and I instantly protested, even though she was sober yet I couldn't just let her drive, because it's not safe at all.

She didn't let me drive because she was worried about my injured arm, even though I assured her the im totally fine.

And so, we ended up taking a cab, both of us stubbornly refusing to let the other drive.

After arriving at the hospital, I got my injured arm dressed.

Ayezah sat beside me on one of the hospital beds, her concern evident in her eyes. As the nurse finished dressing my arm, she handed me some painkillers to ease the discomfort.

Feeling a bit awkward, I turned to the nurse and asked if she could pass me some cotton. Confused but obliging, she handed it to me before leaving the room.

I shifted my attention back to Ayezah, who had a slight frown on her face. Gently, I brushed the cotton against her stained cheek, wiping away the slightly dried blood that had smeared when I cupped her cheek earlier.

"Umm, I'm sorry about that," I murmured.

Ayezah touched her now clean cheek with her fingertips.

She smiled, shaking her head, and I couldn't help but smile back at her. We sat there, gazing into each other's eyes, a comfortable and soothing silence enveloping us.

Ayezah's POV:

It was early in the morning, and here I am, lying on my stomach on the bed, giggling to myself, like a complete lunatic.

A soft pillow supports my arms as I revealed everything to Laila about yesterday's night on the call.

Even though she was furious with me for leaving the ice rink against her clear instructions and for impulsively going to a bar and getting drunk, her anger melted away when she heard the happiness in my voice. Relief washed over her, and she couldn't help but feel genuinely happy for me.

Her final words before we ended the call were, ' Told ya! He couldn't resist your stunning beauty for too longer.' I couldn't help but chuckle, before we said our goodbyes.

I still can't believe that last night wasn't a dream.

It was real, and every word he spoke felt like magic.

My heart races wildly at the mere thought of it.

After a refreshing shower, I change into a peach-colored crop top with full sleeves, paired with white jeans.

As we returned from the hospital yesterday, it was clear that neither of us wanted to sleep in separate rooms. I could feel Rahil's longing gaze, as if silently pleading for me to join him and sleep in his room.

However, he restrained himself, as if he didn't want to make me feel uncomfortable.

Only if he would know.

I couldn't even muster up the courage to take the initiative, because it would be embarrassing as I was the one who suggested this absolute stupid idea of sleeping in separate rooms and now I hate myself so much because of it.

His clenched jaw and saddened expression revealing the struggle within.

The way he wasn't ready to let go off my hand, makes my cheeks blush, and I can't help but squeal in delight.

"I want to fall in love with you."

His words echo in my mind, causing me to bury my face into the pillow and raise my legs, letting out an exuberant 'oh my god!'

I must be crazy, behaving like a teenager who just found out that her crush likes her back.

But I just can't help it.

Rahil Ahmed khan had indeed made me crazy! with his actions, words and everything.

Last night, if it hadn't been for the throbbing headache from drinking alcohol, I wouldn't have been able to sleep. But I was so tired that I ended up dozing off. Anyway, I woke up early this morning, filled with happiness and excitement.

Now that he's shared everything with me, I also want to share everything with him, like absolutely everything about my past.

I quickly get out of bed and start getting ready, eager to spend the day with him.

"You really think I can do this?" Rahil asked nervously, his gaze fixed on the ice rink in front of us. I nodded, a smile playing on my lips.

After enjoying a delightful breakfast together, I revealed my plan to take Rahil to the ice rink.

Only Laila knew about my ice skating skills; it was a secret I had kept from everyone else.

"Don't worry, Rahil! I'll be your guide," I reassured him with a warm smile.

He looked at me, surprised. "You know ice skating?" he asked, his astonishment evident. "Of course, I do! I've even won a few awards here and there," I replied proudly, watching as he became impressed and stunned.

"Let's go," I said, taking his hand and leading him inside the ice rink. We were already wearing our skates, our overcoats left behind on the long bench outside the ice rink.

As we stepped onto the ice, I could sense Rahil's legs trembling with nervousness. But I held onto his hand tightly, guiding him forward.

As we glided together, he let out " Woah, Woah," almost losing his balance and falling backward.

Swiftly, I turned and skated in front of him, placing my hands on his waist to steady him. In that moment, his hands instinctively gripped my waist, his expression filled with horror at the thought of falling.

I couldn't help but laugh, finding his adorable expression endearing.

"Just relax, I won't let you fall," I chuckled, still holding him close.

I continued laughing, the sound echoing through the air, as I felt his gaze fixated on my face. But as I glanced at him, his eyes held an intensity that made my laughter subside.

Slowly, his arms enveloped my waist, drawing me closer to him, and my laughter faded away completely.

"But I have already fallen," he whispered, his words causing my heart to skip a beat.

Our eyes locked instantly, he gently brushed his fingers along the side of my forehead, tucking a strand of hair behind my ear. All the while, my gaze remained fixed on his face.

He took in my entire face, as if trying to memorise every little detail of my face, his eyes filled with adoration.

" you're so beautiful." the mere words my heart race uncontrollably.

The intensity his eyes held while boring into mine, sent shivers down my spine, and before I could fully comprehend what was happening, he leaned in and pressed his lips against my forehead.

The softness of his kiss lingered for a few precious seconds. His lips remained on my forehead and I could feel his heavy breath on my hair, as he inhaled my hair deeply, leaving me breathless.

"I think we should skate!" I blurted out in nervousness, my voice slightly trembling.

A mischievous smirk danced across Rahil's face, as if he knew the effect he had on me.

He teasingly leaned closer, our lips mere inches apart, and whispered, "Ah huh?"

My heart raced, my breathing quickened. He brushed his lips against mine, and just as I thought our lips would meet, he pulled back with a smirk and said, "Yeah, we should just skate." making my jaw dropped.

oh, oh dear you didn't just mess with Ayezah shah!

I started skating, gliding forward with speed and grace, intentionally leaving him behind. His eyes widened as he struggled to keep up, only to end up falling with a thud on his butt. I twirled around, gliding effortlessly, and couldn't help but burst into laughter.

He sat there, hissing and glaring at me. I sat down beside him, leaning in close to his face, stopping just inches away from his lips.

With a playful tone, I whispered, "Too bad I can't help you up since you said you've already fallen!" I brushed my lips against his, just like he did and moved back immediately.

In the blink of an eye, a surprised squeal escaped my lips as I attempted to stand up. But before I could regain my balance, Rahil firmly grasped my arm and effortlessly pulled me towards him.

We both tumbled back onto the icy surface, with me landing on top of him. His arm instinctively wrapped around my waist, and with a playful tone, he uttered, "You really are something!"

without a second's hesitation, he smashed his lips on mine, kissing me madly, as if im the very air he needed to breathe urgently.

I responded eagerly, kissing him back with the same intensity and fervor.

The kiss on the ice rink transformed into an intense make-out session, leaving both of us breathless and yearning for more.

We stopped immediately because we couldn't possibly go any further here right?

Now, we find ourselves awkwardly seated on the long bench outside the ice rink.

I steal a glance at Rahil, only to find him nervously scratching the tip of his nose with his forefinger, his gaze avoiding mine.

Wait, could he possibly be blushing?

My heart races as I continue to gaze at him, captivated by his adorable shyness.

Suddenly, he clears his throat and musters the courage to ask, " you wanted to tell me something? "

Oh right, I completely forgot that I brought him to the ice rink at the first place to share everything with him.

"Yes, it's about why I acted that way the previous night," I reply, taking a deep breath and mentally preparing myself.

Concern fills his eyes as he immediately reaches for my hand, intertwining our fingers. "You don't have to if you're not ready," he says, his voice filled with genuine care, his thumb stroking the back of palm in soothing manner.

"I want to," I assert with determination

I don't want to keep any secrets to the most important person in my life, I want to share every part of me, every vulnerable piece of my being to the man I love with my whole heart.

Chapter 10

Rahil's POV:

I listened attentively as she spoke, noticing the slight tremble in her hand which was interlaced with mine.

She took a deep breath and began, "You would have known from the way I acted that night that I have a trauma with fire. I had overcome it through therapy, but seeing those massive flames suddenly ignited memories within me." I gently squeezed her hand, silently encouraging her to continue.

Her gaze remained fixed ahead, and I couldn't help but admire her stunning side profile.

She continued, her voice filled with a mix of vulnerability and strength.

"I was only 5 years old, and I distinctly remember it was an early winter morning when I woke up. The house was empty, and I asked one of the house helps where my mom was. She told me that my mom was out for some work, and my dad was often away on business trips. I felt a sense of boredom without my mom around, so I decided to occupy myself with puzzles, something I loved back then when I was a kid."

As she spoke, I could feel the chill in the air. She continued, her voice quivering slightly, "It was so cold, you know. Although i was wearing t-shirt and a sweater upon it, it felt really cold, i was always cold actually. so I went near the crackling fireplace in our drawing room. It was always lit during the winter months."

She paused, swallowing hard, and I could see the pain etched on her face as the memories flooded back.

I could feel the weight of her words as she shared it to me.

"I was just a kid back then, completely unaware of the danger that lurked within the warmth of the fireplace. Lost in the world of puzzles, I found myself inching closer and closer to the crackling flames. The heat grew intense, but I was oblivious, as I basked in the cozy embrace of the fire's warmth. I felt relieved that I wasn't feeling cold anymore."

My heart sank as the thought of what would have happened next.

"It was then that a searing sensation on my back jolted me from my puzzle-induced trance. Panic surged through me as I discovered my sweater had caught fire. I screamed, standing up and started crying loudly. The house help rushed to me, swiftly removing the burning garment away."

Tears welled up in her eyes, and I couldn't help but feel an ache in my chest.

"The aftermath left a lasting scar on my upper back, a burn scar that forever prevents me from wearing backless outfits." She shook her head slightly.

" Since that day, fire became my greatest fear. As I was very young back then, I couldn't sleep for months, haunted by the vivid imagery of flames engulfing me, the burning sensations etching my back, into my memory. I always ended up crying my heart out at hugging my mom tightly at night." She smiled slightly, through her teary eyes.

" My mom..." she started but paused, her smile turning a little sad.

"My mom, she was the nicest person ever! She loved me so much.....or at least that's what I believed until I reached the age of 7." A tinge of sadness crossed her face as she continued to say.

"You know, my mom was the sweetest soul. She was very lovely. Her passion was ice skating, and she was a true champion on the ice." I could hear the admiration and love in her voice as she spoke of her mother.

"She wanted me to follow in her footsteps, and while I was definitely interested in skating, I just wasn't as skilled as she was. There were other kids whose parents were friends with my mom, and they would bring home countless medals. Meanwhile, I always seemed to fall short. It frustrated my mom immensely! She couldn't stand the thought of her friends boasting about their kids' achievements while feeling pity for me because I couldn't skate well."

"You know, talent comes inbuilt, and no matter how hard I worked, I couldn't meet my mom's expectations. As her friends continued to mock her, she grew more restless and furious. And then..." She paused, swallowing hard, as if summoning the strength to share the next part of her story.

" my mom.. she started using...using my fear against me to threaten me and to make me work hard on my skating skills. I didn't like practicing in mornings because it would be freezing cold but she would scare me with the lighter which she carried always with her and threaten me with it, I just turned 7 back then, I was a kid and I was really scared of my mom suddenly acting like that, you know since then she turned completely opposite, she was not like my sweet and lovely mom anymore. She said that her love had spoiled me a lot." She gulped and I couldn't believe what I just heard.

Sometimes parents don't even realise that they are seriously hurting there children to get their motives achieved.

They become so selfish and stoop so low in scaring their children to work hard for their own satisfaction, that they don't even realise that their own child has serious trauma with it.

" I loved my mom so much and I didn't blame her for that, I was weak and incompetent, she only wanted good for me so she did that right? but you know when I finally learned it well and brought certificates and medals, she wasn't there to appreciate me...she... she died before that. " Her chin wobbled and I felt my heart breaking into million pieces.

"The last happy memory I have with my mom is from my 6th birthday. I remember her giving me this beautiful snowflake pendant." She held onto the shiny pendant tightly which she always wore, a radiant smile gracing her face.

"This pendant is something I will always treasure. It's the only clear and joyful memory I have with my mom." As she spoke, a tear rolled down her cheek, which I immediately wiped away.

My heart was aching with each passing seconds, hearing her every word.

" I was 11 years old when she passed away. I would just sit, hugging my knees and stare at my medals and certificates for hours and hours, wondering why would my mom prioritize external recognition over my emotional well-being? That why she played with my feelings so horribly when she knew I seriously feared fire a lot.

Wasn't I her only daughter? Didn't she love me anymore? " Her voice trembled as she continued.

" It was my competition day. She had sent me with driver in morning to start early morning practice and when she was coming to attend the competition, she met with an accident and died, while I won the competition here and was so happy to show my first ever gold medal to her. But when I went home, she was no longer with us."

" The last..The last memory I have of her is her threatening me to go to the morning practice.." She broke into loud sobs and started crying loudly, i immediately wrapped my arms around her tightly.

She broke down crying on my chest while I kept tightening my hold on her. A tear slipped down my eyes, and I wiped it off harshly.

My chest burned, and my heart ached for her. How could a mother do something like that to her own child? I felt the need to break something. I felt so damn furious.

After crying for a few minutes, she moved back, sniffing. " You know what's the most ironic part of all this? " she said.

" My dad never knew anything about this even now he don't. He loved mom a lot, like really a lot, and I didn't have the heart to tell him all this because I knew he would blame mom for whatever she did to me and I didn't wanted him to stop loving my mom or spoil her picture perfect of being the best wife and mom in the world."

I felt my chest tightening more hearing her. How could she be so selfless? Even after all that her mom did to her she still wants her dad to keeping loving and respecting her mom?

She was too pure for this cruel world and at that very moment i realised that she deserves the world but the world doesn't deserve an angel like her.

" My dad has always been the best dad for me. He was always there, though he wouldn't spare a lot of time for me. But when he did, he would play with me and bring me my favorite food, snacks, and toys. However, he was often away from the house because of business, and I was all alone. " she continued, now smiling through tears.

" You know, in all of this, I didn't realize when I developed this playful nature and the tag of Playgirl. I was really attached to mom, and after what she did to me, I was scared...scared that people I got attached to would eventually find out about my trauma and use my fear against me. So, I never had any long-lasting friends or any long-lasting relationships, all the boyfriends I had were just for fun. I didn't plan on falling in love because loving someone means breaking all your walls and telling them every vulnerability part of you but I didn't wanted to do that. I didn't let anyone know about my fears." She smiled and looked at me, brushing her fingers on my cheek.

" until I met you. I don't know how did you manage to make me fall in love with you, I guess I just couldn't resists your charms." She chuckled, shaking her head.

I looked at her, feeling a lot of emotions running all together into.

She believes me. Yess she does, because She loves me. ALOT! I could literally feel it right now.

Ayezah's love was fierce. She can love you so fiercely that it would burn you to know the intensity, depth and selflessness of her love.

And despite me rejecting her twice, she still agreed to marry me, because that's how deep she can go when she loves someone.

How could someone possibly be this pure and kind?

Right now I feel the luckiest man on this entire planet.

My heart pains so much for her. I feel like someone is slicing my heart, seeing her in pain.

My heart screamed and cried for her. Why such a pure soul like her has to go through all this? What was her fault in all this?

" Hey, why are you crying? " She cupped my cheeks, wiping my tears away and only then I realised that I was actually crying.

I immediately knelt infront of her and took her palms in mine startling her.

" Thank you thank you so much.." I swallowed.

" Thank you for sharing it all to me. I promise I will never ever hurt you. I'll prefer killing myself before even letting the thought of hurting you cross my mind. " I kissed her knuckles one by one in utter urgency.

" Thank you for trusting me and loving me.."

" I promise to love you back with all my heart, to take away all your pain, to make you forget all your dreadful memories and make new happy memories with you. I'll cherish you Ayezah, you are way too precious, you don't deserve anything you went through. "

" I will love you with my whole being." I said my voice cracking, and she looked at me with tears filled eyes and shut her eyes crying loudly letting her tears fall freely and holding my palms tightly.

In that moment, I swiftly stood up and sat on a bench, pulling her onto my lap. Her legs dangled to one side as I held her close. She immediately wrapped her arms around me and hid her face in the crook of neck, crying loudly.

I tightened my hold on her, my one arm wrapped around her waist and another hand stroking her hair.

Her each sob, each sniff and each tear, suffocated me to no extent, tightening my chest with passing seconds, it felt like someone was squeezing my heart with long pointed sharp nails.

"Shhh, babie, don't cry. Everything will be okay," I whispered, cupping her cheeks gently and breaking the hug, wiping away her tears, i kissed her wet eyes one by one as she closed them.

As I held her in my arms, In that moment, I made a solemn promise to myself.

I would do whatever it takes to ensure that she never experiences pain or sheds another tear again.

Her happiness became my new purpose in life and I vowed to love her with every single cell of my body and protect her until my last breath.

Chapter 11

Ayezah's POV:

Comfort. warmth. Good. Nice. Amazing. Bettter than ever.

All these words weren't enough to capture the emotions coursing through me at this very moment.

It was as if I had stumbled upon a hidden sanctuary, a place where all worries melted away. The warmth enveloping me was like a gentle embrace, a cocoon of solace that whispered promises of eternal bliss. It felt like i could just live here for the rest of my life.

My cheek, pressed against a strong, yet tender chest, could feel the steady rhythm of a heart beating in sync with mine.

Two arms, wrapped securely around me, provided a sense of safety and belonging that I had never experienced before.

With a slow flutter of my eyelids, I opened my eyes, only to be met with the sight of the most breathtakingly handsome face I had ever encountered. A contented smile tugged at the corners of my lips as I lazily snuggled even closer, my arm encircling his torso.

But then, in an instant, my eyes snapped open, a furrow forming on my brow.

Wait, we are sleeping together?

I glanced around, taking in our surroundings.

my eyes slightly widened realising that we were still on the long bench outside the ice rink.

My half of the body was lying on top of his, and he was sleeping soundlessly.

I couldn't help but notice that I was wearing my long overcoat and his overcoat was wrapped over me, like a blanket, keeping me warm.

we really slept here the whole night? oh my god!

My heart ached at the thought of him sleeping in just his t-shirt. I couldn't help but worry that he might have felt cold, while keeping me warm the whole night.

The last memory I had was of pouring my heart out, tears streaming down my face, as I was crying horribly, being seated on his lap.It was a release of emotions that I had bottled up for years.

Laila had witnessed my tears before, she has seen it all, but with Rahil, it felt different, it felt like all the walls I had built around my heart had crumbled completely. I exposed my raw, vulnerable side to him.

I'm so glad I opened up to him because I vividly remember how his arms enveloped me tighter with every sob that escaped my lips.

His jaw was clenched, as if my crying was killing him.

The way he gently kept stroking my hair, And oh, the countless kisses he planted on top of my head, each one felt like a silent declaration that he would protect me.

Though he didn't utter the words, I could feel it in my core that he would shield me from any harm, no matter the cost.

And I would do the same! I would do anything for him to keep him safe and by my side.

I, too, would go to any lengths to protect him because I love him so much that I can't even begin to explain it in words. It's a love that runs deep and fills my heart to the brim. It's a love that has consumed me completely.

I just love him so damn freaking much.

He stirred ever so slightly in his sleep, and in that very moment, he pulled me completely on top of him, making my eyes slightly widen.

with a lazy grace, he opened his eyes, meeting my gaze with a soft, affectionate smile playing on his lips.

"Am I really that handsome?" he asked and only then I realised that I had been staring at his sleeping self, for god knows how long.

His morning voice, husky and deep, sent a shiver down my spine, making it hard to find my words.

I couldn't help but swallow, feeling the heat rise within me. "You ...were awake?" I whispered, my voice barely audible.

He hummed lowly and oh boy, what's with him sounding so hot and sexy this early in the morning?

Ayezah! Get a grip.

" Well, when your gorgeous wife has been staring at you, how long can a man resist?" he remarked, causing a flush to spread across my cheeks.

We locked eyes for few seconds, before he closed his eyes once again, a contented smile gracing his lips. He held me even closer, if that was even possible.

"Are you okay? How are you feeling?" He softly asked.

A smile bloomed on my face as I pressed my cheek against his chest, feeling a sense of contentment like never before. "Never felt so better," I replied, my voice filled pure happiness.

He placed a gentle kiss on top of my head, chuckling lightly.

I titled my head up, resting my chin on his chest, and he looked down at me. "Aren't you cold? I mean sleeping in that uncomfortable position, and that too on a cold bench? " I asked, concerned.

His smile grew as he brushed his finger on my forehead, tucking a few locks of my hair back.

" who said it was uncomfortable and cold?" he replied, his voice filled with warmth.

"Actually, when you slept, I thought of carrying you-" I cut him off immediately.

"No way, mister! Your arm is injured and needs to heal, remember?"

He chuckled. " I know, I know."

I squinted my eyes, passing him a glare.

" Then why didn't you wake me up? "

" well, seeing you so serene while you slept, I couldn't bring myself to disturb you, you looked so much at ease. " He explained with a smile, planting a gentle kiss on my forehead.

"But Atleast you could have taken your overcoat, It's freezing, and I already had mine on."

" Don't worry, I had the best sleep of my life with you in my arms. It was so cozy." his voice was filled with so much contentment, making my heart do a little flip. I couldn't help but smile at him.

He squeezed me closer, cradling me a little in his embrace, and I let out a giggle, tightening my arms around him and resting my head on his chest.

This couldn't get any more perfect.

After we left the ice rink, Rahil asked me out for a breakfast date and i gladly accepted.

We then had a delightful breakfast date at the nearby cozy cafe.

we sat there, randomly talking about few stuffs here and there, laughing our hearts out while enjoying our chocolate-filled crispy croissant.

The flaky pastry melted in our mouths, perfectly complemented by the rich, velvety hot chocolate topped with fluffy marshmallows. The cold morning weather added a touch of magic to the moment, making it the most coziest breakfast of my life.

The day went by smoothly, and i couldn't stop smiling from ear to ear throughout the day because it was spent with someone who brings immense joy to me.

It feels unreal how just the day before, I poured out my heart to him, releasing all my pain and worries. But now, in his presence, all of that seemed to vanish, with him I feel like I don't have to worry about anything.

He had this incredible ability to make me feel like the happiest person in the world.

I love him so much that I feel like my heart is going to explode.

The evening approached and I found myself seated in front of the dressing table in my room, getting ready for the dinner party at Addin's place.

It was Noor's idea to invite everyone for dinner at her place. Najma and her husband were also joining us.

with a gentle stroke of the blush's brush against my cheek, I smiled, looking at the reflection staring back at me in the mirror, satisfied with the way I look.

I had chosen to wear traditional attire. My appearance consisted of a stunning long black anarkali, adorned with intricate embroidery.

The top boasted a mesmerizing display of craftsmanship, with full embroidered sleeves.

The black pants beneath were almost hidden, concealed by the floor-length top.

To complete the look, I draped a heavy black satin embroidered border dupatta over one of my shoulder blades.

For accessories, I opted for simple yet dazzling diamond studs. As for my neck, I decided to let the dress's exquisite embroidery take the spotlight, resembling a glistening diamond necklace, and ofcourse I had my snowflake pendant on.

I did some minimal makeup and styled my waist-length hair by gathering it on one side, letting it flow over my shoulder, and lightly curling my brown highlights.

I sprayed my favorite perfume and grabbed my trusty black sling bag before heading outside.

As I made my way downstairs, I couldn't help but notice Rahil patiently waiting for me in the living room.

I descended the stairs slowly and gracefully, brushing my fingers against the smooth railing.

I caught a glimpse of Rahil glancing at his brown wristwatch, his eyes subconsciously flickered towards me for a brief second before looking back at watch.

And just next second, with a swift motion, he snapped his head up, so quickly that I doubt his neck hasn't strained.

His gaze locking onto me, as he roamed his eyes from up to down and then stopped his gaze, connecting our eyes. He looked into my eyes with such intensity that it made my heart race insanely.

Feeling a rush of warmth spreading through my cheek, I reached the bottom of the stairs, mustering a shy smile in his direction. He continued gawking at me.

I couldn't help but feel a bit self-conscious, as tug a few strands of my hair behind my ear, feeling something unfamiliar : shyness.

What's with you, Ayezah? Shy? Seriously? This is so out of character!

I took a quick glance at him and my heart skipped a beat. He was dressed in a loose cream shirt that perfectly complemented his dusty brown dress pants.

His fluffy hair was casually tousled, yet neatly styled, adding to his irresistible charm.

How does he manage to look so adorable and effortlessly hot at the same time?

He stood there, his face seemed quite expressionless and gaze fixed on me. It felt as if he was starstruck or lost in some sort of daze?

I cleared my throat, nervously licking my lips before mustering the courage to speak. "Let's...go?" My voice came out as a mere whisper, barely audible.

He blinked a few times, as if awakening from a trance, before averting his gaze. I noticed the visible movement of his neck muscles as he swallowed, his jaw tensing slightly.

Then, he lightly scratched his forefinger on his nose, Finally passing me a small sweet smile.

He extended his palm towards me, and I couldn't help but press my lips into a smile.

As I took his hand, my eyes widened slightly when he swiftly pulled me closer, wrapping his other arm around my waist.

My other hand instinctively held on his shoulder blade for support, the closeness between us made my heart race.

In the next moment, he released my hand which was holding his palm and gently held my chin, caressing it with his thumb pad.

He dipped his head down a little and pressed his soft lips on mine, making a delightful tingling sensation in the pit of my stomach.

He skillfully sucked on my bottom lip, almost drawing out the moisture from my lip gloss. As he pulled back, he left a lingering peck on my lips.

"No doubt you look stunning in everything you wear, but when you don traditional attire, you become the most haseen thing I've ever seen," he whispered huskily, his words brushing against my lips.

[haseen : beautiful]

Our breathing charged due to the close proximity, and I could feel his warm breath on my face.

My heart fluttered at his words, causing my already flushed face to resemble a boiled crab.

I cleared my throat, trying to conceal the huge grin that was spreading across my lips.

I moved back slightly still in his arms, looking here and there, avoiding making eye contact, feeling a sudden rush of shyness.

"I didn't knew that Ayezah could even shy away like this," he said, his voice filled with amusement.

I brushed a lock of hair off my forehead, nervously licking my lips before responding, "No, I'm... not shy..." I stammer, scolding myself internally for doing so.

He chuckled, and I glanced at him. " And I didn't know that you could say such romantic things," I remarked, and he shook his head.

"I can't help it, it just comes out naturally and effortlessly ever since I married a certain someone so gorgeous," he replied, causing me to blush some more.

"Okay, so you're getting smooth now, huh?" I teased, wrapping my arms around his neck as he pulled me closer by placing his hands on my waist.

"Am I?" he asked, smiling, and I nodded, saying a playful 'ah-huh.'

We stood there, gazing into each other's eyes for a few precious seconds. I gently brushed my fingers against his cheek, cupping it softly, I tilted my head and planted a lingering kiss on his cheek.

I could feel him closing his eyes and letting out a contented sigh.

Smiling against his cheek, I basked in his signature masculine scent, feeling a wave of comfort wash over me.

"So, let's go?" I asked, raising one eyebrow. He flashed a playful smile and pressed a quick, hard kiss on my lips.

"Yeah, now let's go," he chirped, his huge grin contagious. I couldn't help but chuckle, shaking my head. He gently intertwined his fingers with mine, and we made our way outside the door towards the car.

_______________________________________Thanks for reading <3 please don't forget to vote, comment your reviews and do share my book with your reader friends. I love you all ⊠⊠

Heyy beautiful people !! Hope y'all are doing great! My exams are still going on, but I managed to take out some time to write three chapters.

So, if you could help me out by getting me 200 votes and 100 comments on this chapter, I'll be able to post the next chapter soon, probably by tonight or tomorrow. This chapter was more of a filler, but the next one is gonna be a blast!

Chapter 12

Ayezah's POV:

The penthouse door swung open, revealing Noor with a gorgeous smile that could light up the room. She was dressed in a stunning sage green floral satin full-length dress, looking as pretty as ever.

"OMG, you look so gorgeous!" she exclaimed, pulling me into a tight hug. I embraced her back, smiling widely.

She has always been a sweetheart.

" c'mon not more than you! " I replied, pulling away.

I noticed Addin approaching from behind Noor, donning a casual black hoodie and pants. His hands were tucked in his pants pockets. Rahil quickly joined him, giving him a side hug and a fist bump.

Suddenly, Rahil's words from that night when I got drunk and he told me about how Addin actually cared for me, flooded my mind.

"Well, that night, when Addin called me, he was warning me that if I ever hurt you in any way, he wouldn't hesitate to break my neck!"

The words echoed in my head, and strange warm, fuzzy feeling enveloped me.

but why didn't this idiot tell me about all this when I went to his office the very next morning and grilled him?

Although Addin and I weren't particularly close, we had crossed paths many times during family events. We always found ourselves playfully arguing and teasing each other. I secretly enjoyed getting under the skin of that grumpy creature. But that day, when Rahil shared his perspective on Addin, I realized there was more to him than met the eye.

Deep down, I sensed that Addin was like a hard shell, tough on the outside, but inside, he had a heart of gold.

And honestly I'm so grateful to him and to Noor because without them, we wouldn't have been able to get married. I wouldn't have married the man I love so much.

It felt as though I had gained a brother, someone who cared for me like his own sister. It was a newfound feeling, and it oddly brought me immense joy.

I don't know what got into me at the moment, but the next thing I did, shocked everyone.

I snaked my arms around Addin's torso, and rested my head on his chest. I felt him instantly froze as he stopped talking mid-sentence to Rahil.

I quickly pulled away, not wanting to make the situation any more awkward than it already was.

Noor and Rahil exchanged wide-eyed glances, clearly taken aback by my unexpected gesture.

Addin, on the other hand, looked like he had just seen a ghost. He cleared his throat and blinked, trying to process what had just happened.

"What the fuck was that? Stay away from me," he grumbled, his voice filled with confusion.

Annoyed by his reaction, I retorted, "Shut up! It was just a hug! You don't have to grumble about everything!"

"And c'mon now can't I even hug my brother?" the words rolled off my tongue on their own and the realisation made me hit my own head on the wall.

Addin's expression turned incredulous.

" Are you high or something, Ayezah?" Addin asked, clearly flustered by the situation.

Meanwhile, Noor and Rahil couldn't contain their laughter, and they both busted out laughing covering their mouths with their palms as they exchanged amused glances.

" Typical, brother-sister things, Oh my god!" Noor said, her laughter filling the air.

"I know, right?" Rahil chimed in. Addin and I exchanged awkward glances, unsure of how to react.

"This is so damn good, Noori!" Najma chirped, showering Noor with compliments. I savored the bite of my butter naan, soaked in the rich, flavorful butter chicken, with a mouthful, I said "Can't agree more, Noor. This is just wow." Noor thanked both of us, smiling widely.

Seated around the dining table, we all indulged in the delicious feast that Noor had prepared, a spread of mouthwatering desi dishes.

Suddenly, Najma burst into laughter, catching everyone's attention.

"Sorry, but I remembered the last time we had dinner at Bhai's place," she managed to say between her laughter.

" oh god yess! That was hilarious." Her husband joined in laughing, and Rahil shot them a glare.

Curiosity got the best of Noor, and she frowned, leaning closer to Najma and asking her about it.

After a few whispered words in Noor's ears by najma, Noor's face lit up, and she too erupted into laughter, leaving me feeling a little flushed.

I shot a glare at Najma. "Sorry, Bhabhi, you both were too cute that day! " she chuckled.

Then, Najma turned her attention to Rahil, her mischievous grin widening. "Oh, and by the way, Bhai, I can expect to become an aunt soon, right?" she asked innocently.

Rahil choked on his water, his ears turning pink, clearly caught off guard. He shot Najma a glare, attempting to regain his composure.

"Najma... stop talking so much while eating," he stammered, finally managing to take a sip of water. I couldn't help but press my lips together, finding his nervous state utterly cute.

Rahil Adorable khan.

I quickly pushed the urge back to just pull down his face and kiss him breathless.

I cleared my throat and focus my attention back on food.

"I said no, Najma!" Rahil stated, his annoyance evident in his voice. We were all now gathered in the living room after the dinner. Noor and Addin occupied the front couch, while Rahil and I sat across from them. Najma and her husband settled comfortably on the side couches.

Najma winced as she pleaded, "Bhai, just one song! It's been so long, please." Rahil contemplated for a moment, then suggested, "If you want to listen to music, we can play some. And also, there's no guitar here."

" I have your old guitar, since you left it at my place long time back." Addin said, with a smirk on his face.

So, right now, Najma was insisting Rahil to sing a song and make us all hear. I remembered how Rahil used to talk about his love for playing the guitar when we were friends four years ago, but I had never actually heard him play or sing.

The sight of a guitar in his room had always piqued my curiosity, making me even more excited to finally listen to him.

"You know, bhabi!" Najma exclaimed excitedly. "Bhai sings and plays so well! He's too good. But he's literally the shyest person on earth, and right now, I guess he's shying away because of you." Najma's words made me burst into laughter, unable to contain my amusement.

Rahil's face flushed, as he stammered, "It's not... like that..."

Najma, rolled her eyes sideways towards her brother and motioned to me secretly, urging me to pursue her brother. I frowned at her and She motioned even more insistently this time by slightly widening her eyes.

This girl i tell you!

I leaned closer to him and playfully said, "please, sing a song. I'm dying to listen to you!" I purposely spoke dangerously close to his face, causing him to blink and blush even more. His eyes wandered across my entire face, and in a dazed state, he replied, "Okay."

"YAYAYA!" Najma squealed and Rahil seemed to snap out of his daze, clearing his throat and looking away, trying to regain his composure.

Addin got up and brought the guitar.

Rahil gently cradled the guitar in his arms, its smooth curves fitting perfectly against his body.

" There's this song playing in my head since the evening. I just can't get it out of my mind. So I'll be just singing that one now." He paused for a moment, his eyes flickering to me.

He looked down at the guitar and his fingers gracefully danced across the strings, producing a soft melody. The sound filled the room, wrapping around us like a warm embrace. I couldn't help but smile, captivated by this awesome man's talent already.

The melody continued to flow from the guitar for few precious seconds.

" Tum ko paya hai to jaise khoya hoon"

And at that very moment he looked up and locked eyes with me, making my breath hitch in my throat and my smile slowly faded away.

" Kehna chahoon bhi to tumse kya kahon "

The intensity in his gaze was so powerful that it made my heart race uncontrollably, almost as if it wanted to burst out of my chest.

" kisi zaban mein bhi woh labaz hi nahi ki jeenmein tum ho kya tumhein bata sakun "

Not once did his eyes leave mine, causing a flurry of butterflies to dance in the pit of my stomach. His lips moved, whispering the lyrics to the melody in his soothing voice and his fingers danced effortlessly on the guitar strings.

" main agar kahoon tumsa haseen kaynaat mein nai hai kahin "

A slow smile spread across his lips, it was so breathtakingly gorgeous that it held the power to melt me like a puddle in an instant.

" Tareef yeh bhi to sach hai kuch bhi nahi."

" WOW BHAI OH MY GOD!!! "

As soon as he finished, Najma squealed with delight, throwing herself into her brother's arms, engulfing him in a tight embrace.

Her giggles filled the air, creating a joyful atmosphere that echoed with applause from everyone around.

But for me, time seemed to slow down in that moment. My heart raced in my chest, I could literally hear the song still resonating in the background.

I watched as Rahil, with a wide grin on his face, embraced Najma back, their laughter blending harmoniously.

Rahil's eyes met mine, his smile soft and tender. He held onto Najma, while his gaze lingered on me.

The ride back home was incredibly awkward, with an almost tangible tension hanging in the air.

As we reached the top of the stairs, we stood there, uncertain of what to do next.

Are we still going to stay in separate rooms?Damn you, Ayezah! it's all your fault to begin with. Why do have to ask for staying in separate rooms?

Rahil looked around, nervously cupping the backside of his neck. "Umm, goodnight then?" he said.

"Yeah...well good night," I managed to reply, my own hesitation palpable.

Rahil blinked, seemingly unsure, and turned to leave.

I sank down, my gaze fixated on his retreating figure. Suddenly, he spun around, catching me off guard. I straightened up, my heart leaping with anticipation.

He opened his mouth as if about to speak, but quickly closed it.

" ummm that I-"

Please say it, just for once. Please.

my hope crumbled when he said, "If you need anything, then do tell me." I let out a sigh, nodding, as he turned away and left in haste.

I sighed for the umpteenth time, sulking and lazily applying moisturizer to my bare arms and face.

I just took a warm shower, dried my hair and slipped into onion pink silk shorts and crop top which had full balloon sleeves.

"I mean, couldn't he say it at least once?" I muttered to myself.

"We're literally husband and wife! We should be sleeping in the same room." Frustration filled my voice as I huffed and continued talking to myself.

"Okay, I could have said it too! But it's so embarrassing, since it's all my fault, AAHH!" I groaned, slamming the moisturizer shut.

"Oh God! I must be going crazy! I'm actually talking to myself," I cried out, burying my face in my hands.

After a few minutes, I found myself standing near the door of my room, taking a deep breath.

"Just go and tell him that I'm ready to share the room. That's it! Don't be embarrassed," I reminded myself.

He had said it was okay to embarrass myself in front of him because he's my husband and he wouldn't mind.

Gathering all the courage, I slowly opened the door to my room, only to find him doing the same with his room, which happened to be right in front of mine. The spherical round staircase stood between us.

I blinked in surprise, my eyes widening as I didn't expect him to emerge from his room. Our gazes locked, and I could see the same astonishment mirrored in his expression.

Slowly, he made his way towards me, his footsteps echoing softly in the hallway.

"Do you need anything?" he asked.

I swallowed nervously.

Just say it Ayezah!

" Ah, yes..I actually....i... I.. I need some water... There's none in my room," I stammered, my words stumbling out in a jumbled mess.

Even foolishness has some limits! What the hell is wrong with me?

"I'll get you some- " he started to say, but I interrupted him quickly, not letting him finish. "No, no, it's fine. I'll just go to the kitchen!" I insisted, my voice a little too eager.

He nodded. Silence creeped the air for few seconds.

"What are you doing here?" I blurted out, catching him off guard for a moment.

After a few seconds of hesitation, he replied, his words slightly stumbling. "Ah, nothing.....I.. I just came to check up on you," he said, his voice carrying a hint of uncertainty.

Silence once again created its room between us with a mixture of awkwardness and tension.

" well then..I'll get going," he said after few seconds, his voice filled with hesitation and nervousness.

"Oh yeah, me too..Good night," I replied, mirroring his uncertainty.

He waited for me to leave, and I smiled forcefully muttering a 'ah yess.' and started moving towards the stairs, he began making his way towards his room.

I was descending the stairs, my heart pounding, chewing nervously on my bottom lip and tightly clutching my delicate snowflake pendant.

But then, something inside me snapped.

"Okay, fuck it!"

I was about to turn around, But before I could, a gasp escaped my throat as he out of nowhere swiftly pulled my arm and pinned me against the wall on the staircase.

Time seemed to freeze as his mouth smashed onto mine without missing a beat.

He started kissing me as if it was a matter of life or death for him, I could feel the desperation into the kiss.

I wasted no time in reciprocating, sucking on his lips as if they were the very air I needed to breathe.

My fingers went behind, tangling in his silky hair, as his arm wrapped around my waist, drawing me impossibly close.

Our bodies pressed against each other completely.

I tugged on his hair and he groaned lowly into my mouth.

We kissed as if we were starving for ages, our heads tilting and turning, sucking each other's lips as though we had been deprived of each other for an eternity.

Reluctantly, we broke apart, gasping for air. He pressed himself against me, his arms caging me against the wall.

Our foreheads touched, our noses brushing against each other, as we both struggled to catch our breath.

"Move into my room, forever. I can't bear the distance, even if it's just a room away. I want to wake up to your beautiful face every morning, and fall asleep watching you sleep peacefully. Please, just be with me." His voice, husky and filled with longing, whispered against my lips, making my already racing heart, race even faster, to the point where I felt like it would just jump out and fall right at his feet.

I raised my hand and brushed my fingers against his cheek, and cupped his jaw, caressing his cheekbone softly.

" you don't have to say please. You have no idea how desperate im to move into your room." I whispered, breathless and titling my head, I pressed my lips on his, kissing him.

I pulled away and he cursed in his hot voice.

" Fuck! You drive me absolutely insane, Ayezah! I can't get a grip of myself, it's so difficult.." I silenced him again by smashing my mouth on his and kissing him madly, he wasted no seconds and responded to the kiss eagerly.

"No one's telling you to get a grip of yourself! " I whispered, playfully smirking, as I ran my hands along his well-build clothed chest feeling his perfect muscles, in a seductive way.

He arched an eyebrow, his smirk mirroring mine.

"Damn! You are already so irresistible and now you are tempting me to no extent." he huskily confessed.

Without hesitation, I wrapped my arms around his neck and jumped into his arms, wrapping my legs around his torso.

He chuckled, and held on the back of my bare thighs firmly, keeping me in place.

Tilting my head, I pressed my lips against his, in a soft, tantalizing kiss.

He pulled back and playfully whispered, " so Mrs khan, shall we head to our room then?"

" Are you ready? "

" Always ready, Mr khan." I couldn't help but giggle.

He started climbing the stairs while still carrying me in his arms, he had this adorable huge grin on his face that just melted my heart.

I couldn't resist reaching down and gently cupping his cheeks, feeling the warmth of his skin beneath my fingertips.

With each step he took, I playfully showered his lips with sweet noisy pecks, causing him to chuckle.

Finally, we reached his room, or should I say, our room.

Chapter 13

- -

Rahil's POV:

As I entered the room, holding her still in my arms, my heart raced with anticipation.

with a gentle motion, I laid her down on the bed, feeling the soft thud as her body made contact with the mattress. Her beautiful silk locks cascaded around her.

Her chest rose and fell with charged breaths, mirroring my own condition.

I couldn't tear my gaze away from her captivating amber eyes, which danced with raw desire.

Time seemed to stand still as I hovered over her, my elbows softly dipping on either side of her head.

In an instant, our foreheads touched, our noses brushing against each other's, intensifying the electric jolts running between us.

our breathing becoming more ragged and charged with each passing moment.

Unable to resist the magnetic pull, she arched herself up, her lips claiming mine in a hungry, passionate kiss.

The kiss was very wild with all dances of tongues and bites involved, which made something twitch inside my pants.

Her arms snaked around my neck, pulling me closer, as if she wanted to fuse our bodies together. I reveled in the sensation of her warm, soft form pressed against mine, the heat between us igniting a fire that consumed us both.

Her sweet, intoxicating scent enveloped me completely, filling my lungs and clouding my mind in a blissful haze.

She pulled away to catch some breath, and I immediately nuzzled my nose into her hair, inhaling the most addicting smell of her hair and then I started kissing the side of her face urgently, moving down and nuzzling my face into crook of her neck.

Her skin was incredibly smooth, like the softest silk, her scent was driving me at the edge, making me lose all sense of control.

I felt completely captivated and trapped. A trap from where I would never want to break free.

I pressed my lips softly on her neck, smooching her smooth skin, and started leaving open mouth kisses all over her neck and throat.

Unable to resist, I dig my teeth softly into her flesh, and she moaned lowly. I nibbled on her skin, leaving few of my artistic marks on her beautiful slender neck.

I moved down and looked at her perfect collar bones, as soon as I put my mouth on it, she whimpered out my name.

Definitely weak spot.

I smirked slightly, and placed a noisy kiss on her collarbones, followed by sucking on them.

"Rahi.. Rahil." She moaned out my name, in such sultry hot voice, which turned me on more than I already was.

I trailed my lips down kissing her slightly exposed chest desperately and a grunt escaped my throat because of the cloth, which restricted my mouth to be on her warm, smooth skin.

Next moment her top went flying on the ground, as I swiftly took it off.

I sucked in a breath, gawking shamelessly at her perfect round breast, barely covered by her cream-coloured lace bra.

Dammit, So fucking hot!

I looked up at her and she smirked down at me, playfully wriggling her eyebrows, as if asking me 'like what you see?'

This girl is really something!

I flashed her an amused look and a chuckle escaped my throat.

She grunted as if I had ruined the moment and grabbed my t-shirt, swiftly throwing it away more like almost tearing it, as if it had frustrated her to no limits.

The next moment she switched are positions, hovering over me, her eyes scanning my body with raw desire, while my eyes shamelessly falling down and locking onto her tempting cleavage.

Her hands roamed all over my body, from my shoulders to my chest, abs and then she replaced her hands with her lips, kissing my neck, chest and abs, so desperately as if it's the only thing she needed to survive.

I closed my eyes, feeling her warm mouth all over my body, my breathing getting charged and hard.

So fucking good!

She bit my neck, sucking on it like some mad hungry vampire and I let out a grunt of pleasure.

Damn this woman! Her touch is paralysing me.

The way she is so dominating without even trying is simply so sexy!

I pulled back a little and she groaned, cupping the backside of my neck with her palm and pulling me close immediately.

I pressed my lips on hers, biting and sucking on her luscious lower lip, I whispered against her lips.

" Let me have every inch of your body first, and then I promise you can have all of me as well! I'll gladly submit to you." At this point I don't even know what I exactly blabbered out.

I'm desperate. I'm high on her. I'm vulnerable.

I need her. All of her.

I didn't give her any second more to process my words and un-clasped her bra. Her tits bounced out and my eyes darkened.

Before I know, im sucking on her hardened nipple like a thirsty creature. My palm flew to grab her other breast, kneading it, and feeling its softness. I pushed her down on the bed, and buried my face entirely in her chest.

She pulled at my hair, and whimpered out my name.

" Fuck it Rahil, just get inside me now! " She groaned, ordering me in her sultry voice.

Oh no no babie.

I raised my head from her chest, " You can't order me darling! I'm taking the lead, and im going to slowly enjoy every bit of you! If you really want me inside you, then beg me. Beg me and let me know that you're just as desperate as I am. " I hissed against her nipple, and bit on it, nibbling it between my teeth and teasing it for few seconds.

she arched her back moaning out my name.

" Rah..Rahil.. please.."

I moved to her another breast, giving it the same attention just like the other one.

I took it whole in my mouth and left it with a pop sound.

I kissed her nipple and pinched the other swollen one, and she dig her nails into my arms.

I moved down, leaving noisy kisses all the way till her navel. And yanked her bottoms down, along with her panties.

My lips were busy smooching the skin of her stomach, while my fingers ran over her perfectly smooth thighs, moving to her inner thighs, i brushed my knuckles on it.

I parted her thighs gently, my mouth still nibbling on her flat stomach.

I looked up at her, and she gazed back into my eyes. Her eyes were hazy.

I roamed my eyes all over her naked beautiful self, lying under me being a perfect mess.

" You're so extremely beautiful, so fucking perfect! "

I kissed her thighs, moving down.

I dipped my head down, and rubbed my thumb over her core lips and next second my mouth is replaced with my thumb.

" Fuck Rahil! " she moaned, as I feasted on her little crotch, sucking and biting her sensitive skin, desperately.

" yess babie! You are going to fuck me only." I hissed, eating her out.

" oh god! " she cried out, clutching my hair and pressing me more inside her.

I smooched it, before looking up.

" so fucking flavoursome." I licked my lips, and smirked at her.

She grabbed my hair, and pulled me up, kissing me, furiously.

As I got lost in the kiss, she took advantage and swiftly switched our positions.

" You are so frustratingly slow." She hissed, pulling back from the kiss and dipped her knees on either side of my waist and started unbuckling my pants hastily.

I blinked at her bold move. She threw my pants away along with my boxers, and gawked at my hardened member.

She smirked at me playfully, as if flashing me an impressed look and heat rushed to my neck.

This woman is unbelievable.

Her hands brushed against my throbbing member, and I groaned, throwing my head back.

She cupped the backside of my neck with her palm, and pulled me to look into her eyes.

" You're mine Rahil Ahmed khan! All mine and only mine." She grunted, possessiveness dripping her voice.

She bit my lower lip, grinding against me.

Her perfect delicious tits bounced as she grind and holy shit that was my last straw.

I entered inside her without warning and she screamed out my name.

I kneaded her breast with one palm and the other one cupped her jaw, I smashed my lips on her, swallowing her screams.

I slowly started moving and felt her walls clench around me, and my jaw tighten.

She dipped her face into my neck, while I kept moving in an animalistic pace.

Fuck!

This is the best feeling ever, so warm, so good, so damn amazing.

She held onto my bicep, digging her nails and bit my neck, muffling her moans.

After few seconds of thrusting in and out, I felt myself close.

Before I could, she released all over me and I followed behind her, releasing inside her.

She placed her head on my chest, clearly exhausted and I dropped a kiss on her head.

She then raised her head, and placed her palms on my bare chest, resting her chin on them.

She gazed at me with hazy yet sparkling eyes and flashed me her widest grin.

" I love you." She murmured ever so softly, her grin not wavering a bit.

My heart skipped a beat. And I blinked at her, my throat ran dry.

" I—" she didn't let me complete and pressed a kiss on my bare chest.

She placed her head back on my chest, saying.

" you don't have to say it back just for the sake of saying it. Say it when you actually feel it."

Chapter 14

Ayezah's POV:

" Woah! " I let out a giggle of delight as the sweet melody flowed from the guitar, my fingers delicately caressing the strings.

I was comfortably seated on Rahil's lap, A smooth silk white bedsheet wrapped around me, covering my chest to my lower body, while my bare shoulders were on display.

My back was pressed against Rahil's chest, his pants on but his upper body bare.

The guitar was cradled in my arms, while his arms encircled mine, gently guiding me in playing the music. I continued to produce more melodies as my fingers danced across the guitar strings.

We were seated in the spacious balcony of our room, positioned on the floor near the railing. The early morning hours painted a slightly dim atmosphere, with the sun yet to rise.

The cool air brushed against us tenderly. The view from our room's balcony was the back yard of the penthouse, we could catch glimpse of the house pool glistening in the distance.

"You were so amazing last night," I giggled again, my eyes fixated on the guitar as I delicately ran my fingers across its strings, with a huge grin on my face.

I sensed a gaze on the side of my face and turned to find Rahil tilting his head and staring at me, his eyes filled with amusement that soon transformed into a mischievous glimmer. A gorgeous smirk slowly crept onto his face, causing my eyes to widen slightly.

Oh no, no, no!

"Was I?" I felt flustered suddenly as his smirk continued to grow.

"I meant... that you sang and played...so wonderfully last night at Addin's place." I stumbled over my words, mentally kicking myself for doing so.

Ugh, how embarrassing can I get?

He raised an eyebrow, squinting his eyes at me.

"Okay, well, you were also amazing in bed last night," he chuckled, leaning his head into the crook of my neck and planting a soft kiss.

"I know, right?" he smirked some more against my skin.

uh-huh! Cocky much, I see.

I rolled my eyes, and refocused my attention on the guitar.

"By the way, can I ask you something?" I said, my voice laced with curiosity and excitement.

He hummed, his warm breath tickling the strands of my hair as he nuzzled closer, inhaling my hair.

His fingers gently swept all of my hair to one side. His lips brushed against my bare shoulder, making me shudder.

He planted numerous kisses on my shoulder,Slowly, his lips trailed a path, moving from my shoulder to the expanse of my bare back, leaving a trail of electrifying kisses on my bare back.

I turned around, titling my head back.

I mustered the courage to speak, my voice slightly trembling. "Umm, just don't look at my upper back too much," I murmured, my words laced with vulnerability.

He frowned, his eyes filled with concern.

"You know, the scar—" I started, but he cut me off, his lips finding mine in a gentle peck, silencing my self-doubt.

"It isn't ugly," he insisted, his voice filled with conviction.

I sighed, feeling the weight of his words slightly lifting the insecurities that had plagued me for so long.

"But still, it's...kind of, you know—" I trailed off, my voice tinged with uncertainty.

He interrupted me with another tender kiss, his lips pressed against mine, his eyes speaking volumes of adoration, he held for me.

"I told you, every single part of you is extremely beautiful, Ayezah," he whispered, his voice filled with sincerity.

"You are perfect in every way. The most gorgeous person, inside and out. I don't know why you restrain yourself from wearing backless dresses because, honestly, the scar on your back is just as stunning as you are."

My heart thumped loudly against my ribcage, as if it were trying to break free from its confines.

The words he spoke resonated deep within me, infusing my being with a comforting warmth that spread like a cozy blanket on a chilly night.

Could it truly be possible to love someone even more when you already believed your love for them had reached its limits?

This man before me has the incredible power to make me fall in love with him every single second.

The love I feel for him is so immense that it brings tears to my eyes. I fight back the overwhelming urge to cry, swallowing hard as I throw my arms around him, burying my tear-stained face in the crook of his neck, taking in his soothing signature scent as I sniffle softly.

His arms immediately envelop my body. we sit there, locked in each other's tight embrace. He gently placed his palm on top of my head, his touch tender as he caresses my hair.

we remain like this for a few precious seconds, simply holding each other.

Eventually, he pulls back, concern etched on his face.

Softly, he asks a small, 'Are you alright?' His knuckles brush against my cheeks, wiping away the tears with a gentleness that eases my heart.

With a smile, I nod, my face lighting up. In return, he smiles back, his eyes filled relief.

" so you were going to ask something?"

I nod eagerly, remembering my question. " Oh yeah, yeah! I wanted to know how you learned to play the guitar and sing? " I inquire, curiosity dancing in my eyes.

well, he had talked to me about his love for music, but he never mentioned how or where he learned it.

"Actually, I took music classes when I was young. I've always had a passion for music, especially playing the guitar. It's more like a hobby for me," he explained.

"I can play the guitar pretty well, but I'm not the greatest singer," he added with a modest smile.

"Nah, I don't agree. Your voice is so soothing, I absolutely love it. I could listen to you sing all day," I grinned at him, unable to hide my joy. He leaned in and kissed my forehead, chuckling softly.

"Well, I don't usually sing, but if it brings you joy, I'll sing for you all day," he said, his words causing a flutter of butterflies in my stomach.

My cheeks turned a rosy shade, and I couldn't help but break into a wide grin. He kissed both of my cheeks, chuckling, his laughter filling the air, along with my giggles.

The whole day enveloped us in warmth and coziness as we basked in each other's company.

we talked for hours, we laughed our hearts out together like nothing in the world worries us or matters anymore, we ate delicious meals together, we watched some movies together while cuddling, we kissed, almost every single chance possible.

The day seemed to slip away, and before we knew it, evening had arrived.

We ones again found ourselves on the balcony of our room, sipping on hot chocolate, after the dinner.

we discussed our honeymoon plans and Greece was the destination we chose.

we were seated facing each other and engrossed in the conversation about how beautiful Greece is, and at that very moment I bend forward, intending to wipe away the chocolate mustache adorning Rahil's upper lip, but next second I'm seated on his lap, our mouths locked in a fervent, hungry kiss. We kissed as if the time itself was running out.

My legs were on either side of his torso, His back was pressed against the balcony railing as we were seated on the floor just like how we sat in the morning.

His strong arm encircled my waist, holding me in place, while his other hand roamed desperately on the contours of my back, igniting a trail of desire.

I broke the kiss, gasping for breath, my chest rising and falling. He wasted no time and attacked my jaw, his lips and teeth exploring every inch of my skin.

waves of pleasure rippled through me, causing soft moans to escape my lips.

His lips trailed down my neck, and in one swift motion, my off-shoulder crop top was lowered, my bra was unclasped and thrown away, revealing my bare skin to his hungry gaze.

He didn't even pause for a second. His mouth remained on my neck, his lips and tongue leaving a trail of desperate kisses and tantalizing bites on the skin of my neck.

His warm palms found their way to my breasts. His skilled hands kneaded them, a surge of pleasure shot through me, causing my back to arch involuntarily.

I discarded his t-shirt, revealing his chiseled shoulders and perfect abs. My hands roamed eagerly over his sculpted body, tracing every contour and reveling in the warmth of his skin.

with open-mouthed smooches, I planted kisses on his chest, each one drawing out a groan from deep within him, his head thrown back against the railing.

" Ayezah.." he moaned out.

I grabbed the back of his neck, pulling his face down to mine, our lips crashing together in a wild, mad kiss.

Next second, with a sense of urgency, he swiftly lowered his pants along with boxers, and in sync, I shed my lowers with the same desperate need.

Before I could fully comprehend the moment, he plunged himself inside me, his lips sealing mine, eating up the moans that escaped me.

As he began to move, a wave of pleasure coursed through my body, causing me to dig my nails into his biceps, anchoring myself to the overwhelming pleasure that consumed us both.

Oh, dear god, the sensation was beyond words. Every inch of him felt so incredibly good.

Our bare chests pressed together, the heat radiating between us, intensifying the passion that fueled our every movement.

with a relentless pace, he continued to thrust into me, driving me to the brink of ecstasy.

My moans and whimpers of pleasure filled the air, mingling with the sound of our bodies colliding together.

I wrapped my arms around his shoulders, hugging him closer, and softly biting his earlobe, his name escaped my lips in breathless whispers into his ear.

He slightly pulled back and dipped his head down, his lips finding my eager hardened nipple, while still deep inside me.

with raw hunger, he took my sensitive bud into his mouth, savoring it as if it were his most cherished delicacy.

The warmth of his breath and the gentle suction of his lips on my nipple, made me feel high and dizzy.

As he tilted his head, his lips and tongue moved to my other breast, lavishing it with the same intensity.

His mouth then refused to detach itself from my breasts, as he alternated between sucking, biting, and nibbling on my nipples.

Each flick of his tongue and every gentle nip, made me fist his hair.

He continued his assault, causing my nipples to swell and become even more sensitive. I was left in a breathless, moaning mess, surrendering to the overwhelming pleasure that consumed me.

He is so fucking great! I must just die with so much pleasure he is giving me right now.

"Oh, god, babie! I think, I'm utterly addicted to you," he husked against my lips, his voice dripping with desire, as he continued to move inside me.

"I can't seem to get enough of you either, Rahil... You're absolutely amazing," I whispered, my fingers gripping his shoulders.

He kissed the top of my breasts, his lips trailing down to nuzzle into the valley of my cleavage.

with a deep grunt, he picked up his pace, and I couldn't help but hug his head, my hands fisting his hair.

The pleasure intensified with each second, and it felt as if I was seeing stars and in that very moment, we both climaxed together, our bodies panting for air.

He gently pressed his forehead against mine, a smile playing on his lips. His damp hair, glistening with sweat, cascaded over his hazy eyes.

His thumbs found their way down to my breast, caressing my swollen nipples, as if he was soothing away any lingering pain.

"I could do this every day and night," he whispered breathlessly, our noses touching, his thumb still working its magic on my breast.

I raised an eyebrow, a playful smirk dancing on my lips.

"Well, I wouldn't mind either. You're quite the wild one in bed, Rahil! Sly as a fox, pretending to be innocent when you're anything but," I teased.

With a mischievous grin, he met my gaze. "Oh, darling, this side of mine is reserved solely for my gorgeous wife," he declared, his smirk deepening.

He dipped his head down, his lips softly pecking my swollen buds one by one.

I looked around, and then it hit me.

We had just done it in the fucking balcony?

It was almost night, and as I gazed out into the open space of our private house pool area and backyard, a rush of excitement coursed through my veins. Though I knew no one would be there, the thrill of being exposed, sent shivers down my spine.

He gently cupped my face, his touch causing my eyes to lock onto his.

He pressed his lips against mine in a deep, noisy kiss before lifting me effortlessly, my body exposed and vulnerable in his arms.

His hands firmly gripped my bare ass, holding me close as he carried me inside our bedroom, passing through the huge glass-sliding door of the balcony. our discarded clothes lay completely forgotten on the ground.

with a gorgeous smirk spread across his face, he whispered, "Let's have a round two on the bed. It's much more comfortable, you know." I wrapped my arms around his neck, my head shaking in both agreement and excitement, as I held him close.

Chapter 15

Laila's POV:

" Umm, Subways are seriously the best ever!"Ayezah squealed in delight, munching a mouthful of her delicious pepper chicken subway sandwich. It was the lunch break, and we decided to grab a bite together at the nearby subway.

I took a big bite of my own mouthwatering barbecue chicken subway sandwich, chewing on it I asked, "So, when are you going on your honeymoon? " A mischievous grin spread across my face.

Ayezah's face lit up with a wide smile.

"Soon, I just want to take care of the business deals and everything before we go," she replied, her excitement palpable.

It had been a month now since Ayezah and Rahil jij got married, and they had recently returned to the work from their wedding holiday.

In our three years of friendship, I had never seen Ayezah radiate such genuine happiness. Her smile was no longer forced; it was a reflection of the joy in her heart.

I remembered all the times Ayezah had shed her precious tears for her selfish and uncaring mom, who was blinded by external recognition so much that she neglected her own daughter's mental health.

But my Ayezah truly and dearly loved her mom, despite everything. The way she still wears the pendant given by her mom speaks volumes. Not everyone could do that, knowing how much her mother's memories hurt her, but she tries to hold on to the good ones.

She says that, after all, that woman was still her mother, and no matter what, she can't hate her. It breaks my heart to see how pure she is.

Seeing her now, filled with genuine happiness, warmed my heart. She had finally found her bliss.

And I would literally do anything to protect her happiness.

Ayezah was my only family. I lost my parents when I was very young in a plane crash. My grandparents took care of me, but then they too passed away soon, leaving me all alone in this world.

The so-called relatives, heartlessly turned their backs on me, deeming me a burden simply because I was a girl.

Fucking stupid society. It's frustrating how they often sees girls as burdens.

I was mature enough to make my own decisions, so with the money my grandparents left me, I left Pakistan and moved to Australia to start a new life.

It was in this foreign land that I discovered Ayezah. She radiated goodness like a sunbeam, illuminating my path. In Pakistan, I had known loneliness, but with Ayezah by my side, everything transformed into colourful wheel of belonging and love.

Ayezah made everything better. She became a sister, a best friend, and my family. When her father told her to move to London, she took me with her, and I gladly went because she was all I had.

So there's this thing that's been bugging me for the past few days now.

The tacky red hoodie person.

Surprisingly, it's not Alexander like we initially thought. I actually confronted that piece of shit myself and gave him a piece of my mind, threatening him that I won't hesitate to slit his throat if he doesn't stop this stupidity soon.

And he denied being the red hoodie person.

Alexander wouldn't dare to lie, especially when he had a knife to his throat. He's not brave enough to lie in such a situation. so I'm certain he wasn't lying about not being the red hoodie person.

Over the past few days, I've noticed a car following Ayezah from her office to her home. It's quite concerning me, especially since we usually head home together.

Ayezah is always so excited to go back to the love of her life, basically returning to her home, that she seems to not notice the red car that always chases behind her.

Every time, without fail, I spot that red car patiently waiting for her in the parking lot and the person in the tacky red hoodie is always inside! The crazy thing is, they change their number plate every single day. How in the world do they have so many number plates?

I'm determined to find out who this person is, no matter what it takes.

I don't want to burden Ayezah with this information. She is so happy these days, I can't take that away from her because of some assholes.

My gut tells me it could be her business rival or some other despicable individual.

I'll find out who it is, and once I do, I'm going to disrupt their peace, just like they disrupted mine.

"LAILA???" Ayezah's loud voice snapped me out of my thoughts. "Umm..yeah?" I stuttered in response.

"What's wrong? I've been calling you for so long," she frowned.

I smiled and shook my head. "I was just thinking about something."

A mischievous grin spread across Ayezah's face. "Thinking about something? Or someone?" she teased.

I closed my eyes and groaned. "Ayezah! not again."

" Why? Just say yes already! " she winced, and I held my forehead.

so here's the deal, Yesterday, after the meeting at Rahil jij's office, since Ayezah's company and Rahil jij's are already business partners, we all decided to go to a cafe.

Adam ABSOLUTE IDOIT Hussain, had the audacity to propose me to be his girlfriend. Right there, in front of Ayezah and Rahil jij.

I won't deny that I felt flustered, with butterflies in my stomach and my heart almost tripped down the stairs. But I won't admit it aloud.

Adam is Indian. It's not that I'm racist or anything, but it's just strange considering the historical tensions between India and Pakistan.

My grandpa was a retired army officer, who used to tell stories about the deep-seated animosity between the two nations. And It weirdly bothers me.

I don't know, maybe I'm just being straight up stupid but I can't help it. It gives me somewhat uneasy feeling.

I don't know how that annoying piece of shit managed to make me fall for him with his stupid, flirty lines.

Was it his ridiculously handsome face or maybe his natural ability to be a charmer?

I've never been particularly drawn to cute boys until Adam Hussain came into the picture. But it's frustrating that this difference in nationality comes between or it's just me who lets it come between.

"Cummon, it's clear in your eyes that you too like him back! Quit playing hard to get," Ayezah grumbled.

I shot her a look and replied, "Shut up! I ain't playing nothing like that, okay? I just don't like him, he's so dang annoying."

"Yeah, yeah, sure!" she said, her voice dripping with sarcasm. I narrowed my eyes at her, warning her to back off. But she couldn't resist teasing me further. "Annoying enough that you were all pink and red yesterday after he proposed to you!" she teased, wiggling her eyebrows mischievously.

" I'll chop you into pieces, if you don't shut it already," I warned and stood up from my seat, stomping outside angrily. Ayezah leaned back, laughing loudly, and called out, "Wait for me!" as she hurriedly followed me.

A pair of stunning green eyes locked onto my face, the gaze piercing through me as I focused on driving.

"I already told you not to stare at me like a creep," I hissed at the idiot sitting beside me in the car on the passenger seat.

"I can't help it-"

"One more cheesy line from you, and I swear I'll kick you out of this moving car," I threatened, cutting him off before he could continue. He simply grinned back at me like a stupid that he is.

I shot him my best glare before redirecting my attention to the road ahead.

Right now I was chasing the red car that had been tailing Ayezah for the past few days. The sky was gradually darkening.

This evening, right after office hours, I made a bold and impulsive decision of catching that freak in red hoodie.

I knew that calling the cops might have been the logical choice, but I couldn't risk Ayezah finding out.

So, I chose to take matters into my own hands and handle it myself.

If this person is some kind of psycho, well, once they meet me, they'll know who the real psycho is!

How dare they stalk my best friend?

As soon as Ayezah arrived home, the red car suddenly changed its route. I had to be extremely cautious because I didn't want to raise any suspicions with Ayezah. I couldn't afford for her to catch even the tiniest glimpse of my car, as it would surely make her suspicious. After all, my usual route home is completely different from hers.

"Ummm! So, is it a yes?" Adam asked, his voice filled with slight hesitation.

I frowned and looked at him, "About what?" I asked.

"Being my girlfriend? I mean, you didn't call me for that?" he questioned.

I didn't wanted to go behind that freak alone because it would be quite foolish of me to do so.

What if I found myself in real shit and there was no one around? What if the psycho tried to harm me? Who would call the cops? These thoughts flooded my mind, pushing me to call Adam because, other than Ayezah, I didn't have any friends or acquaintances, and strangely, I found myself trusting Adam.

So, I called him and asked him to meet me, but he got so excited that he didn't even let me finish speaking. When he arrived, I didn't have much time to explain everything.

"No-" I started, but he cut me off with a loud yell.

"NOOO??? Whyyyy?? I thought you would say yes right away, but you left without a word yesterday, and I understand because you needed time to think- " he rambled on. This time, I interrupted him.

"Adam, I meant that I called you for some other reasons."

I was driving him somewhere in the car since almost 25 minutes now, and this oblivious guy didn't even bother to ask where I was taking him.

He just kept gazing at me with dreamy, heart-eyed expressions, which was quite distracting, but I managed to regain my composure.

"So, it's about Ayezah!" I began, and proceeded to tell him everything about the creepy person in the tacky red hoodie. He listened intently, nodding along.

I finished telling him everything while carefully driving and closely following the car, making sure not to lose sight of it.

I also warned him not to spill any of this shit to Rahil under any circumstances.

"So you aren't refusing, huh?" he teased, wiggling his eyebrows mischievously and flashing me a teasing smile.

At first, a frown started to form on my face, but it quickly transformed into a scowl.

I had just shared something so serious and important with this guy, and all he seemed to focus on was my answer?

"Okay, okay, I'm sorry!" he said, chuckling as he looked at my scowl.

Then, he curiously asked, "So, how are you so sure that the person in the red hoodie is a woman?" I paused for a moment, gathering my thoughts, and replied, "Well, I'm sure because I once caught a glimpse of perfectly manicured, feminine hands on the steering wheel." His face contorted into an 'oh' expression.

" And why did you ask me to tag along?" he asked.

I couldn't help but roll my eyes at his question. "Why can't I? Are you the busiest person in the world or something?" I retorted, a hint of sarcasm lacing my words.

He chuckled, shaking his head, and replied, "Well, nope! Even if I'm busy, I don't mind taking some time out for you."

" I'm all yours, princess." He winked at me.

" please, imma throw up! " His laughter filled the air as he shook his head in amusement.

"I know, I know. You called me because you trust me, don't you?" he said, his voice warm and reassuring. And he was right. I did trust him, more than I cared to admit and also deep down, I couldn't deny that his willingness to be there meant a lot to me.

Or Maybe I just wanted a reason to be with him.

Wait, Did I just say that I wanted to be with him? was I actually going crazy?

" Oh, dream on! I called you because I needed a scapegoat, you know, like if any danger comes, I could just throw you in front and get rid of you forever." I said, trying to brush off my previous thoughts.

His laughter echoed, and he threw his head back, thoroughly amused by my words.

The car has stopped right in front of a small, cracked, shabby, and dusty old gate. It's been about five minutes, and neither the hoodie bastard nor us have made a move.

I kept tapping my fingers on the steering wheel, feeling increasingly impatient. What on earth is he doing in there? Come out, you coward! I screamed internally.

All of a sudden, I jerked back in place when I felt a warm palm on my hand which was on the steering wheel, anxiously and impatiently shaking slightly.

" calm down, princess!" Adam assured me with a calm look etched on his face.

I strangely felt a sense of calmness seeping inside me from his simple gesture.

"Ewww! What you tryna do?" I exclaimed faking annoyance, and slightly jerking his hand away from mine, coughing I turned my head towards the window, hiding my flushed cheeks.

" uh princess yo-" Adam started but was soon cut off when I whispered yelled loudly.

"Alert! Look, he's out." I squinted my eyes as I scrutinized the man from afar. I slowly gestured for Adam to come out of the car, but a thought struck my mind.

"No, no, get in!" I whispered urgently, gesturing for Adam to get back in the car as I saw him stepping out on the other side.

I can't take him to follow me into danger. What if the freak tries to harm him? That wasn't part of my plan. So, I think it's safer for him to stay in the car and help me when I'm in dire need, rather than coming along with me. I can't risk anything.

Adam ruminated for a while and then squinted his eyes at me as if scrutinising me.

" ain't no way I'm letting you go there alone," he said ever so casually.

" ain't no way I'm taking you along," i protested.

"Well, it's dangerous, you jerk. But if you still want to join, sure, I wouldn't mind. It's up to you if you want to die virgin because ain't no way we are making it up alive." I said trying to scare him but nonetheless it didn't work.

" firstly, who told you that I'm a virgin, princess?" He walked towards my side of the car and leaned over me, causing my back to press against the car door, all while wearing a smirk

my breath got knocked out at the proximity, and my heartbeat accelerated.

" From the way I know you and your personality it doesn't seem that you've been laid ever anytime. " I said pressing a tight sweet smile on my face and nodding at him.

He rolled his eyes at me and shot me a look of pure annoyance. And I did a small victory dance inside my head, because that's what you get for always pissing of Laila siddique.

I pushed him away and started walking towards the gate where the bitch was standing with a phone pressed to his ear, probably on a call with someone.

Adam followed me, pissing me off to no extent. Can't he for once listen to me quietly? Ugh!

"Look, princess, I don't care what happens. If I live, I'll live with you. If I die, I'll die with you. So, yes! I'm coming along, and you won't say a word about it." Adam said, his tone filled with warning.

I scoffed at his audacity, " you know what! you're too cheesy for your own good! Also I shouldn't have bought you here with me in the first place." I said with a scowl etched on my face.

without ny further debate, I let him follow me. The hoodie freak opened the gate and started walking in, Adam and I followed him with slow, sneaky steps.

we quietly followed the person without uttering a word or making any noise.

I quickly scanned the area, and my eyes widened in surprise. It was a shabby, run-down garden with not a single plant or flower in sight. The earth was cracked, and there was wet mud everywhere, as if someone had intentionally watered the garden.

The person suddenly stopped, and for some reason, I had a feeling that they knew we were following them. Their head subtly tilted towards the left corner, where I was, but they continued walking nonchalantly.

I felt my breathing tighten for a moment, but then I brushed it off and started taking slow, quiet steps.

Once again, the person stopped, and I saw a small, bushy, old, worn-out, shabby, and dusty cottage-like hut.

" Back off! " a manly, deep husky voice reached my ears and I felt as if the hair behind my neck stood up.

Did I hear it right? a manly voice? A women speaking in a manly voice? oh no stupid Laila this seems to be kind of fucked up.

I scoffed loudly at the person's audacity, " you filthy coward, a complete piece of shit! do you really think you can scare me by that? Turn around bitch or bastard whoever you're," I yelled furiously.

Adam held onto my arm and whispered a 'calm down' in my ear but I completely ignored him, because I'm having another personal beef with him for following me behind forcefully.

The person laughed like a maniac, which only confirmed my suspicions that they were a complete lunatic.

" you a mere girl, who the fuck are you? just get out of here before I do something that will lead to serious consequences." the manly voice threatened, still facing his back to me cowardly.

Taking a deep breath to calm myself, I jerked Adam's hold on me and quickly approached him/her and forcefully pulled the hoodie's cap with one hand while placing my other hand on the shoulder, making him/her finally turn around.

There we go! It's a man with sharp eyebrows and dark eyes, half of his face covered with a black thin mask.

But wait a man? a man with pedicured nails? Really? my brain hammered and I swiftly gazed at his hands only to see manly normal rough-looking hands.

I got lost in my thoughts, wondering if the person in the red hoodie could be the same girl I saw before with perfectly manicured nails, because I'm damn sure it was a feminine hand.

Did we chase the wrong person? Maybe we misunderstood something.

As I was contemplating whether we had chased the right person or if we were completely off track, lost in my thoughts, suddenly I felt an intense pain at the back of my head. It was as if someone was forcefully pulling out all of my hair from the roots and scalp.

I looked at the man who had a firm grip on my hair, causing me to hiss and yelp in pain. I desperately tried to free myself from his harsh and tight hold.

"Fucker! How dar-" Adam's words were cut off as blood started to ooze out from his mouth. I froze on my spot and my eyes widened in pure shock.

The man had stabbed a huge, thick and sharp dagger on Adam's waist, exactly near to his lower abdomen and stomach. My heart stopped at the dreadful sight.

Adam let out a harsh hiss of pain, and the pain I felt when he gripped my hair doesn't even compare to what he's feeling now.

I couldn't help but gaze at the sharp dagger piercing Adam's waist, with blood staining his white office shirt. My pulse quickening with each passing second.

The man's grip on my hair loosened and I noticed his hands shaking while he held the dagger. Swiftly, he discarded the dagger from Adam's body and threw it on the ground.

Adam fell to the ground with a loud thud, and the man seemed terrified by his own actions. He took a step back, visibly shocked, as if realizing what he had just done. I was completely in state of shock, my body locked on its own and I couldn't process anything in that moment.

I could only hear Adam's painful hisses echoing in my ears. My mind felt foggy, and my heart felt heavy. It felt like my legs were glued to the spot where I was standing.

I knelt down to where Adam fell clutching his wound which was constantly bleeding. My heart clenched at the sight of him and I felt like shredding the man into two.

" Adam.." I say, my voice cracked, shaky and mere whisper.

" I'm okay Laila, he's running away, go after him, " Adam pointed towards the man that was running away by now and my jaw tightened.

" No you are not okay-" he cut me off.

" Just go after him dammit.. " He hissed and clutched his wound, and my heart clenched even more.

" Don't worry I'll take care of myself...please go after him." He insisted between hissing and I bawled my fists.

" I'll be right back! " Swallowing I ran towards the man who was running away from the backyard of the ground, my jaw clenched and eyes darkened.

I mustered all my strength and landed a harsh kick on his back, causing him to jolt and fall to the ground.

Learning martial arts was some use today!

Rage and fury burned in my eyes, and there was no way I was going to spare him now.

" What the fuck bitch? " He growled hissing in pain.

I strode towards his side and gripped his collar tightly with both of my hands, raising him to his feet. The intensity in my eyes could have pierced through steel as I locked my gaze onto him.

" How fucking dare you?? " I yelled.

With a swift and forceful motion, my clenched fist connected with his jaw, making his head turn sideways with the force. I then tried to pull off the mask from his face, but he jerked, tripping on something and falling on the ground.

Chuckling like a lunatic that he is, he stood up and strode towards me hastily, punching me harshly across my jaw. It felt like I almost broke my jaw bone. I hissed holding my jaw, and I could taste blood on my lower lip.

I kneeled him in the balls with all my force, and he bent over screaming and holding for his dear life.

I planned on continuing and beating the shit out of him with all my strength until I heard Adam's loud hiss which made me snap my head towards him, I immediately rushed to him.

I snapped my head back only to see that the fucker had escaped.

Chapter 16

Adam's POV:

She is beautiful. so freaking beautiful. it's like she stepped out of a fairytale or something because every time I gaze at her, I'm in awe of her perfection.

I always find myself wondering if I'll ever tire of staring at her, but the truth is, I could do it all day and night and still wouldn't get enough.

You know, they say you don't believe in love at first sight until you experience it yourself, and it's absolutely true. I believed it when it happened to me.

I can vividly recall the exact moment, the date, and the day I first laid eyes on my Laila.

It was a day when Rahil sir's company was collaborating with one of his acquaintances, or more like an old friend. I clearly remember how Rahil sir's eyes sparkled with excitement, as if this collaboration meant the world to him. He was so incredibly happy, as if he had never been this thrilled to collaborate with any other company before.

We were in the meeting room, I was seated on one side of Rahil sir's chair, absentmindedly twirling my pen in anticipation of the boring meeting ahead.

A stunning lady entered the room, and Rahil sir's face lit up with sheer delight as he stood up to greet her. In that moment, I snapped out of my sulking mood and shifted into professional mode.

As the gorgeous lady moved slightly, my eyes caught a glimpse of someone behind her, and my breath hitched at the mere sight.

There was a person with focused eyes, her slim tablet held firmly in her hands, typing away with a sense of urgency.

Her vibrant red locks framed her diamond-shaped face, gently brushing against her cheeks as the rest of her hair was stylishly tied back in a high, messy ponytail.

Her attire exuded professionalism : a black turtle neck top paired elegantly with brown dress pants, cinched at the waist with a thin belt.

But it was when she finally lifted her eyes from the tablet that my heart skipped a beat. It actually felt like time stood still as our eyes met, and in that instant, my heart threatened to burst out of my chest.

Raven eyes, a small nose, plump strawberry lips, and perfect dark eyebrows adorned her captivating face.

As if these features weren't enough to drive me crazy, she unexpectedly flashed me a small greeting-like smile. My heart skipped several beats as I inhaled deeply, trying to suppress the silly grin that was desperate to break free from my lips.

I couldn't help but stare at her unapologetically, my excitement evident as I started grinning like an absolute goner.

However, her smile faded, her brows furrowed, and she shot me a hard glare which screamed 'look away you weirdo'

Oh goodness, is she annoyed?? so adorable.

She greeted Rahil sir, and he introduced me as his secretary to them.

My grin widened even further, and she looked at me as if I had escaped from a mental asylum.

A low chuckle escaped my throat and Laila gave me a look before focusing back on the road as she was driving to who-knows-where.

The destination didn't matter as long as I had the precious opportunity to be with her. Since our first meeting, we had to stay in touch as secretaries, constantly coordinating meetings and schedules. I was over the moon, honestly.

She was absolutely adorable when she got all riled up, and I loved provoking reactions out of her.

I couldn't resist flirting with her whenever I could. She was a force to be reckoned with, a fiery and captivating woman. Her reactions only fuelled my desire.

She used to threaten me, saying she'd complain to my boss, but I couldn't care less. My job was important, sure, but wooing Lailahad taken center stage in my life.

I may not have known what I wanted from life, but one thing was crystal clear : I wanted her. Only her.

I never knew I had that natural flair for flirting within me. You see, I've always been known as the happy-go-lucky person, goofing around and spreading joy to everyone.

I didn't have any flirty tendencies until certain red-headed came into the picture.

" I already told you not to stare at me like a creep," Her voice broke me out of my trance.

I was about to throw a full-on flirtatious line, but she quickly silenced me with her humorous threats, leaving me unable to suppress a chuckle.

A tinge of disappointment washed over me when she revealed that she hadn't called me here to say a simple 'yes.' I had hoped she was about to give me her answer.

Never before had I felt such nerves coursing through me as I did when I proposed to her yesterday, asking her to be my girlfriend.

If it were up to me, I would have directly asked her to be my wife, but I cherish my life very dearly.

So, I opted for the safer route of asking her to be my girlfriend. However, her piercing gaze almost killed me, you know like if looks could kill and all.

And as expected, she left without uttering a single word in response.

Deep down, I know she has feelings for me as well, but there's something holding her back, something I can't quite put my finger on.

She told me about how Ayezah has a stalker and all the shit about the mysterious figure in freaking red hoodie.

The depth of her love and care for her best friend warmed my heart, knowing that she was willing to put her own life at risk. I knew she could go any lengths for her loved ones.

That's just how amazing my Laila is, y'all. She's absolutely perfect in every way.

I think I fell even more in love with her in that moment, as if I'm continuously tumbling and falling deeper into a love that feels impossible to escape.

Suddenly, the red hoodie dude abruptly halted his car in a shady and unsettling location, that creep the fuck out of me.

At first, Laila didn't object to my accompanying her, but later she insisted that I stay inside the car. I couldn't believe it. Did she really think I would let her face that freak all alone?

To tease her, I playfully circled the car, and the sight of her cheeks flushing as I leaned closer to her, made my heart race.

I love the effect I have on her.

Even when I touched her hand inside the car, she jerked away as if my mere touch burned her. And if she thinks I didn't notice her flushed cheeks back then, she's completely mistaken. I can see through her attempts to hide her reactions.

we cautiously approached the figure in the red hoodie. The stupid dude got her all riled up in mere seconds.

She strode towards him with such intensity, as if she will finish his very existence. I tried to calm her down, but the moment fucker decided to put his hands on her, a surge of rage coursed through my veins, shattering my composure.

Before any words could escape my lips or I could do anything, a searing pain pierced the side of my waist, causing a sharp gasp to escape my mouth.

The world around me blurred slightly as crimson droplets trickled from my lips and the wound.

The way that bastard's hands trembled as he flung the knife made it clear that he had no intention of causing harm in the first place.

It was even more fucked up than it initially appeared, so I urged Laila to go after him. Maybe she could catch a glimpse of his face. I knew she was skilled in martial arts and she fought the fucker with all the strength and might, until I hissed because the pain got a little unbearable and she immediately rushed to me back and the coward of a bastard ran away.

I could feel the searing pain coursing through my body as I pressed my palm tightly against the wound, to stem the flow of blood. A sharp hiss escaped my lips as Laila knelt before me, her eyes wide with concern and worry etched across her face.

"Oh my god! You're bleeding so much!" Her voice was cracking and filled with fear.

My gaze shifted from my wound to Laila's face, and a surge of anger coursed through me.

The fucker had hurt her. He hurt my Laila.I clenched my jaw, feeling a burning rage building within me. I noticed a trickle of blood escaping from the corner of her lower lip, and my heart ached at the sight.

If only I weren't weakened by my own wound, I would have grabbed the dagger that lay on the floor, the very same dagger that had pierced my flesh, and I would have chased after him, hunted him down and sliced his hands off for daring to hurt her.

She gently placed her palm on top of my hand, which was tightly clutching the wound, causing me to hiss once again. She immediately retreated her hand back.

"Oh god, I'm so sorry! Did I hurt you?" Laila's voice trembled with guilt and regret. Her eyes were filled with a myriad of emotions, shimmering with unshed tears.

In that moment, I raised my other clean hand and tenderly cupped her cheek. I carefully wiped away the blood from the corner of her lips.

" You.. you are hurt.." I managed to say ignoring the pain.

A single tear escaped from her eyes, tracing a path down her soft flushed cheek. She placed her other hand on top of mine, the one that was pressed against her cheek, and began to cry loudly, her eyes tightly shut.

Suddenly she hit my shoulder lightly, causing my eyes to widen in surprise.

"Why? You're bleeding so much, and all you care about is my mere wound? Why, Adam?" Her voice was filled with anguish as she continued to sob, her eyes still shut tightly.

I mustered a faint smile. I struggled to speak, the pain making it difficult, but I managed to utter those words clearly.

"Because I love you."

She opened her eyes, her lashes glistening with tears, and stared at me in disbelief and something else twirling in her beautiful raven eyes.

" Oh God! How could you say it just like that? You are such an idiot, I hate you! "

I smiled as next second her arms flung around my neck, and fresh tears cascaded down her face. I suppressed a wince as her body crashed into mine, though she was careful, it still stung slightly. Without hesitation, I immediately wrapped my other clean arm around her, relishing in her warmth and delight of her citrusy scent.

She wept, clinging onto me for a few precious seconds, and I rested my head in the crook of her neck, taking in the comforting aroma of her with each breath.

Suddenly, she pulled away, and I already longed for the warmth, scent and softness of her body, despite the intense pain coursing through my lower abdomen.

"We need to go to the hospital! Come on," she urgently got up, Swiftly wiping away her tears with the back of her hand and helped me to my feet.

She wrapped my arm around her neck for support and I limped towards the car as she guided me.

Laila drove me to the hospital with such an urgency and high speed that I thought we would surely end up in an accident.

We finally reached the hospital, and without wasting any time, I was taken in to get my wound stitched and dressed.

The doctor informed me that I had lost a significant amount of blood, and the fact that I hadn't fainted was quite surprising.

He then prescribed some meds and painkillers, and I was hooked up to an IV for an hour to replenish my blood.

Throughout the entire process, Laila never left my side. She sat there, softly sobbing, her eyes fixed on me all the time.

As we arrived at my apartment, the car came to a halt, and a heavy silence filled the air. The entire ride back, Laila didn't utter a single word, hell she didn't even threaten me to look away when I was staring at her continuously. Her grip on the steering wheel was so tight that her knuckles turned almost pale.

She let out a small sniffle, unclicked her seatbelt, and turned towards me, fully facing me.

"Umm... I-I'm really sorry for today! It's all my fault. I shouldn't have taken you there! I feel so stupid for going after that freak without any protection. I'm so sorry that you had to..." Her words were interrupted by tears streaming uncontrollably down her cheeks.

I unclicked my seatbelt, leaned forward, and gently cupped her tear-stained cheeks.

"Shhh," I whispered, wiping away her tears and gazing into her beautiful eyes, glistening with pearls.

"I'm sorry, Adam." she whispered, her voice barely audible.

I pressed my forehead against hers, "Stop saying that and stop crying please! It's not your fault. In fact, I'm glad you took me with you! I'm glad that you're not hurt badly and that you're safe. That's what matters the most."

She gazed into my eyes, with some different kind of emotions swirling within hers.

She lightly hit my shoulder, "Stop saying such things so casually!"

I couldn't help but smirk.

"Why? does your heart flutter, princess?" I teased. She sniffled and shot me an annoyed look.

"No."

I chuckled softly. "I see you're quite good at lying." I continued caressing her soft cheeks, and she closed her eyes, leaning into my touch, causing my heartbeat to pick up its pace.

We stayed like that for a few seconds, our foreheads pressed against each other.

"By the way, why are you so sad? Didn't you want a scapegoat? You also told me you wanted to get rid of me for forever, right?" I asked, feigning innocence and wanting to tease her a little.

But to my surprise, she didn't look annoyed. Instead, she softly gazed at me, tears shimmering in her eyes.

She cupped my cheeks too with her delicate palms. "No! I never want you hurt, Adam! Never ever. It stings me too to see you in pain, and it stings more thinking that it was because of me."

My heart race uncontrollably. Then, she looked a bit hesitant, her expression flushed with a mixture of emotions.

" I like you, Adam! I like you a lot."

Oh.my.god.

She admitted it! Laila Siddique admitted her feelings for me.

Is it a dream? If yess then I'll never want to wake up please.

my heart felt like it was going to burst out of my chest right then and there.

I was speechless, caught in a trance, just staring at her.

She broke the silence, "Say something, I'm feeling embarrassed now!"

I snapped out of my daze and without thinking twice, I leaned in and placed a long kiss on the corner of her mouth.

She froze for a moment, and I pulled back to look at her. She stared back at me, blushing slightly. So freaking adorable.

This girl was going to be the death of me, i'm telling you.

I kissed her forehead, cheeks and chin excitedly, making her giggle out loud.

I stopped at her lips, her smile faded slightly, and she gazed at my lips, mirroring my own action.

And in the next second, she pressed her lips against mine, making me close my eyes with the feel of her soft petals.

I kissed her slowly, savoring the taste of her sweet lips, as if each moment was way too precious.

The gentle pressure of her teeth on my bottom lip sent a shiver down my spine, and I couldn't help but part my lips. Our tongues intertwined together, sucking each other's breaths out.

The kiss was passionate and electrifying, leaving us both breathless, our chests rising and falling in sync as we pulled away to catch our breath.

Our eyes locked and I whispered breathlessly against her soft lips, "So, it's a yes, right?"

My lips brushed against hers in a gentle caress.

She placed a lingering smooch on my lips, making me shut my eyes automatically and her hands gracefully wrapped around my neck, pulling me closer in an embrace that spoke volumes.

"No."

"No?" I couldn't help but raise an eyebrow.

She pressed her lips together, a mischievous glint in her eyes, as if trying to suppress a laugh.

But her lips couldn't hide the subtle smile that tugged at the corners of her mouth.

"Well then, how about wife?"

she shot me an annoyed look and pushed me away slightly.

I couldn't help but chuckle loudly, the sound of joy filling the air as I leaned forward and connected our lips once again.

Chapter 17

Ayezah's POV:

Life feels unbelievably perfect, beyond what I could have ever imagined.

I never thought I could feel so alive and amazing. But that's exactly what happens when you're living with your favorite person, the one you love.

Rahil is everything and more than I could ever ask for. He has turned my life into a fairy tale, filled with perfection and beauty.

Each passing day and every second, I find myself falling even more in love with him.

Right now, he's sulking like a babie in my arms, trying to snuggle into my chest. We're sitting in front of the dressing table in our room.

Rahil is seated on the stool, and I'm seated on his lap, with both my legs on one side. His strong arms are wrapped around my waist.

He's wearing only grey trousers, which showcase his abs and well-built muscles. His veiny hands are a treat for my eyes. As for me, I'm wearing a fluffy black bathrobe, with nothing beneath it.

The scent of his fresh, clean shower gel fills the air, and no matter how much I inhale, I can't get enough of it. It smells so good. He smells so good.

His hair is still glistening with water, and I'm doing my best to gently pull his face away from my chest and dry his hair with a hairdryer.

"Rahil!" I hiss, my fingers gripping his face gently but firmly. He responds with a lazy, annoyed look, his eyes narrowing slightly.

"What? Do we really need to attend this party? I'm exhausted! Working all day and being away from you is already torture enough, and now we have to endure business parties too? Come on, the evening is my favorite time when we're back home together, just the two of us. I don't want to share that precious time at some stupid party." He grumbles, hiding his face in my chest once again.

Can you believe the change he's undergone?

Ever since we had that sex in the balcony, everything seems different.

Since that balcony scene, we've both been acting like sex maniacs unapologetically, having sex at every chance we get.

And he's become so obsessed with me, just as I am with him.

"Wait a minute," I say

" When did these parties become 'stupid parties'?" I raise an eyebrow.

" Ever since they started interrupting my precious alone time with my wife."

I couldn't help the heat raising to my cheeks.

"But come on," I continue, my eyes sparkling with excitement. "We really need to attend this party, especially since it's such an important opportunity for you to collaborate with the company you've been pursuing for so long. Don't you still love the thrill of collaborations?" I ask, knowing Rahil's sharp business mind always craves new ventures and profits.

"Nah," he says, a mischievous grin spreading across his face as he lifts his head from my chest.

"Collaborations don't excite me anymore, not since the last time I collaborated with your incredible company." I laugh, ruffling his hair slightly damp hair and grab the hairdryer, resuming to dry his hair.

He stays still this time, allowing me to dry his hair. His gaze remains fixed on my face for a few seconds, and then I notice the subtle shift in his eyes.

They become fixated on a particular spot, I follow his intense gaze and find him staring at my cleavage, which peeks through the folds of my bathrobe.

His neck muscles work as he gulps, and next instant I feel the gentle brush of his finger against my cleavage, causing a shudder to run throughout my body.

with deliberate intent, he slowly parts open the bathrobe, granting him complete access to my cleavage.

Next second he dips his head down and presses his lips on my cleavage, making me shut my eyes immediately. Goosebumps erupts my skin and my bottom lip curls under my teeth, feeling his warm lips on my sensitive skin.

He then dig his teeth into the flesh and I whimper out his name.

" Rahil.."

He keeps nibbling on the sensitive skin of my cleavage, sending bursts of pleasure coursing through my veins.

My eyes shot open in a sudden realization.

"Oh no, Rahil!" I exclaimed.

" I'm wearing a dress with a slightly deep neckline."

He leaves a trail of tender kisses and smooches on my cleavage before lifting his head, "So what?"

" Everyone should already know that you're off the limits, so they better not even think about glancing in your direction, let alone inappropriately. The mere thought of some loser daring to look at you the wrong way makes my blood boil," he says, his voice brimming with intense possessiveness.

"Whoa, hold up there! Where's my calm and sweet Rahil? What have you done to him?" I playfully tease, raising an eyebrow.

"He's gone," he grins mischievously, and I can't help but shake my head in amusement.

"But seriously, possessive much, huh?" I tease again, a playful smirk on my face.

"When it comes to you? Absolutely."

His words stirred something deep within me, creating a delightful fluttering sensation in my stomach. I shook my head, trying to regain my composure, and leaned in to kiss his lips. He responded eagerly, deepening the kiss.

His hand reaches for the knot of the bathrobe, attempting to open it but I hold his wrist halting his movements.

I reluctantly pulled away earning a deep groan from him, my lips still tingling from the connection.

"We'll be late," I whispered against his lips. He tries chasing my lips for another kiss but I title my head back a little, giggling.

I peck his lips once more before quickly getting up from his lap.

He grumbled something like ' I truly hate business parties now.' and I couldn't help but smile as I made my way to the walk-in wardrobe to change.

Rahil extends his arm gracefully as soon as we step out of the car. I smile, delicately wrapping my hand around his strong bicep.

He's dressed in a sleek black suit that seems to have been tailored specifically for his body, hugging him in all the right places.

His dark hair is styled with precision, each strand perfectly in place and he's looking as handsome as always.

As for me, I'm wearing a sage green silk gown that drapes gracefully around my figure. The gown is sleeveless, with delicate thin straps resting on my shoulders, giving it an elegant and feminine touch.

Of course, I didn't go for the deep neckline. I mean, seriously, it would've been so embarrassing because the hickey he left on my cleavage was really noticeable and dark. No matter how much makeup I tried to use, it just wasn't doing the trick.

My hair cascades down in loose waves. For my makeup, I've opted for a minimal yet bold approach. I've carefully applied the wink eyeliner, and added green eyeshades to complement the color of my gown.

To complete the look, I've adorned myself with silver accessories and silver heels.

" You know we can still ditch the party if you want." Rahil whispers in my ear.

I glance up at him, my eyes reflecting a mixture of amusement and affection, and gently shake my head, refusing his tempting offer.

"You look too hot and irresistible! I wanna gobble you down." He whispers again, causing my eyes to widen in surprise. His words ignite a spark within me and his warm breath on my earlobe only intensified the sensation.

"You're getting bolder these days!"

" Learning from the best, afterall." He shrugs nonchalantly, a mischievous glint in his eyes. I can't help but smirk, raising an eyebrow and giving him an exaggerated 'oh' face.

I look ahead, my eyes narrowing as I spot a scene that catches my attention.

Adam steps out of his car and opens the door of the passenger seat, extending his hand towards a lady.

A wide grin spreads across his face as he delicately kisses her knuckles.

wait, who the hell is she? Don't tell me he moved on from Laila so soon—

My thoughts come to a halt as I notice the hair colour of the lady.

Red head? Laila?

My doubt is cleared when the lady turns around.

It's Laila.

Adam extends his arm, and she wraps her hands around his biceps, planting a tender kiss on his cheek. He playfully clutches his chest, as if he might have a heart attack from the overwhelming joy. She laughs, her head thrown back in pure delight.

Oh!

I absolutely can't believe this! Just yesterday, this girl was claiming she had no interest in him, and now she's with him?

What's pissing me off for real is she didn't bother telling me about it. Me! Her best friend, the one who literally shares everything with her.

Dear bestfriend, you have landed yourself in big trouble now. You are so going to be dead meat.

I shoot death glares at my so-called best friend, who's sipping on her blue lagoon mojito like she ain't got a care in the world.

Earlier in the parking lot, we walked up to them, and Adam proudly declared that they're dating. Rahil seemed way too happy, like, weirdly happy.

Laila's face went all pale when she saw us, and I've been glaring at her ever since. Rahil and Adam are chatting up with some business partners, so I took the opportunity to corner Laila near the bar.

"Quit sucking on that damn straw and spill," I say.

She clears her throat, looking all nervous. "You know Adam, right? He's so annoying. He wouldn't leave me alone until I said yes, so yeah, yesterday I said yes...yeah," she stammers.

I narrow my eyes at her. "You expect me to believe that you just randomly said yes out of nowhere when I distinctly remember you being annoyed even with the idea of him just yesterday? Something's fishy here. What changed overnight that made you suddenly say yes? " I ask, sounding like a damn detective to my own ears.

Her face pales like a white paper and she appears nervous some more.

Laila and nervous? There's definitely something going on.

" Nothing's fishy! You're just being silly," she laughs, her laughter sounding forced and only making me more suspicious.

"Come on, you should be happy! You wanted me to say yes, right? Well, I finally said yes. And guess what? I actually like him and I was just playing trying hard to get. You should be happy for me," she says, trying to convince me.

"Oh, right, or more like strangle you for not telling your only best friend," I retort sarcastically.

"Oh wait a minute! Who's that bitch getting all cozy with Rahil jij?" Laila's attention suddenly shifts behind me.

I turn around to see Rahil laughing with a lady. The lady stands tall, her figure accentuated by a stunning deep red gown with a daring slit on the side. Her face remains hidden as her back is turned towards me.

As I observe her, I can't help but notice how dangerously close she stands to Rahil, her hands brushing against his arms whenever she gets the chance.

My gaze fixates on her hand, which now rests on his shoulder, that has perfectly manicured red nails.

My hands balled on my sides on their own. Rahil's eyes meet mine and he smile at me but it soon starts fading away when I narrow my eyes, glaring at the hand resting on his shoulder.

Rahil's smile fades completely, replaced by a frown as my glare intensifies.

He quickly creates a safe distance between himself and the lady, jerking her hand away as if he hadn't even realized she was touching him, putting a halt to my mind that was racing with thoughts of ways to spoil her perfectly manicured hand that dared to rest on his shoulder.

The lady slowly turns around, her piercing blue eyes locking onto mine. Her chocolate brown hair cascades down her shoulders, framing her face. As she looks at me, an unsettling feeling settles in the pit of my stomach. Suddenly, her lips curl into a wide, eerie smirk.

Rahil, sensing my unease, guides her towards me, all the while keeping a safe distance. He stands by my side, his arm wrapping around my waist, offering me a reassuring smile.

" Ms. Smith, meet my gorgeous wife, Ayezah," he introduces with pride.

Her smirk widens, and she continues to give me those unsettling stares.

" Nice meeting you Ayezah! I'm rose, rose smith." She forwards her hand for a handshake.

Trying my best to remain composed, I extend my hand to greet her. Her touch sends a chill through my fingers, causing me to quickly pull back.

" Ms. Smith is the one my company is collaborating with. She's a remarkable businesswoman," Rahil explains. I nod, attempting to smile, though it's clear that my discomfort is evident.

Glancing at Laila, I notice her glaring at the strange lady, studying her intently.

" I'll be right back." whispering this into my ear, Laila suddenly stomps off to god knows where.

I refocus my attention on Rose, who is now engrossed in a conversation with Rahil about business. The way she looks at him is different, from the way she looks at me. While she gazes at me with a creepy aura, her gaze towards Rahil is even more unsettling.

Rahil then excuses himself to talk to some other business partners, leaving me and that creepy rose alone. She continues giving me those creepy looks, and I try my best to ignore her.

She then comes to stand next to me near the bar and orders herself a glass of wine. The bartender hands her the wine glass, and she twirls it while looking at me.

"We finally met," she says, making me frown. Finally met? What does she mean?

"I must say, Rahil is very handsome and nice. You're lucky to have such a gracious man as your husband."

"Well, yes, My husband is really nice and handsome, and I'm aware that I'm very lucky to have him. Thanks for the reminder, though," I say, faking a sweet smile, which she returns with a smirk.

"Your welcome!" she says with a twisted smirk, her eyes gleaming with a hint of madness.

"By the way, don't you think someone like you doesn't deserve someone like him?"

Take a deep breath and stay calm. You don't want to create a scene at the party. This bitch is simply trying to get a reaction out of you.

I can feel it that she is doing this on purpose and I refuse to let her get under my skin.

With a calm yet cutting tone, I reply, " I'm not quite sure what you mean by 'someone like me.' But let me tell you, It's not about what someone deserves, but rather the connection and happiness they share. And trust me, the bond between my husband and me is something truly extraordinary."

"And how about you mind your own fucking business?" I'm ready to storm out. I can feel the anger bubbling up inside me, ready to explode.

But just as I'm about to storm away, she says something that makes me freeze in my tracks. "Oh yeah business! well what are the chances of you divorcing Rahil or Rahil divorcing you, maybe?"

This bitch

Anger boils inside me to a very great extent as I hear her spewing absolute nonsense. Who the hell does she think she is?

and what on earth is this psycho's problem? What the fuck does she exactly want from me?

Chapter 18

Rahil's POV:

Life becomes like a beautiful painting, and your favourite song, when you find that special someone who makes your heart overflow with happiness.

It's having a person who truly gets you, who's always there for you. Someone you can come home to after a long, exhausting day.

A person who fills the void of loneliness. A person who transforms a house into a warm and welcoming home. Being with them is like finding a safe place.

Ayezah is that person for me. She's not just my person; she's my everything.

I didn't realize how deeply I'm smitten and obsessed with my wife until my eyes keep going back to her. I want to gaze at her endlessly, never wanting to look away. Throughout the day at work, I eagerly await the evening, just so I can go back to my home, my wife.

I can't help but look for her all the time, even when I'm talking to other people. I just want to be with her.

It's a feeling beyond words. I'm consumed by this obsession, this desire to always have her within my gaze.

Even now, as I converse with a some important business partner, my eyes instinctively search for my gorgeous wife, who is not currently in my sight.

I scanned the crowd, my eyes eagerly searching for the stunning lady in green, but to my dismay, she was nowhere to be found.

A frown creased my forehead as I realized she wasn't anywhere in the massive hall. Perhaps she had gone to the washroom? But why hadn't she told me? Wait, hold on Rahil, why are you acting so clingy? Can't she go to the washroom alone? what the hell is wrong with you?

I refocused my attention on the business talk, trying my best to push thoughts of my wife aside, but it proved to be an incredibly difficult task. She was always on my mind, occupying every corner of my thoughts. Time seemed to slip away, and an entire hour passed with no sign of her. My heart started to race, worry creeping in.

Without wasting another moment, I pulled out my phone and dialed her number. To my dismay, she didn't pick up. Panic began to well up inside me.

I made my way towards the washroom, waiting anxiously outside for what felt like an eternity. Each woman who exited the washroom was not my wife. I sent her a text, desperately hoping for a reply, but none came. What on earth was happening?

Frustration and concern coursed through me as I continued to call her, my steps quickening as I rushed outside. Along the way, I bumped into Adam and immediately questioned him that if he had seen Ayezah anywhere. He hadn't seen her either. I informed him that I was leaving and hurried towards the parking lot, still dialing her number.

My heart pounded loudly in my chest, refusing to calm down. Why did I have this sinking feeling that something was wrong? Where could Ayezah have gone without telling me?

As I walked into the parking lot, I could hear the thunder rumbling and see the rain pouring down. It was raining hard and I got drenched in no time, but I couldn't care less about being wet. My mind was racing, thinking only about one thing: finding out where on earth my wife had gone?

Take a deep breath, Rahil! Stay calm and think carefully. Where could she possibly go?

In a flash of realization, I remembered Laila. With a sense of urgency, I dialed her number. At first, there was no response, but I didn't give up. I called her again, and this time, she answered.

"Heyy Laila, is Ayezah with you?" I blurted out.

" Heyy Rahil jij....yess Ayezah is with me." Her words felt like a balm to my anxious soul.

I closed my eyes, letting out a sigh of relief, feeling the tension in my heart ease, and my chest rise and fall with each calming breath. "Okay, where are you guys? Why did you leave so suddenly? Why didn't Ayezah inform me? And why isn't she picking up her goddamn phone?" I bombarded Laila with questions, my tone tinged with anger at the end, a result of the panic and worry that had consumed me.

" We're at my apartment...Ayezah is staying with me tonight. You see, I wasn't feeling too well...so we had to leave in a hurry. Unfortunately, Ayezah didn't get a chance to inform you and her phone is dead as well."

"Oh, are you okay?" I asked.

" Oh yes, yes! It's just a pesky fever, nothing more. And don't worry, Ayezah is perfectly fine too."

"Can I talk to her? Could you pass the phone to her? " I requested.

There was a brief silence before Laila responded, "Oh, she's in the washroom at the moment. She'll give you a call once her phone is charged.....Alright, Rahil jij, I need to get some rest. I'm really tired. You should head home too and drive safely, okay?" Before I could say anything else, the call abruptly ended.

A frown crept upon my face as something felt off. Laila's voice and behavior seemed peculiar, but I brushed it aside anyway.

Today, Ayezah is staying with Laila, and that thought made me a bit gloomy.

"It's okay," I reassured myself.

"she'll call once her phone is charged. Now, stop acting like a darn toddler and get moving." with a sigh, I made my way to the car and drove back home.

I showered and changed into fresh warm clothes.

With a lazy motion, I reached for the towel and lazily rubbed it through my damp hair.

As I settled onto the bed, memories of Ayezah drying my hair earlier flooded my mind, a bittersweet reminder of her absence. I couldn't help but let out a groan, feeling the ache of missing her already.

I knew that Laila needed her, but I need her too. Her presence had become an integral part of my life, and the thought of spending even a single night without her felt unimaginable.

Since she moved into my room, my heart had been filled with an overwhelming happiness, and I never anticipated a day where she wouldn't be by my side, peacefully sleeping.

With a frustrated sigh, I tossed the towel aside and let myself collapse onto the bed, my arms sprawled out and my body sinking into the mattress.

I lay there, gazing up at the ceiling, lost in thoughts, more like her thoughts.

The wind outside howled and the distant rumble of thunder added to my already gloomy mood, making it even gloomier.

I reached for my phone on the bedside table, while still lying in the middle of the bed, and called Ayezah.

However, disappointment washed over me as her phone was still off. Seriously, how long does it take to charge a phone? Ayezah should really consider buying a new phone or better yet, I'll buy her a new one with a larger battery capacity.

With the frustration mounting, I tossed the phone to the side and let out a groan.

Ugh I really miss her man.

Just as I resigned myself to the gloominess of the moment, my phone suddenly rang, breaking the silence. A spark of excitement ignited within me, and I eagerly grabbed the phone, a smile forming on my lips.

However, that smile quickly faded when I saw the caller ID.

It was Adam. Reluctantly, I answered the call.

He asked me if I found Ayezah, and I told him that I did. I explained that she is with Laila, who was feeling a bit unwell, so they left.

I could hear the panic in his voice as he frantically prepared to go outside. But I reassured him that the weather wasn't ideal for driving at this time, and more importantly, Laila was fine. I suggested that he could visit her tomorrow morning. He said he would call Laila to confirm whether he should go or not, and then he ended the call abruptly.

I waited and waited for Ayezah's call, which felt like hours. I tried calling her a few times as well, but there was no answer. I figured she must have fallen asleep.

Oh Lord, Rahil, let her sleep. She must be tired, and you should get some rest too.

I tossed and turned, unable to find sleep. I had grown accustomed to a warm presence beside me.

Her soft frame pressed against my body, my nose nuzzling into her hair, her gentle scent of flowers filling my nostrils and soothing my senses, lulling me into a peaceful slumber. Now, I felt a chill in the air and discomfort.

I looked at the empty side of the bed and made a face. I grabbed the pillow that still carried her gentle flowery scent and brought it closer to my nose, nuzzling and inhaling deeply.

Her scent somehow managed to calm my restless heart, and before I knew it, I drifted off into a peaceful slumber. As I fell asleep, I made a mental note that the first thing I would do in the morning is visit her.

I slumped in my office chair, sulking and endlessly scrolling through my phone.

I couldn't visit her in the morning, no matter how much I longed to. I knew I couldn't just barge in like some clingy mess, unable to spend even a single day apart.

So, I decided that I would see her in the evening instead. After all, she would be back home by then, right? I mean, Laila is okay now, I suppose?

But you know what's really getting on my nerves and frustrating me? She still hasn't called or texted me, and that's really bothering me. Is she so caught up in taking care of Laila that she forgot about her own husband? Not cool. Okay, am I actually feeling jealous of Laila now? Ugh, I can't believe myself.

It was lunch time now and my stomach growled loudly. I barely had breakfast because I'm used to having it with my wife, and today, without her at the dining table, it felt incredibly empty.

Sulking, I made my way to the nearby restaurant to quickly grab something to eat, making sure not to forget my phone on the way.

The entire day slipped away as I found myself glued to my phone, like a teenager addicted to their screen.

Not a single call or text came from her. It's alright. She'll be back home in the evening, and I'll make sure she makes it up to me for leaving me hanging like this.

A mischievous idea suddenly sparked in my mind, causing a smirk to spread across my face as I made my way towards my car, ready to drive home.

I decided to send her a text, asking if I should come to pick her up. But once again, she didn't see it, so I figured out that she would come back on her own.

I didn't want to bother Laila since she was sick, not wanting to come across as some selfish jerk. But when it comes to Ayezah, I can't help but feel a bit selfish. She has this way of making me want her all to myself, not wanting to share her with anyone else.

Ugh, congratulations, Rahil, you're officially going insane. I always knew this girl was driving me crazy, but this level of crazy? Oh, God! I seriously need some help.

As I arrived home, I quickly changed my clothes.

Feeling wave of boredom washing over me, I thought why not prepare Ayezah's favorite spaghetti? The one she loves so much when it's cooked by me.

So, I busied myself in the kitchen, preparing a delicious dinner for her. I waited and waited, but there was no sign of her. My patience, which was already hanging by a loose thread, finally snapped when the digital wall clock clicked to 8:00.

That's it. Call me clingy, call me selfish, but I need my wife back now.

I threw on my overcoat, snatched my car keys, and made my way outside. I hopped into the car and began driving towards Laila's place, Determined to find answers about all the ghosting part and bring Ayezah back home where she belongs.

Chapter 19

Ayezah's POV:

Fear. I've always despised that word with all my heart. No matter how much I try to convince myself that I'm tough, fear always manages to get the best of me. It's like this relentless monster that lurks within, ready to pounce at any moment.

I wish this night never fucking happened. I wish I had never crossed paths with Rose. If only I could rewind time and erase this night from its existence, I would do it in a beat.

But it's done. There's no going back, no undoing what's been done.

The fear has consumed me, it's taken hold of me, squeezing the life out of my spirit, numbing my senses and driving me to the brink of madness.

The fear ruined my childhood and now it's determined to seep into my present and future as well, tainting every step I take. It's like a relentless beast that won't rest until it's devoured every ounce of my happiness.

The fear of fire, messed up my childhood. It was like this dark cloud that hung over my younger self, leaving me with memories that still give me chills.

And now, here comes this new fear, threatening to wreck everything.

It's the fear of losing him, the person who means the world and beyond to me.

" Killer. you're nothing but a heartless killer. What do you think will happen when your beloved husband discovers your dark secret? He'll want nothing to do with you and leave you."

Rose's words echo in my mind like a broken record. I find myself walking aimlessly, rain pouring down on me, and thunder rumbling in the distance.

The world around me blurs, making it hard to focus on anything—the honking of vehicles, the crashing thunder, and the glaring headlights.

I don't even remember how I ended up leaving the party. I'm lost, unsure of what to do next.

" Killer, you're a murdered and a home wrecker. Rahil will abandon you."

No. I'm not a killer or a home wrecker. I'm not.

Rahil won't abandon me or leave me, right? He trusts me. He loves me.....doesn't he?

" even if he doesn't leave you! I'll make sure I snatch him away from you 'cause you don't deserve to be with him. After all, you're a home wrecker, a bloody murderer. I'll end Rahil so he can be free from your grip, even if it means I become a killer myself. I'll seriously do it. Either you disappear or he leaves you. If not, then I sure as hell kill him."

I nearly strangled the fuck out of her for even daring to think of hurting my Rahil. what the fuck does she think of herself?

If it wasn't for her maniacal laughter, I wouldn't have snapped out and released her, and would sure as hell choke her to death.

And would actually end up becoming a killer.

Rose is a psycho, no doubt about it. I just met her tonight, but the madness in her eyes and the way she spoke, tells me she's a psycho.

It's not like I didn't argue or fight with her. I did. I fought tooth and nail with her.

And no matter how hard I try to protect Rahil, I can't compete with a mentally ill psycho. You never know when they'll snap.

why? why did this mess have to happen with me? Haven't I gone through enough already? Why me? I thought I could finally be happy.

" Stay away from Rahil! Get out of his life, or else I'll definitely end him. I'll do whatever it takes to separate you from your happiness, just like you did with mine."

Her words keep going on and on. The rain pours so hard that the droplets start stinging. I clutch my head and squeeze my eyes shut.

STOP, PLEASE. STOP THIS. Let this be a nightmare and let me wake up in Rahil's arms. PLEASE.

Just as I open my eyes, I see a flash of a vehicle. I'm too numb to move, my limbs are locked.

Move Ayezah. Move.

I cannot. I'm not able to.

Am I going to die? Maybe if I die then Rose will be satisfied and leave Rahil alone.

A hand grabs my elbow and yanks me with great force. I stumble into that person, almost knocking us both to the ground.

"What the actual fuck is wrong with you? Why the actual hell are you doing here?" Laila's voice pierces through the rain, snapping me out of my thoughts.

I gasp for air, my heart pounding in my chest. The rain continues to drench us both as Laila grips my shoulders tightly.

"Have you lost your mind, Ayezah? Why on earth are you walking on this busy road like it's a damn park, and in this fucking rain? What the hell are you even thinking—"

Before she can continue, I interrupt her.

"Can you please take me to your home?" my voice barely audible and my gaze fixed on the ground.

What's wrong with me? Was I really willing to give up on my life just now like some weak pathetic coward?

Laila's eyes search mine as she makes me look up at her.

"What's wrong?" she asks, concern etched on her face.

"Please, just take me to your home, and I'll explain everything, I promise." I plead, my chin quivering, tears threatening to spill.

"Okay, okay, just breathe," she reassures me, pulling me into a tight hug. I cling to her, my arms wrapped around her, as tears mingle with the rain, streaming down my cheeks. "I'll call a cab, alright?" she says, gently breaking the hug.

"Whoa! I can't fucking believe this shit! Are you fucking serious right now?" Laila snarls, her voice filled with disbelief.

I told her everything.

After we arrived at her place, she gave me some time to freshen up and lent me her clothes.

I showered and changed. Throughout the shower, I couldn't keep the thoughts away of whatever happened tonight.

The worst part about me, the part that drives me insane, is being an overthinker. I'm a master at it. I can't seem to control this never-ending thought train, no matter how hard I try.

So I knew I have to share it with Laila before my mind explodes.

Once we're both in fresh clothes, we settled in her living room. She prepared a steaming cup of coffee for me, but I can barely take a sip before abandoning it on the coffee table.

Laila's face contorts with anger, " No but I seriously can't believe this shit! That bitch has fucking manipulated you so well! "

"At first, I couldn't believe her either, but when I saw the picture, everything became clear." I say.

" It's not your fault, Ayezah. Nothing is. She's a fucking psycho for fuck sake."

I nod, tears welling up in my eyes.

"I know I'm not a killer. But she'll hurt Rahil if I don't leave him. She made it clear that she will and she looked dead serious about it. But I can't leave him, Laila. I just can't. I won't be able to survive without him. I fucking won't. And I would rather take my own life than even think about any harm coming his way, leave alone because of me. What do I do?" vulnerability was evident in my voice.

Laila's expression softens as she looks at me.

" You don't have to Ayezi. Why would you leave your husband for some psycho bitch? "

" And are you really scared of that little psycho shit? I can't believe you, Ayezah. Where's my friend who was all confident and badass?" she questions, her voice tinged with disappointment.

"It's not about being scared of her laila. It's about challenging a psychopath. I can't risk it. and surely not when it comes to Rahil. " I hiss, frustration seeping through my words.

"I'll do anything it takes to protect Rahil. Literally anything. Even if it means cowering away like some fucking weakling." I gritted out.

"Fine then, how about I take care of this bitch myself?" she suggests, her tone turning murderous.

"No, no, Laila! You can't get involved in all this!"

"I can't risk your life, no way."

Laila let out a heavy sigh, her shoulders slumping.

" I knew it was some bitch." She muttered under her breath, causing a frown to crease my brow.

"What do you mean you knew?" I asked.

Laila blinks, caught off guard.

"Ah, I mean... ah, nothing," she stammered nervously, her attempt at deception clear as day.

"Okay, I know you're hiding something from me. Tell me!" I gave her a firm look.

Laila hesitated for a moment, then reluctantly complied. "It's really nothing—" I shot her a hard glare, cutting off her dismissive statement.

I had been suspicious of her ever since she arrived with Adam, today evening.

"Okay, so it's like I kind of followed the person in the red hoodie, who turned out to be that stupid Rose, because I knew she was stalking you," Laila confessed, her words sending a shock through me.

She continued to tell me about what happened with her and Adam the previous night, how they followed my stalker who happened to be Rose as she admitted it to me herself and I told that to Laila.

And then the shit went really down when Adam got stabbed by some man, who no doubt had to be someone Rose sent to deceive them.

My heart sank, and tears streamed down my face as I realized the danger they had willingly put themselves in, for my sake.

I immediately pulled Laila into a tight embrace, my tears flowing uncontrollably.

"I'm so sorry..Laila," I managed to say between hiccups.

"Heyy, no, please. It's not your fault. I didn't tell you this because I knew you would blame yourself." She gently pulled back from the hug, wiping away the tears with her palms, that stained my cheeks.

"You are not to be blamed okay? I made the choice to go there on my own, Ayezi."

"But why would you risk your life for me, you idiot." I ask between my sniffles

"Why not? I would do it again in a heartbeat. You are my only family, Ayezi,"

" Remember when I first arrived in Australia? I was so lost and broken. I found solace in your friendship, you made me happy, Ayezi. "

" when I had lost every hope, you were there. You became my family when no one else was. So, of course, I would stand by your side, always." she concluded.

I threw my arms around her once again, overwhelmed by all the emotions, and buried my face in her neck.

"I love you, Laila," I whispered against her neck.

"You are truly one of the greatest friends one could ever have. I will forever be grateful to have you by my side."

If it wasn't for her, I couldn't imagine how I would have managed or how much of a mess I would be.

"I love you more, and I'm grateful as well." She tighten her arms around me.

" ehhh—Now, let's not get too emotional, okay?" She gently pulled back, and I noticed tiny beads of tears glistening in her eyes.

My lips curled upwards little, as I nodded.

Laila's phone rang, and she grabbed the device from the coffee table.

My heart began to race, pounding against my chest, as I read Rahil's name flashing on the screen. A gulp escaped my throat, and Laila looked at me, her eyes silently questioning what to do next.

"Don't pick it up," I blurted out.

"But he must be worried. You just left without saying anything."

She was right. Rahil must be worried sick. I was so lost in my thoughts, I hadn't even considered how my sudden disappearance would affect him.

My phone remained in my clutch, and I was too consumed by my swirling emotions to even bother checking it.

Just as I was about to say something more, the ringing abruptly stopped, and a wave of relief washed over me. But, within seconds, the phone began to ring again.

"We can't let him worry, Ayezi. He genuinely gets worried sick about you. I'm picking up the call," Laila declared.

My hesitation lingered, and I swallowed hard, knowing that she was right. "But..." I began, my voice trailing off.

"Don't worry, I've got this." she answered the call and put it on speaker, allowing Rahil's voice to fill the room.

"Heyy Laila, is Ayezah with you?" Rahil's panicked voice pierced through the air, tugging at my heartstrings. In that moment, I felt a wave of guilt wash over me, realizing how much I had made him worry. I felt like a bitch for doing so.

Laila smoothly handled the situation, while I remained silent, my ears tuned in to Rahil's soothing voice.

But then, his desperate plea broke through, "Can I talk to her? Could you pass the phone to her?" His words filled with desperation, caused a lump to form in my throat.

I knew that if I spoke to him, I would definitely and completely break down.

Laila glanced at me, and I shook my head. Understanding the turmoil within me, she nodded.

"Oh, she's in the washroom at the moment. She'll give you a call once her phone is charged... Alright, Rahil jij, I need to get some rest. I'm really tired. You should head home too and drive safely, okay?" She abruptly ended the call.

"I feel guilty and bad for doing this to him. I'm such a worst person, right?" my voice trembled badly, as I fought back tears.

Laila's hands gently enveloped mine.

" No you are not. It's okay, Ayezi. Everything will be fine," she assured me.

I cried, clutching onto Laila's hand.

I hate myself for doing this to Rahil. I hate this fucking pathetic and helpless feeling.

Later that night Laila received a call from Adam. He wanted to know if she was alright or if he should rush to her side right away, the panic and worry was evident in his voice.

Laila, assured him that she was fine and told him not to come because of the horrible weather. He insisted that he wants to see her and was ready to drive here but Laila refused immediately.

To put Adam's worries to rest and assure him, she decided to video call him. They had a lovely conversation and I went all aww about how much Adam loves and cares about Laila, they both are so sweet, literally.

I couldn't help but playfully tease Laila with mischievous looks, and the way she blushed confirmed my doubts that she loves Adam.

Because best friend isn't someone who blushes so easily.

Seeing their love and affection for each other made my heart swell with happiness for her.

However, I felt a pang of sadness hit me when the thought of certain someone crossed my mind.

I didn't sleep the whole night. Laila was right by my side, knowing that I wouldn't be able to sleep and would overthink myself to death.

She stayed awake for me, skillfully distracting me by sharing stories about random things, like how she and Adam got together. I have to say, I'm one hell of a lucky person to have someone as caring as her.

As the morning slowly arrived, I could see that Laila was struggling to stay awake. I felt a pang of guilt for keeping her up, so I insisted that she go to sleep and promised to rest as well.

Of course, sleep eluded me and it was nearly impossible to sleep without being entangled in Rahil's arms.

However, I managed to take a short nap, exhausted from the events of the previous night, but soon restlessness overcame me. That's when I thought of heading to the ice rink, as it always helps me think better.

I rummaged through Laila's wardrobe, finding some clothes to wear. Putting them on, I left for the ice rink in the early morning.

The crisp air greeted me as I arrived, and the sound of my skates gliding across the ice filled the silence. I skated and skated, losing track of time until it was almost 10:30 in the morning.

Despite the physical exertion, my mind remained clouded with thoughts. With a sigh, I made my way back to Laila's apartment.

When I returned, Laila was still asleep. I decided to shower and change into some comfortable, loose-fitting long-sleeved t-shirt and pants and made my way to the kitchen to cook breakfast for both of us.

I had planned to skip the work today, and it seemed like Laila had the same idea. Anyways I'm the boss, so she can take the leave without any worries.

After preparing a simple breakfast, I managed to eat a few bites. However, my appetite quickly vanished the moment I switched on my phone and saw Rahil's countless missed calls and texts. My heart sank once again as I read his messages right from my lock screen.

There were numerous texts from Rahil, asking where I was. Then it went to why I hadn't been in touch with him. He even mentioned my phone's battery, suggesting he would buy me a new one with a better capacity. Scrolling down, I found more messages that tugged at my heart.

Rahil : Are you already asleep? Did you have dinner? You better not skip your meals.

Rahil : You said you loved the pasta made by me. If you were here, I would have cooked it for you. But it's okay I'll make it for you tomorrow.

Rahil : I really wanna talk to you. Please reply, I miss you so much :(

Rahil : Its so uncomfortable to sleep without you. I miss you.

Rahil : okay, I know I'm acting like some clingy jerk, but hey, at least text me back. Just one text to let me know you're alright. Please?

My chin wobbled with a mix of emotions as I read his messages.

Rahil : I have this sudden urge to kiss you and hug you, it's impossible to sleep without cuddling you, really...I just miss you so fucking much.

Rahil : I guess you are asleep. Its okay. I hope Laila's fine. Good night zah <3 I really, really, miss you, man. Rest well, okay? You must be tired from the party.

Zah! That's the nickname he gave me, and it never fails to make my heart flutter. He even calls me his tigress, but little does he know that I'm nothing near to a fierce tigress.

I'm a fucking pathetic, stupid coward who tries to put on a strong facade.

There are few more new texts which are sent just an hour ago.

Rahil : Good morning, babie! Are you awake? Did you sleep well? How's Laila doing? Are you guys heading to work today?

Rahil : Don't tell me your phone still isn't charged? If that's the case, then it's high time that you buy a new one, actually no, I'll buy you a new one.

Rahil : what's wrong? Why aren't you answering any texts or calls?

Rahil : Are you ignoring me? why? I miss you. Please reply.

The whole day goes by and he keeps texting and calling me. I ignore him, completely acting like a bitch because I don't know what to talk him or where to even begin with.

Rahil : so you still ghosting me huh? It's fine. I'll make sure you make it up to me in not so appropriate way. *smirk emoji*

Rahil : ugh I miss you.

Rahil : okay, I know Laila is your bestfriend and all, but hey, I'm your husband. You can't just completely avoid me like this. I'm seriously hurt and offended now.

I chuckle slightly, tears welling up in my eyes.

Rahil : you are coming back in evening right? I can't wait for the evening to arrive. I just miss you so much that I actually can't wait anymore to hug you tightly, shower kisses all over your face and just nuzzle my nose into your hair and keep inhaling your addictive flowery scent until I get my fill because again I fucking missed you like crazy and I'm still missing you like crazy.

Me too Rahil. Me too. I fucking miss you like crazy as well. I miss you so much.

It's almost evening now, whole day I locked myself in Laila's room, reading Rahil's texts from my lock Screen.

He constantly texted me and I have been glued to my phone, all day.

I have figured out that I'll ask Addin's help for all this messed up situation, my cousin is the best option.

I couldn't risk telling Rahil everything. what if he leaves me after knowing the truth? no he won't, right? Still, I can't help but feel a bit anxious about this whole situation. I think I need some more time away from him so I can think about all this—

My phone screen lit up.

Rahil : Should I pick you up from Laila's place?

After few seconds there is one more text.

Rahil : I guess you are coming on your own? Drive safe, okay?

Then there's silence for straight half an hour, before my phone buzzes with another text.

Rahil : why aren't you home yet?

Because I'm a fucking coward.

Tears sting my eyes.

what is wrong with me? what am I even doing? why am I making him wait like this? who gave me the right to?

Rose was right, I don't deserve him.

Later that evening, the thought of stepping out the room and lending a helping hand to Laila with dinner crossed my mind.

She had given me the space I needed throughout the day, understanding how much I like my alone time, when I had things to sort out.

Just as I was about to make my way out of the room, a sudden commotion erupted outside.

"Rahil jij?" Laila's voiced reached my ears, causing my heart to slam against my ribcage harshly.

Freezing, my hand remains in mid-air, gripping the doorknob.

"Where's Ayezah?" His deep, resonant voice, intensified the rapid beats of my heart. And just like that I'm not ready to face him.

I knew I would do something foolish and maybe somehow end up potentially hurting him.

Chapter 20

Ayezah's POV:

"Where's Ayezah?" My heart raced insanely, refusing to calm down.

I grip the door knob tighter as I hear Laila's voice from outside.

"Ah, she's actually resting inside the room,"

"Resting? Is she alright? She hasn't replied to any of my texts or calls at all. It's not likely of Ayezah to do so. Even when we used to go to work, we would always text and call each other. She has never ghosted me like this. I know something is seriously wrong." My grip on the door knob tightens even further, my knuckles turning white.

" I guess her phone.. isn't charged yet." Laila says, unsure of her words and I can hear how much she's struggling to answer him.

"Oh, come on! Do you take me for a fool? What phone takes this long to charge?" Rahil's voice is filled with frustration.

" ummm... maybe she didn't plug it to charge.."Laila stammers, trying to find an explanation.

Okay that's enough Ayezah. You can't possibly hide from him forever.

I need to face him somehow.

with a racing heart, I slowly twist the door knob, my throat tight with fear. I swallow, closing my eyes and taking a deep breath.

I slowly move outside of the room, gently closing the door behind me.

As I stepped forward, I instinctively reach out to adjust the sleeves of my long-sleevedt-shirt, tugging it down, feeling anxiety bubbling inside me.

From where I stood, I could catch a glimpse of the living room. His back was facing me.

Laila's eyes met mine.

My heart skipped a beat as he turned around, following Laila's gaze.

His warm brown eyes gets locked with mine instantly, increasing the pace of my heartbeat.

Nervously, I bit my lower lip, my fingers unconsciously clutching the snowflake pendant around my neck in a tight grip.

"Ayezah!" Rahil's voice rang out, filled with both relief and concern.

He rushed towards me in a beat, his hands firmly gripping my shoulders. His eyes searched mine, as he pours out a torrent of questions.

"Are you okay? What's wrong? Why haven't you been responding? Please tell me you're okay," he pleaded, his words tumbling out in a rush.

He was dressed in simple black t-shirt and jeans, looking so gorgeous as always.

my gaze wandered over every inch of his face, taking in the familiar handsome features that I had missed so dearly, as he continued to speak.

Rahil then suddenly fell silent, his eyes roamed all over me and then wandered all over my face, mirroring my own actions.

Our gazes met, a mix of emotions swirling in both of our orbs.

One moment he is gazing at me and next second his arms get wrapped around my shoulders.

Rahil envelopes me in a warm and tight embrace, crushing my body completely against his.

I stood frozen in place, my hands resting motionlessly at my sides.

The clean scent of his body wash filled my lungs, causing my eyes to shut on their own.

His presence, his touch, his smell, everything overwhelms me so much that I feel the need to cry my heart out.

And It was then that I realized just how insanely I had missed him.

He holds me even closer, inhaling my neck deeply, as if trying to absorb me completely into him.

"Please just once tell me that you're okay." he breathes out against my neck.

No Rahil. I'm not okay. I'm really not okay at all. I missed you so much.I'm sorry for not answering any of your texts or calls. I truly am sorry.

I want to pause this moment here and never want to resume it ever again. I want to be in your arms, I want to be with you, always.

I want to engrave you into me so deep that no one could ever take you away from me. I want to be by your side, always.

I love you so much that it had started to ache physically. I love you Rahil. I love you so much that I don't recognise the person I have become.

I want to scream all these words loudly but not a single sound escapes my throat.

" stay away from Rahil. Leave him! Or else I'll do it for you. I'll end him. I'll take him away from you, and no one will be able to stop me from doing so, not even you."

Rose's words echoes in my head and then keeps fucking echoing like a broken record from a horror movie, until I push Rahil away harshly.

The shock, disbelief, and hurt that crosses his face make me want to slap myself hard.

I want to protect you Rahil. I'm sorry. I don't want to hurt you.

But aren't you doing exactly that right now?

My heartbeat accelerates to an abnormal level and my breathing becomes charged.

"what's..wrong?"

Rahil asks, his voice filled with cautious concern.

Summoning all my courage, I close my eyes, taking a moment to gather myself for the harsh words I'm about to throw his way.

"Exactly what's fucking wrong with you?" I snap.

"Why are you being so clingy and annoying? Can't you give me some space and let me stay at my best friend's place for a while? You're suffocating me. And why the heck do you keep asking if I'm alright? Can't you see that I'm perfectly fine? I can't believe you're acting worse than some clingy toddler." I manage to say it all in one breath, surprised that my voice didn't crack.

Rahil looks at me, his eyes filled with utter shock and disbelief, as if he didn't expect this at all. He looks at me as if can't believe his own ears.

He looks at me as if he's seeing me for the first time, as if he doesn't recognize me.

I'm sorry. I'm so sorry.

He swallows visibly, his gaze fixed on me. After a moment, he lowers his head and mutters, "I'm sorry. I didn't mean to be clingy and annoying. I didn't realize I was suffocating you." It takes every ounce of strength to hold back the sob threatening to escape.

"It's just that I missed you so much," he says, his voice barely audible. I look up at the ceiling, pressing the back of my hand against my mouth to stifle my tears.

Rahil looks up at me again. "You can stay with your friend. I won't bother you. But if possible, please come back soon. I can't bear to be without you for too long."

why? just why is he so nice? why can't he be rude and make this all a little easy for me? why can't he just snap back at me? like I did.

I really don't deserve him.

I turn around without glancing his way and dash into the room, my heart pounding in my chest, unable to bear the sight of his fallen and hurt face any longer.

I swiftly close the door behind me, Leaning against the door, I slide down. My back pressed against the door as I bring my knees closer to my chest.

Tears stream down my face, uncontrollably. I press the backside of my trembling hand against my quivering lips, trying to stifle the sobs that threaten to consume me.

I hate myself. I hate myself so much for doing this with him.

Why am I such a colossal coward? Why does fear always have the power to ruin everything I hold dear? And why do I allow it to control me?

As I sit there, crying my eyes out, it feels as though time stretches on endlessly.

After a while, a soft knock on the door interrupts my thoughts.

My sobs come to an abrupt halt, and I strain to listen as his voice, filled with both sadness and understanding, whispers through the door.

"I'm going to go now," he says.

"Take care of yourself. And remember, you can always call me if you need anything." There's a brief pause, the silence heavy with unspoken words, before his footsteps gradually fade away, leaving behind an echoing emptiness.

Leaning my head, I press the side of my face against the door.

I gently reach out my palm and place it against the door, still leaning on it, I squeeze my eyes shut, to allow the remaining flow of tears.

I'm sorry, Rahil. I love you. I really, really do.

R a h i l ' s P O V :

Gosh, why would I be so annoying? Anyone would obviously lose their cool with such clingy behavior.

I mean, seriously, who acts so foolishly and fails to give someone space? I genuinely despise myself for making her feel suffocated. What was wrong with me? It's been over a month since our marriage, and she hasn't even visited her dad. She's always by my side, and I should have realized that she needed some breathing room.

I can't believe how stupid I was, acting like some obsessed, possessive toxic husband who can't bear to let his wife out of his sight for even a second.

Although I'm truly obsessed and possessive about her—which I can't help, but I'm not toxic.

I understand the importance of personal space, but she could have just told me, and I would've understood.

Her sudden outburst didn't shock me would be an understatement of the century.

Ayezah has always been incredibly kind and sweet to me. She never snapped at me, not even when I rejected her twice!

So imagine my surprise when she suddenly snapped at me.

But honestly, I deserve it for acting like some annoying, clingy creep.

And here I am again, standing right outside of her company's building the very next day, holding a lunchbox in my hand that I prepared myself for her.

Just yesterday I was having a serious beef with myself for not giving her enough space and yet it didn't stop me from coming here.

It's not like I didn't try. I really did made an effort to push those thoughts away and resist coming here.

Okay, whom am I even kidding? The first thing I did when I woke up this morning was prepare spaghetti, so I knew all along that I would end up here.

Seriously Rahil? I can't believe you. You deserve a real beating.

Running a hand through my hair, I let out frustrated groan. I'm dressed in my formals and I came here straight from work as it is lunch break now. As I stand here, I can't help but feel a little nervous.

Should I just pass the lunchbox to the guard and leave? What if she thinks I'm being clingy again?

But I'm just here to pass her the spaghetti she's been craving for a few days now.

And also to ensure that she eats well. I'm not asking her to come back or demanding her time. I just want to make sure she takes care of herself, especially after that incident on our first night of marriage when she nearly fainted due to not eating properly.

A soft smile tugs at my lips as I get flashbacks of our first night.

It was then that I prepared the same spaghetti for her, and since then, she's become a big fan of my 'spaghetti.' I have never being so proud of my great cooking skills until now.

My mind was abruptly pulled from its wandering thoughts as I caught sight of a commotion inside the building.

A furrow formed on my brow as I observed several individuals in the reception area running around in urgency.

Even the guards stationed outside, just a minute ago are no where in sight now.

I went inside the building, near the reception. The receptionist was engrossed in a phone call.

"Yes, it's the top floor of the CEO's cabin. we urgently need the fire brigades.." her voice echoed in the background, the words 'fire' and 'CEO's cabin' piercing through the air. My heart skipped a beat.

Fire brigades? why?

The CEO is my Ayezah and her cabin has caught fire? No, it can't happen, right? Maybe I misheard something.

My fingers trembled around the lunch box as I swallow hard, gathering the courage to approach the receptionist, who had just concluded her call and was hastily dialing another number.

"Excuse me... Did I hear correctly that there's a fire on the top floor?" I managed to utter, my voice barely above a whisper.

The receptionist turned towards me, her expression grave.

"Oh yes! Not the entire floor, mind you, just the CEO's cabin. It seems to have been caused by an electrical issue. Unfortunately, the fire alarm and sprinkler system failed to activate..." Her voice trailed off as the lunch box slipped from my grasp, crashing onto the floor.

My legs carried me swiftly towards the elevator on its own, my heart pounding in my chest like a wild stallion.

No, no, no, not the fire please. It fucking terrifies her.

She's all alone there. She will be fine right? She has to be. I won't let anything happen to her

I'm coming to you, Ayezah. Please stay safe and remain calm for me. I need you to be unharmed.

I press the elevator button desperately numerous times but it wasn't opening.

I dashed towards the staircase, urgency fueled my every step as I ascended the stairs, skipping a few in my haste.

"Please, be okay, please." I muttered repeatedly, like a madman.

My heart refused to relent, its relentless race intensifying with each passing moment.

It felt as if my very sanity was slipping away.

Get a grip of yourself. Ayezah needs you.

After what felt like an eternity, I finally reached the top floor, my breathing ragged and my body drenched in sweat.

As I moved forward, the thick smoke billowed out, enveloping me in its suffocating embrace.

The panicked voices and frantic footsteps echoed through the air. The floor appeared eerily empty, with only a handful of people scattered about.

Without wasting a moment, I sprinted towards Ayezah's cabin, my heart pounding in my chest like a wild drumbeat.

As I neared the door, a sight that struck fear into my very core greeted me.

Bright Flames roared ferociously, dancing hungrily upon the surface of the office door.

I took a deep breath, summoning every ounce of courage within me, and with a swift kick, I burst the door open.

The inferno loomed before me, its fiery tendrils reaching out like a beast hungry for destruction. I closed my eyes, shielding my face with my arms, and forged ahead, coughing and gasping for air.

"Ayezah!" I yell loudly.

I caught a glimpse of her figure, curled up in a ball on the floor, completely surrounded by huge scary bright flames.

Her body was visibly trembling with fear, as she hugged her knees more to her chest. Tears streaming down her face.

From across her desk, I could see the agony etched onto her beautiful face, smudged with traces of black soot.

My heart shattered at the mere sight of her.

"Rahil..." she whimpered, her voice trembling with both relief and despair. She was completely trapped between the relentless flames, across her desk.

"Go away! Oh God, how did you even get here? Go away... I'm going to di-die... and I don't want you to end up with me dead," she cried out between sobs, her words a desperate plea.

The flames roared with fury as I tried to approach her.

"No, you won't die. I won't let you," I yelled back and tried to approach her.

But the fire surrounding her seemed to grow higher, its fierce heat pushing me back.

"No, go away!" she cried out, her voice strained and filled with desperation, followed by a fit of coughing.

" I ain't leaving you fucking alone." I attempted to reach her from the other side, only to have the flames surge directly towards my face, forcing me to stumble back once again.

"Ayezah!" I screamed as she collapses onto the floor.

With a renewed sense of urgency, I desperately tried to move closer to her, but the fire roared with such intensity that I could feel its scorching heat searing my skin, causing me to fall to the ground.

Through the flickering flames, I caught a glimpse of Ayezah's gaze fixed upon me, her eyes barely open.

"I love you... and I'm sorry," she whispered, her words barely audible amidst the deafening whoosh of the fire.

And then she closes her eyes.

No. No. NOOOO

"No, no, please, no!" I scream.

The flames engulfs her whole form, and I scream so loud that it feels like my throat got ripped apart.

"NOO!"

The side of my face remain pressed against the floor, as I let my tears mingle with the scorching heat.

The heat gets too much until it's burning my skin but I stay limp, staring at the flames infront of me that has engulfed my everything.

Chapter 21

Rahil's POV:

I jolt awake, my eyes snapping open with a gasp that echoes through the room.

As I sit up, I reach out into the air, desperately grasping for breath, my mouth open wide. My body is drenched in sweat, causing my t-shirt to cling uncomfortably to my back.

My heart pounds relentlessly, as if it's on the verge of bursting.

My chest rises and falls rapidly, my breathing ragged and uneven.

Nightmare. It was just a nightmare.

It felt so fucking real, that my body is still trembling uncontrollably.

It felt so real that i can still feel the terror in my every bone. I can still feel my skin burning, as if it's ablaze.

I turn my head to the side, only to be greeted by emptiness and coldness, just like it has been since one week now.

It's been a whole week without Ayezah, and it feels like I'm just merely existing instead of living.

I haven't been able to get any sleep either because it's nearly impossible to get some comfortable sleep without her being all wrapped in my arms and now that her sweet flowery scent has faded from the pillow, I find it difficult to sleep at all.

I've respected her need for space and stayed away. Though I did check up on her through few occasional texts, which she ignored completely, and contemplated to call her a plenty of times, trying my best not to come across as clingy or suffocating. But her absence is suffocating me instead.

I take a deep breath, switching on the lamp next to the bedside table, my body still trembling and my heart refusing to slow down. Each breath feels heavy and charged with anxiety.

"Come on, Rahil," I tell myself, trying to calm down.

"Ayezah is okay. She's safe." Yes, she has to be. I close my eyes, but the scene from the nightmare where fire engulfs her whole form flashes before my eyes, making me snap them open in pure horror.

No. nothing has happen to her.

She. is. fucking. Safe.

The image of her trembling form, curled up and crying, surrounded by fire, keeps replaying in my mind, and I can't bear it any longer.

I grab my phone in a hurry from the bedside table, almost knocking all the things kept on the table down, because of the trembling in my hands.

with a insanely racing heart, i dial her number. I start chanting, "Pick up! Pick up! Pick up!" like a madman, my desperation clear in my voice.

I keep dialling her number, again and again and fucking again.

But she doesn't pick up and the restlessness within me grows tenfolds.

I don't give a damn that it's 2:30 in the morning. I need to see her. I need to know that she's all okay, safe and unharmed. Otherwise, I'll die. I'll fucking die.

I dash out of the penthouse, not bothering to grab an overcoat as the frigid breeze slams into me like icy daggers.

My heart is racing, and I drive like a madman, pushing the limits of speed, my hands gripping the steering wheel very tightly.

The nightmare still lingers in my mind, hauntingly vivid and real.

The nightmare made something crystal clear to me.

when the fire engulfed her completely, I wanted to die then and there. I wanted to follow Ayezah. I didn't had any desire to live anymore.

and that's when I realised that, If it's end of her, then it's end of me.

Ayezah has become my everything. Literally. without her, there is no me.

If anything were to happen to her, I'm killed automatically.

The ache in my heart and the mere thought of losing her make me realize the depth of my feelings.

I'm in love with her. I have always been.

But at this point, It's not just love; it's something far beyond that.

It's so strong, so powerful that it has consumed every fiber of my being.

It's become the very air I breathe.

The more I realize I can't live without her, the tighter it becomes for me to breathe.

The mere thought of the nightmare becoming a reality suffocates me. I pressed the accelerator harder, my knuckles gripping the steering wheel so tightly that it turned as white as paper.

My heart thumped wildly, like a maniac out of control and my breaths came in ragged gasps.

I attempted to focus on my breathing, desperately trying to calm down. I lightly tapped my chest, hoping to alleviate the burning pain, but to no avail.

Nothing seemed to work. Absolutely nothing.

All the way to Laila's apartment, I persistently keep dialing Ayezah's number, only to met with frustration of her switched off phone.

Laila! She'll pick up, I should call her yeah.

With a mix of hope and anxiety, I dial her number, my finger hovering over the screen.

But to my dismay, she doesn't pick up. I keep trying.

my heart pounding in my chest, matching the rhythm of the ringing tones. Finally, after a few missed calls, she answers.

"Laila, is Ayezah okay? Is she right beside you, sleeping peaceful-ly?" I blurt out, the words tumbling out of my mouth in a rush. My breathing is heavy, filling the silent car with its presence, and I'm certain Laila can hear the desperation in my voice.

"Rahil jij?" she responds, her voice groggy and slow, as if she just woke up from sleep.

"Tell me, please." I plead, unable to contain my restlessness.

"But what happened?" Her voice is laced with confusion and concern.

"Just tell me if Ayezah is fine!"

"Okay, calm down first, Rahil jij!" I exhale heavily.

"I'm at Adam's place, and Ayezah is at my place. I can assure you that she is fine—"

I interrupt her, my urgency overriding any sense of politeness.

"Okay, can you please tell me the password to your apartment?" I ask, my words rushed.

"Umm, yeah, sure," she replies through the call.

After she shares the password, I apologize for disturbing her in the middle of the night and quickly end the call.

As soon as I reach the apartment, I hurriedly make my way inside.

I unlock the door with the password and it clicks open, stepping into the dimly lit space.

My urgent footsteps echoes in the silent living room, with each step, my heart pounds in my chest.

I reach the room, my hand trembling as I grasp the doorknob. Slowly, I turn it, and the door swings open, revealing a darkness that threatens to consume me.

Panic grips my soul as I realize the bed is empty.

Just as despair begins to settle in, a commotion breaks the silence, most probably coming from the balcony within the room.

The glass sliding door glimmers in the moonlight, slowly opening.

And then, her voice, like a soft melody in the night, reaches my ears.

"Who's there? Laila?"

My eyes search the darkness until they find her, standing at the entrance of the balcony. The moonlight caresses her figure, casting a gentle glow upon her delicate features.

I take in every detail, from the way her hair cascades down her shoulders to the subtle curve of her lips.

She is okay. She is safe. Breathing and unharmed.

Relief floods over me and my back presses to the door, as I sink down to the floor near the doorway, my body still trembling a little.

The nightmare got me real bad.

The room fills with the sound of my ragged breaths, echoing in the stillness. I close my eyes, attempting to steady my racing heart, feeling the rise and fall of my chest as I take deep, calming breaths.

she furrows her brows, her gaze fixed upon me. she cannot see my face, and I can sense her confusion.

" Whoa, hold up there! who the fuck are you and how did you get in here? " It's clear that she thinks me as some random creep who broke into the house in the middle of a night.

Without wasting a moment, I swiftly rise from the floor and stride towards her.

As I draw closer, her hand instinctively rises, poised to strike, but her beautiful amber eyes widen like a pair of soccer balls when the moonlight falls on my face and her hand remains suspended in the air.

The realization dawns upon her, and her astonishment is palpable.

Not giving her a chance to process the situation, I wrap my arms tightly around her waist, and hug her with such a force that causes her to stumble backward onto the balcony.

My face buries deep into the curve of her neck, and as her delicate flowery scent envelops my senses, a wave of relief washes over me.

I feel my racing heartbeat gradually calm, and my breaths become steady.

I press her soft body more into mine by her waist, while her hands remain suspended in the air, frozen in surprise and her back rests against the balcony's railing.

"Rahil..." she murmurs softly, her voice barely audible as I bury my nose deeper into the warmth of her skin.

In that moment, my vision blurs slightly, as the vivid memory of the fire that consumed her entirely flashes through my mind, causing me to instinctively tighten my arms, pulling her soft body even closer to mine, if that's even possible.

My hands, on their own, begin to explore the contours of her back, tracing the gentle curve of her waist, the delicate slope of her hip, and the smooth expanse of her entire back, desperate enough to feel her, to ensure that she is real.

"Rahil... what happened?" she tries to pull back, concern lacing her voice, but I refuse to let go, my arms tightening around her further more with pure urgency and fear.

"Please don't move... please... can you just hold me for a little while?" My voice cracks, revealing the depths of my vulnerability.

She goes still, probably realising the pain in my voice and after a few seconds that feel like an eternity, her arms find their way around my neck, pulling me closer, and without wasting a single second, I snuggle more into her.

Her hand finds the back of my head, her touch gentle and soothing, as if trying to calm the storm within me.

We stay like that for who knows how long.

Her delicate touch, like a feather caressing my soul, draws my attention away from the warmth of her neck.

With tenderness in her eyes, she gently pulls my face, guiding me to meet her gaze.

Her palms, soft and warm, cradle my cheeks. I surrender to the sensation, closing my eyes and leaning into her touch, desperate to hold onto this moment, as if I were a starving soul finally finding nourishment after days of hunger.

I open my eyes and gaze into her enchanting amber orbs, and then take in her beautiful delicate features, my eyes wandering around her whole face.

"Heyy, what's wrong? Why are you crying?"

It's only then, when she tenderly wipes away a tear that slipped from my eyes, that I become aware of the fact that im crying.

I squeeze my eyes shut and let the tears fall freely.

"Rahil, please tell me what's wrong? you are making me worried now." Her voice cracks, her palms still cradling my cheeks.

She gently caresses my cheek, coaxing my eyes open to meet her glassy gaze. I can see tears welling up in her eyes too.

" Tell me first that you're all fine and unharmed." I sniffle and take a step back, even though she stands before me, looking perfectly beautiful in black satin night suit. I just can't help myself.

"I'm fine, really," she reassures me.

I bite my lower lip, tears threaten to spill once more, and I can't hold them back any longer.

I fall to my knees, gripping her hands tightly in mine. Pressing the back of her hands against my eyes, I cling to her, allowing my tears to flow freely.

"Rahil..." her voice breaks, and she tries to lift me up, but I resist.

"I had the worst nightmare... where.. you were...snatched away from me," I manage to say, my voice trembling and stuttering.

Finally, I look up, locking my glassy eyes with her own.

" Ayezah, you have become my entire being! I would literally cease to exist without you! You have become the very air I breathe. It's suffocating..so suffocating without you that I feel like someone is sucking the breath out of me. "

" I understand your need for space but Please, don't keep your distance from me. I promise to give you enough space, I promise not to be too clingy, but right now, I can't help it. I want you. no, I need you." Her chin wobbles badly and she struggles to hold back her own tears.

" You told me to say those three words when I truly meant them, and now I mean them with every single part of me, with every ounce of my soul and from the depth of my heart."

I pause, holding onto her hands as she gazes down at me.

I stare deep into her eyes.

" I love you, Ayezah."

" I love you so much to the point of madness that no one could have ever imagined."

" what I feel for you goes far beyond these three words. They don't even come close to capturing my feelings for you."

" I'm sorry for rejecting you in the past. It was always you, Ayezah. You were always the one for me. I've never felt such strong emotions for anyone else. "

" I've always loved you, but I was too foolish to realise it earlier. And even when I knew I was falling for you, I had no idea it would be so intense."

" I just love you so incredibly much! It's driving me to the point of insanity."

She squeezes her eyes shut and bursts out into loud sobs.

Chapter 22

Ayezah's POV:

They say that when you truly desire something with every fiber of your being, the entire universe conspires to bring it to you.

This very moment, right now, is one I have yearned for with every cell in my body. But I could have never imagined it would be this intense.

I'm not sure if it's because Rahil rushed here in the middle of the freezing night, without any overcoat— only wearing his t-shirt and pants, just because he had a nightmare about me.

Or maybe it's because he told me to hold him tightly, as if his life depended on it.

It could be because he cried, or because I've been away from him for a whole week. Perhaps it's because he fell to his knees and confessed to me, being so vulnerable.

Or maybe because of the depth of his words or the way he gazes at me with such strong emotions swirling in his warm brown orbs.

I break down. I break down into sobs so loudly, that my whole body shakes and trembles.

" Ayezah—" I cut him off, not letting him finish his sentence. Instead, I kneel down, my heart racing, and gently cup his cheeks, tilting my head, I press my lips against his. Hard.

Rose can go fuck herself, I'm done being an absolute coward.

The whole world can crumble, but I refuse to break this pure man's heart. Not when he's showing such vulnerability.

I can't be foolish enough to destroy his mental health, just to save him from any physical harm.

Happy early realisation Ayezah! My subconscious mocks me.

Okay fine, I'm stupid, I know that.

The thought of hurting him any further is unbearable; it would be like tearing my own soul apart.

Without missing a beat, he responds to my kiss, his mouth opening eagerly to meet mine.

He takes my bottom lip into his mouth and sucks on it, as if he's mad at me.

He wraps his arm around my waist so possessively, pulling me impossibly closer as if he wants to glue my body to his. while his other hand gently cups my neck.

He kisses me so desperately, so furiously as if his angry for starving himself from my touch.

I tug at the back of his hair, biting his lower lip, I return the same insanity he's pouring in the kiss.

He groans deeply into my mouth, making me repeat the action again.

We continue kissing, desperately and fiercely.

This whole week without him wasn't easy for me and I've missed him more than words can express.

We kiss like two souls on the verge of losing everything.

Our tongues intertwine, teeth gently grazing, and the sensation of our lips sucking on one another is intoxicating.

Our kiss is mad and noisy in the silent balcony, the cold breeze brushing against us. I don't feel it's chills as the warmth of his body doesn't allow me too.

When it feels like we're both running out of breath, we reluctantly pull away.

Our foreheads pressed together and noses caressing one another.

My breathing comes out charged and heavy matching his, as I try to breathe through my mouth. Rahil's mouth mirrors my own, our chests rising and falling in perfect rhythm.

He captures my lips again in a quick sucking, that leaves me longing for more.

As he pulls away with a noisy smooch, his lips appear slightly swollen, a delicate pink mark adorning the outer edges.

He closes his eyes, grazing his nose against mine, and I can't help but gaze at him.

"I'm sorry," I whisper and he opens his eyes, meeting my gaze.

"For what?" he breathes out.

"For behaving that way with you a week ago, for saying those hurtful words that I didn't mean," I confess, my voice filled with remorse.

He shakes his head, his forehead and nose still pressed against mine.

"No, it's okay," he reassures me.

" I realised that I was actually being too clingy," his eyes closed once again as he continues grazing his nose against mine.

My chin wobbles, and I instinctively bite my lower lip, trying to hold back the sob that threatens to escape.

Shaking my head, I lean into his touch.

"No," I whisper, my voice quivering.

"You weren't clingy at all. In fact, you're the sweetest person I've ever known, Rahil. And I truly didn't mean any of those words I said."

Pausing for a few seconds, I take a deep breath, mustering up the courage.

"There was a reason why I acted that way," I say, my voice filled with vulnerability.

It's okay, Ayezah. Relax. Rahil will not judge you. He's your husband and he loves you. You have to trust him.

Rahil frowns slightly and pulls back, his eyes filled with concern. I gather all my strength and decide to tell him everything, holding nothing back.

"You know your new business partner, right?"

" Ms. smith? " Rahil asks and I nod.

"What about her?" He frowns.

"When I first saw her at the party, I had this strange feeling that she was somehow familiar," I continue, my voice filled with unease.

" And then, when you left me alone with her, she somehow managed to manipulate me with her words and forcefully took me to the rooftop..." I recount every detail of that fateful night, telling him literally everything.

Rahil listens attentively, his face reflecting a range of emotions—disbelief, concern, surprise, and even anger. But none of it is directed towards me. Not once does judgment cross his face.

After I finished speaking, tears started to stream down my face and I bite my lower lip.

"I'm so sorry, Rahil. I'm sorry for being such a coward. I didn't share all of this with you because I was afraid of losing you. It's not that I don't trust you. I do. I trust you more than myself, it's that I don't trust that psycho, Rose." My voice trembles badly.

" Heyy, stop apologising it's not your fault okay?" Rahil's voice is filled with reassurance.

With utter tenderness, he cradle my cheeks, using his thumb pad to gently wipe away my tears.

" But what if she tries to harm you? what am I gonna do? " I manage to ask between my sobs.

He wraps his arms securely around my waist, and pull me to his chest. We still remain in the kneeling position.

"I promise, nothing will happen to me as long as you're by my side." Sniffling, I fist my palm tightly on his shirt, near his heart and bury my face into his chest.

"So don't worry about anyone else and just be with me. I promise, I'll be fine." He pulled me even closer, my head resting against his chest.

Eventually, I calmed down and pulled back slightly, my voice still shaky and hoarse due to crying.

"What are we going to do about her?" I hiccuped.

"Don't worry about her. She'll be taken care of." he assures me, determination evident in his voice.

"She had the audacity to threaten my wife and try to take you away from me. She'll face the consequences." He sounds seriously furious now.

" I'll talk to Addin about it. We make a great team when it comes to handling situations like this."

His words brought a sense of relief, as I had also planned to talk to Addin.

" you know you should stop thinking about all this and just focus on being close to me." He dips his head down near my mouth, and I can't help the smile that forms on my lips.

My heart flutters badly when he seals our lips together in a soft kiss.

and in that moment, I knew that everything would be somehow alright.

Chapter 23

Ayezah's POV:

"what are you doing?"

It's almost early morning right now, and the room is filled with cool darkness of the dawn.

I'm lying on the bed, and Rahil is positioned on top of me.

His one ear is pressed gently against my chest, right near my heart.

"I'm listening to your heartbeat and ensuring that it's beating all fine and that you are actually okay."

His words send my heart racing insanely fast.

"Why is your heart thumping so loudly?" he asks, furrowing his brow and raising his head to look at me.

"That's because you're so close, and your words aren't helping either."

He narrows his eyes at me in playful annoyance.

"Are you really okay?" he probes.

"Yeah, I'm truly fine! You do realise right that you are asking me this for the 1000th time now." Even in balcony earlier, he kept touching me, looking at my whole body and holding me so tightly as if I'll disappear into thin air.

" Was the nightmare that bad?" I ask, when i find him going all silent and blankly gazing at me.

He lets out a heavy sigh, dropping his head back onto my chest and snuggling into me.

"Don't ask. It shook me to core. It felt so real. It was the worst, most horrifying thing that's still sending shivers down my spine." He grunts out.

I wrap my arms around his head, my fingers gently running through the back of his head into his hair.

"What exactly happened?" I ask, curiously.

"I don't wanna talk about it." He whispers, and shifts a little upwards, nestling his face deep into the crook of my neck.

He nuzzles his nose against my neck, presses his lips, smooching the area.

" please." He places few kisses on the curve of my neck and I inhale deeply, nodding.

He stays in that position, gently nuzzling his nose into the curve of my neck and inhaling me deeply, meanwhile my fingers continue to caress the soft strands of hair on the back of his head.

"You didn't say it back." He murmurs against my skin.

"What?"

"The confession."

" You already know it very well."

" But I want to hear it."

"I have said it already before so many times." A mischievous smile played on my lips.

" I want to hear it again. Right now."

" ummm, can you be more precise about it?" I press my lips together.

He lifts his head and his eyes meets mine. My fingers still entangled in his tousled hair.

He rests his palms on either side of my head and lifts himself up a little.

And then narrows his eyes at me. " Fine. I love you."

" I know! You made it pretty clear by saying it so many times earlier." I smirk and he makes a face at me.

I'm enjoying this a little too much.

" Ayezah! " he let out a wince.

A warm smile spreads across my face as I lift my head a little and press my lips to his, in a quick peck, not able to resist his adorable expression. He closes his eyes.

"Okay, I love you too," I whispered, my voice filled with tenderness.

"No, actually, I love you more." I say and he opens his eyes and gazes into mine.

"Nope, I love you more. Definitely."

"Excuse me? Is there some competition going on here?"

" And just a gentle reminder, I fell for you first." I jut my chin out like I'm way too proud of it.

A soft smile tugs at the corners of his lips, and his gaze intensifies.

" But I fell harder." The rush of emotions swirling in his eyes makes it hard for me to catch my breath.

" Damn. fucking. harder." He presses on each word, his voice sounding extra hot, huskier and deep.

My heart starts thumping loudly like a wild horse out of control.

"Did I make your heart race again?" he smirks.

" ofcourse, you never fail to." I smirk back, wrapping my arms around his neck and pulling him closer, he chuckles and shower kisses all over my face.

I giggle along with him, the sound of our laughter intertwining in the air like a sweet melody.

He reaches out with tenderness, his fingers delicately tucking a strand of my hair behind my ear.

I gaze into his eyes, captivated by the warmth and affection that radiate from his gaze.

His one palm still rests on the side of my head, supporting himself. Even though he is draped all over me, he makes sure not to press his entire body's weight on me.

"Why are you looking at me like that?"

I take a moment to gather my thoughts.

"Just thinking, how more of a foolish I can get. I mean, you truly are the nicest person to ever walk on this planet and it pains me to think that I didn't tell you everything earlier and worst, I even hurt you with my words. I'm so mad at myself." I groan, squeezing my eyes shut.

"Do you know what your only negative tendency is, babie?" He pecks my nose gently.

" You tend to overthink everything. It's time to give that pretty head of yours some well-deserved rest." He grazes his nose against mine before planting a tender kiss on my cheek.

The sensation of his touch sends a shiver of warmth cascading through me, like a gentle breeze on a summer evening.

"Actually, you know what,"

Suddenly, he springs up from the bed, leaving me momentarily puzzled and missing the comforting warmth of his body.

With a swift motion, he stretches his arm backside and effortlessly pulls his t-shirt up in one go, discarding it on the floor.

I start to gawk at his Greek-god-like physique, all chiseled and perfect.

" I'm going to fuck the overthinking out of you." He jumps back onto the bed, landing on top of me with a soft thud. I can't help but giggle, my eyes closed at his sudden action.

His head dips into my neck, and a shiver runs down my spine as he places soft, lingering kisses all over.

His lips find the curve of my neck, and with a gentle suck, he moves to my throat. There, he bites, sucks, and licks, igniting a deliciously electrifying sensation that sends waves of pleasure through me.

I can't resist the hunger building within me, and my hands roam eagerly over his sculpted, naked back, hugging him impossibly closer.

A moan escapes my lips, and he responds with deep, primal grunts.

In an instant, he lifts his head, capturing my lips in a breathtakingly urgent kiss.

Our mouths opens together in an eager attempt to eat each other out.

As our lips remain locked, his hands begin to desperately unbutton my black satin night dress shirt.

I raise myself slightly, allowing him to remove my arms from the shirt, all the while still kissing him.

He breaks the kiss and plants numerous pecks on my bare shoulders one by one.

Reaching a hand behind, I swiftly unclasp my bra. With eagerness, he tosses it aside, and his eyes get locked on my exposed breasts immediately.

Lowering his head, he takes one of my nipples into his mouth, his lips and tongue starting their wonders.

Simultaneously, his other hand finds its way to my other breast, kneading it gently yet possessively.

His mouth explores the sensitive flesh of my breast. sucking, licking and nibbling with his teeth, leaving marks all around my nipple.

The sensations ripple through me, intensifying with each passing second.

Just as I begin to lose myself in the pleasure, he switches his attention to the other breast, lavishing it with the same fervor, his tongue tracing maddeningly delicious patterns and his teeth leaving the same marks he left on my other assaulted nipple.

Meanwhile, his thumb strokes my swollen nipple, sending electric waves of pleasure radiating throughout my body.

Overwhelmed by the sheer ecstasy, I can't help but throw my head back, surrendering to the pure sensation coursing through me.

In a swift motion, he removes both his pants and boxers. With a hunger that cannot be contained, he skillfully removes my lowers, his mouth never leaving my breast, still sucking with an insatiable thirst for more.

He plunges into me with a single, powerful thrust, causing my breath to catch in my throat.

He seals my mouth with his, eating the loud moan that escapes from deep within me.

As he begins to move, our breaths mingle, charged and heavy.

"Fuck, I've missed you inside me, Rahil!" I gasp against his mouth.

His eyes darkened. His thrusts become wild, untamed, as if driven by an insatiable beast. Every movement sends waves of pleasure coursing through my body.

"I missed you more, babie!" he growls, his voice dripping with raw desire.

His lips urgently explore every inch of my face, leaving a trail of desperate kisses in their wake.

After several rounds, we both climaxes together and he collapses onto me, still buried deep inside me.

His head rests against my chest, and I feel his rapid breaths against my bare skin.

He inhales deeply between the valley of my breasts.

" I'm never ever letting you go away from me again. Call me clingy all you want, but the fact remains that you are stuck with me for the entire fucking life." He growls out.

Every time he curses, he sounds extra hot.

A smile dances across my lips as I hug his head, my fingers tangling in his silky hair.

"I want you to be extremely clingy with me. I absolutely love it." I say and he pecks my cleavage in response.

Moments later, I feel his breathing begin to relax, his warm breath tickling my bare chest.

I tilt my head slightly to gaze at him, and I'm met with the sight of him peacefully asleep, his arms wrapped tightly around me.

A small smile tugs at my lips, admiring his face radiating a sense of contentment and peace.

Those perfect magical days are back, where I wake up in Rahil's arms, and sleep all wrapped around him.

Two weeks passed in a blur as I returned to my home, where I always belonged to. Right by Rahil's side.

Rahil immediately broke all the ties with that physco's company.

And we did tell everything to Addin. He's got some amazing sources, you know, the kind that can dig up every little details. We told him to dig every peace of information about Rose.

When we shared all this information with Addin his exact words were.

" why fucking bother collecting all the information and shits, when we can just fucking kill the bitch? I have a fucking gun too, Rahil knows about that."

You see my cousin happens to have a short temper. Real bad one.

Rahil looked all awkward and somewhat uncomfortable probably listening to Addin's last sentence, so I frowned and questioned about it.

Addin then revealed it that Rahil has shot and killed someone in the past, but it was a knee-jerk reaction in defence.

I was surprised would be an understatement of the century.

"Zah?" Rahil's voice snapped me out of my thoughts.

"Umm?" I asked, slightly dazed.

"Where are you lost? We've reached your office."

"Ah, yes! Sorry, I was just lost in some meaningless thoughts."

Right now, we were seated in Rahil's car, as he had taken up the habit of driving me to the office and picking me up in the evening.

I don't know what exactly was his nightmare about but I guess it's something related to fire.

He would often remind me to check the fire alarm and sprinkler in my cabin, ensuring they were functioning properly. I didn't press him to reveal the details of his nightmares, as it seemed to disturb him greatly.

"I told you that whenever you'll overthink anything, I'll fuck those thoughts out of your mind! Do you want me to take you right here in the car?" a mischievous smirk played on his lips as he leaned closer.

His boldness seemed to grow with each passing day.

I couldn't help but smirk back, leaning closer to his face.

"As much as I would love that, we both have work to attend." I reply, tapping his cheek playfully.

He let out a groan and I couldn't help but smile, giving him a quick peck on the lips before stepping out of the car.

"Don't forget to come early to pick me up! We have dinner plans, remember?" I reminded him, my excitement evident in my voice.

"Of course I remember, love. Have I ever forgotten anything? In fact, I'll be eagerly waiting for the evening, now." He grins widely and passes me a wink.

I wave at him as he drove off to his own office.

The day flew by at the office, and as evening approached, I couldn't contain my excitement.

I swiftly wrapped up, practically sprinting down to the ground floor. It felt like the first time I was going out for dinner with Rahil, even though we've done it countless times before. But that's the thing about Rahil, every experience with him feels fresh and exhilarating.

As I reached the outside of my building, I waited eagerly, expecting Rahil to already be there, as I had asked him to come early. But minutes passed, and he was nowhere in sight.

Maybe he got caught in traffic? Yeah, that must be it. I shouldn't let my mind wander into negative thoughts.

Stay positive, Ayezah.

Several more minutes ticked by, and still no sign of Rahil. I tried calling him, but it went straight to voicemail.

Worry started to consume me, and I began pacing back and forth, my heart racing. Just as I was lost in my own thoughts, my phone rang, and I eagerly answered it without even bothering to check the caller ID.

"Rahil, where are you?"

I froze when the voice that I never want to hear again, the voice that's haunting my dreams for past few days now, came from the phone.

"Well, hello there, Ayezah! Your beloved man is with me. Didn't I warn you to stay away from him? Since you failed to do so, how about I take care of the task myself? I told you, I'll gladly do it for you."

The phone trembled in my hand as fear coursed through my veins.

No, this couldn't be happening.

" Come to the location I'll provide you soon if you want to bid your precious husband a final goodbye. And don't you dare think about involving the cops or your aggressive fucking cousin who's been breathing down my neck for the past few days. Or else, you won't even get a chance to say that final goodbye," she threatened, before abruptly ending the call.

My hand trembled, and I stood there completely frozen.

It's a nightmare. It has to be.

Please be a nightmare. Please.

Chapter 24

Rahil's POV:

In a twist of fate, like a scene from a cliché kidnapping story, this bitch of a stupid woman named Rose, whom I sincerely hoped to have never cross paths with, and like most of the cliché kidnappers, she too pulled off a cowardly act of kidnapping me.

When I was moving towards my car in the parking lot of my office this evening, With a forceful blow to the back of my head, she made me lose consciousness and whisked me away to a shabby, rundown location that seemed straight out of a horror movie.

And there I was, cliché enough again, bound tightly to a creaky wooden chair. It took me exactly twenty minutes to regain consciousness fully and process everything.

In the dimly lit doorway of this damn haunted house, that physco wearing a vibrant red hoodie stands, accompanied by a man wearing black hoodie.

Of course, she wouldn't have been able to drag me here all by herself.

The room has a small dusty bed at the corner with tattered blankets and a creaky cupboard.

The eerie atmosphere and dim cold lights give off the best creepy feeling.

When Ayezah revealed everything to me about this stupid woman, a wave of anger and protectiveness surged through me.

Only I know the immense effort it took to maintain my composure, and not to go out of character and do something to this bitch.

Only I know how much strength it took me to hold myself back from taking impulsive actions.

But that's the thing, when it comes to Ayezah, I lose all my calm and I so desperately want go out of my character.

The audacity of this bitch of a woman, this intruder in our lives, to dare threaten my Ayezah!

How dare she think she can manipulate my Ayezah and take her away? No one can separate us. No one can keep me from being close to her. She's my wife, my everything, just mine.

And when I say no one, I mean absolutely no one can take her away from me.

Suddenly, the woman whom I despise to core, approaches me with a smirk, her hair concealed beneath the hood of her hoodie.

The man in the black hoodie walks out of the house.

I shoot her a cold, piercing glare.

"Oh, you're awake?"

I remain silent, watching her with a cold, emotionless expression.

"Wow! Where's the polite Mr. Khan who was all smiley and sweet to me just a few days ago?" she mocks.

I don't utter a word, but continue to stare at her with icy eyes.

"Listen, I have no issues with you. You're kind and all, and you're not to blame for anything. But your only mistake is being that fucking bitch's love, husband, and source of happiness."

"Don't fucking curse her." I growl, feeling the anger within me rise.

"Whoa, I see you're so head over heels for her." she says, her eyes darkening.

" Why does everyone falls head over heels for her? " she suddenly leans closer, cracking her head a little side ways.

Fucking psycho.

"Tell me why? Why do you love her so much?" Her voice suddenly turns icy cold.

"What the heck do you mean?" my frustration is evident in my tone.

"She's my wife! Of course I love her."

"Right. Wife." She tilts her head sideways, a peculiar expression on her face.

"Then why didn't he love his wife?"

Before I can even answer, a voice cuts through the air, causing my heart to skip a beat.

"Rahil!" I hear Ayezah's whimper, and my gaze immediately darts towards the door.

There she stands, her hands bound behind her back, held captive by the man in a black hoodie. She's wearing a disheveled brown long coat over white top and pants, her hair a mess, and her face as pale as paper.

No. This is not happening.

"Why the hell did you bring her here?" I snarl at Rose, my anger boiling over to extreme level.

She smirks and straightens herself.

"What do you mean? Of course she'll be here! It's all because of her to begin with. It's her fault. All her fault." she says with a mix of frustration and desperation in her voice.

I grit my teeth, trying to hold back my anger, and respond firmly, "No, it's not."

Suddenly, the man in the black hoodie forcefully drags Ayezah by the shoulder, bringing her closer to us.

"Don't fucking touch her, you filthy scum!" I yell, my voice echoing through the air. The man callously slams Ayezah down onto the dusty floor right in front of me but a little far away.

Ayezah's hair cascades across her face, partially hiding her features.

She manages to lift her gaze and glare at the fucker with all her might.

"What do you mean it isn't her fault? It damn well is! She came between me and my husband! If she didn't exist, me and Sebastian would be living the happiest damn life together." she seethes, taking a step closer to Ayezah.

"Now, tell me, what does she have that I don't? Me and Sebastian were childhood friends, I've loved him since we were knee-high. We were always together, always happy. But then this bitch came into the picture." she points at Ayezah with desperation in her eyes.

" He first laid eyes on her in university. We attended the same damn place. And let me tell you, this woman was a real charmer, flirting with almost every guy in the university. My Sebastian couldn't resist her damn trap and fell head over heels for her. He became downright obsessed." she glares intensely at Ayezah.

"But this woman, she didn't give a damn about him. She didn't even acknowledge his presence. Even when he tried his best to get close to her, I helped him too, because his happiness meant the world to me. But this bitch, she kept ignoring him. Hell, she didn't even recognize him until I showed her his picture." she speaks with an icy tone, her head swiveling around.

"Tell me, Ayezah! why didn't you show any interest in my handsome Sebastian? If you had given him a chance, maybe he would've been happier. He wouldn't have been so grumpy with me, ignoring and blocking me all the damn time." She leans in closer to Ayezah's face, her voice filled with frustration.

"But I was the one who held him when he was broken, all because of you! I married him, thinking I could heal him. He may not have been exactly happy about the marriage, but at least he was with me. At least he didn't block me or leave me. Everything was going perfect until, after so many years, he saw you again at one of those damn business parties." She glares at Ayezah, her eyes filled with anger.

"He went crazy for you again, wanting to leave me. He even had the audacity to ask for a divorce! I was his wife, he was supposed to be with me for the rest of his life! He was supposed to love me! But as soon as he saw you again, he claimed he loved you and could never get over you."

She leans in even closer to Ayezah, her voice filled with desperation. "I told him I'd do anything to become like you. I dressed like you, colored my hair to match yours, wore lenses to mimic your eye color, and even used the same perfume as you. But he still said I didn't come close to being like you. Why? Just because I had a different face? I even went for getting plastic surgery to look like you, but Sebastian found out and told me to stop this madness."

"He called my love for him absolute madness and obsession, saying he loathes me. He even said I disgust and scare him. Why? All because of you." She seethes at Ayezah, her anger burning bright.

"And then one day, he crossed all the limits by leaving me. How dare he abandon me? He was supposed to be by my side for the rest of his life. So, filled with rage, I grabbed him by the hair and took his life. I killed him." she says with a maniacal look in her eyes.

" Fucking liar bitch! You told me he committed suicide because of me!" Ayezah spat angrily, struggling to free her hands.

Rose throws her head back and lets out a chilling, evil laugh.

"Oh, did I? That was just to send you on a little guilt trip." Her voice dripping with malice.

"I mean, how could you be happy with your husband when you destroyed mine? Sure, I was the one who ended his life, but it was because of you. So technically you are the actual killer. If you hadn't shown up at that business party, none of this would have happened, hell if you didn't exist in the first place, none of this would have happened. You're a home wrecker, who tore apart my family. So, why should I let you have any happiness?"

She tilts her head, a sinister smile playing on her lips.

"No. She ain't no killer or home wrecker. You are a psycho bloody murderer. You took down your own husband's life, so quit blaming your sinful deeds on my wife!" I let out a thunderous yell, struggling against the restraints, desperately trying to break free from the chair.

Her head snaps towards me in a twisted, unhinged manner, her eyes burning with a wild intensity as she locks her gaze onto mine.

"I'M NOT! SHE'S THE ONE WHO TOOK MY HUSBAND'S LIFE!" she screams at the top of her lungs, her glare piercing through me like a dagger.

Then, with a swift motion, she turns her head back to Ayezah.

"As much as I want to fucking kill you, I won't. It wouldn't be any fun, Also Once I'm done taking everything away from you, I'll go to my Sebastian. And what if I kill you and you come between us again? no way, I can't risk that. So I'll leave you alive, instead I'll take your happiness, your Rahil with me, leaving you here to rot all alone."

She is fucking mentally ill. She fucking needs serious help.

"You sick psycho bitch!" Ayezah spat, her anger seething through her words.

"Listen to me very carefully. If you lay a finger on my husband, I'll fucking kill you. This time, I won't hesitate or hold back. You might be a psycho, but when it comes to Rahil, I can cross all the fucking limits. I'm done being a coward once and letting you manipulate me, this time I won't, I swear I'll kill you." her anger simmering.

The intensity of her words made my heart race.

Rose lets out an evil laugh.

"Oh, how foolishly adorable you are, Ayezah!" she taunts and with a swift motion, she pulls a gun from the back of her pants.

"You can gladly try to kill me, but before I go, I'll make sure Rahil is far away from you." As she twirled the gun in her hand, she orders the man to fetch something.

Ayezah fought back, yelling and struggling with all her might.

The man returned with a lighter and bottles of kerosene. My mind raced, realizing what this sick mental is intending to do.

Fire? No, Ayezah is here. It will fucking terrify her.

Ayezah's face pales like a white paper and she swallows visibly.

" Thanks for your service, David." And then she swiftly raises her gun in his direction and shoots him right between his eyes

Ayezah's eyes shuts tightly, and a startled scream escaped her lips.

The man's body falls to the ground with a thud sound, his eyes wide open in horror.

Rose swiftly rises to her feet and begins circling me.

"Take one last look at your husband. He's leaving you, just like Sebastian left me because of you!" Her voice drips with venom. As she pours the kerosene in a menacing circle around me.

Ayezah fights desperately. "Don't do it, please," she pleads, and I notice that tears have started to well up in her beautiful eyes.

Rose tosses the empty bottle of kerosene aside and lets out a chilling laugh.

I remained calm this entire fucking time because I know that Addin will track me down.

Earlier this morning, I sensed someone following me, and I suspected this bitch was up to something .

So, I had informed Addin to keep a close eye on me and to call the police if he found me in any unsettling situations.

However, he seems to be taking longer than expected.

The situation is growing increasingly dire.

Not the fire. Please. Not when Ayezah is here.

I'd rather have Rose shoot me directly with that damn gun than put Ayezah through this torture.

She pours another bottle of kerosene over my head. I wriggle in the chair, desperately trying to free myself from the tightly bound restraints.

The pungent smell of kerosene fills the air as she completely drenches me.

" I know all your fears, Ayezah! Even if you try, you can't save your husband from the fire. Fire terrifies you to your very core, all you can do is watch him go far away from you, just the I watched my Sebastian go far away from me." Her gaze filled with madness, fixated on Ayezah.

"Please don't! PLEASE!" Ayezah pleads with desperation, her voice trembles with fear as she struggles greatly against the tight ropes binding her hands behind her back.

"I can't stay here any longer. I need to go to my Sebastian. I miss him so much."

With a flick of the lighter, she ignites the circle of kerosene she had earlier created. The flames erupt with a whooshing sound, engulfing around me.

"NOOOO!" Ayezah's piercing scream fills the air

Rose smiles maniacally, the gun's barrel pressed against her temple. She closes her eyes, a single tear escaping as she whispers,

"Justice is served. I'm coming to you, Sebastian, my love."

In one swift motion, she pulls the trigger, and her lifeless body falls to the ground with a haunting thud.

As the flames encircle me, their flickering dance casts an eerie glow, painting the surroundings in shades of fiery red and orange.

Ayezah, breaks into uncontrollable sobs, her cries echoing through the chaos.

Her body twists and wriggles, desperately trying to free herself.

The moment I've dreaded with all my might, the nightmare that I never wanted to become a reality, is happening.

The only difference is that I'm the one trapped within the ring of fire and not her, so I'm fucking grateful for that.

If I'm going to die here, I want to make sure that Ayezah gets out of here unscathed.

It's my only and final wish.

Chapter 25

Ayezah's POV:

Take a deep breath. Inhale, exhale.

I gasped for air, tears streamed down my cheeks uncontrollably.

The scorching flames surrounding Rahil seemed to suffocate me, their orange glow casting an eerie light and intensifying the heat, making it difficult to draw a steady breath.

"Calm down, Ayezah," I whispered to myself, my voice trembling with desperation.

I cried out louder, squeezing my eyes shut, my desperation growing, yearning to free my hands from the tight ropes that bound them behind my back.

My earlier wriggling and struggling had slightly loosened the ropes, allowing me to slip my palm against the gritty floor.

As I rose to my feet and attempted to approach Rahil, the flames triggered something within me, causing my breathing to become heavy and rapid. My chest ached intensely, and my vision began to blur.

"No, Ayezah! Get out of here! Go away! Stay away from the fire." Rahil's urgent yelling broke through the chaos, bringing me back to the present. My vision cleared, revealing his face etched with concern amidst the blazing fire.

"Noo, I'm not going anywhere without you."I yelled back, the intense heat of the fire making my face all sweaty and sticky.

My head spun, throbbing with pain.

Get a grip. Get a grip.

"No! Just listen—" he started again, squirming in his chair, but I cut him off.

"There's absolutely no way I'm leaving you here to die." I shout, gasping for air, my breathing heavy.

My blurry eyes scanned the room, and I spotted a few tattered blankets on the bed.

I immediately rushed over to the bed. Using the sharp edge of the old metal frame of the bed, I freed my trembling hands from the loose rope. The metal bit into my skin, but I didn't let the pain distract me. I tightly grasped the tattered blankets, clutching them to my chest.

Returning to Rahil, I approached him, the intense heat of the fire causing my skin to crawl.

I squeezed my eyes shut, tears streaming down my face.

"No, Ayezah, don't let your demons win now! You have to save Rahil at any cost." I whispered to myself, mustering up the courage to take another step forward. My whole body trembled, my chin wobbling with fear.

"Just go away!" Rahil kept yelling, but I completely ignored his pleas.

There were two blankets in total. Despite their worn-out appearance, they still had enough thickness to offer some hope against the raging fire.

Without wasting a second, I swiftly placed one of the blankets onto the flames, the crackling fire momentarily subdued in that small area.

As the fire crackled beneath the blanket, I took a step back, tears streaming down my face, and let out a heavy breath, my chest rising and falling with each shaky breath.

With my vision still blurred, my head spinning and my whole body trembling, I mustered all the strength I had left to move closer to Rahil.

With shaky fingers, I began to untie him.

As soon as Rahil was free, he stood up from the chair immediately and I wrapped the one remaining blanket around his shoulders.

But he instantly slipped the blanket from his shoulders and draped it around mine.

I looked at him through my barely open eyes, my head still spinning relentlessly.

His handsome face, glistening with sweat, blurred even further, prompting me to close my eyes momentarily.

In that moment, my body gave way, losing all strength and grip. I began to fall backward, but before I could hit the ground, strong arm encircled my waist and his deep voice reached my ears.

"Ayezah!"

I felt his another strong hand going under my knees, as he effortlessly pulled me off the ground and tugged me closer to hissturdy chest that smelled of kerosene.

I gently rested my head against his chest and my trembling palm fisted his sticky shirt.

Just before everything went blank and black, my cousin's voice pierced the air, filled with anger and frustration, his words laced with numerous curses.

"What the fuck took you so long, Addin?" It was Rahil's voice, yelling loudly.

I also heard police sirens and people rushing in.

My throat feels incredibly dry, like I haven't had a sip of liquid in ages.

Outside, there's a soft sobbing sound that tugs at my heart. I want to open my eyes, but they feel heavy, as if weighed down by exhaustion. A splitting headache throbs through my head, making it feel as though it's been cracked into two pieces.

Summoning every ounce of strength I have left, I slowly flutter my eyes open, only to immediately shut them again due to the blinding brightness.

After a moment, I gather the courage to open them once more, and I see my best friend, with her fiery red hair, sitting at the edge of the bed.

"Laila...?" My voice is barely audible, hoarse and weak.

As I glance around my surroundings, I take in the sterile, plain walls and the crisp white blanket draped over me. I'm dressed in a hospital gown, confirming my suspicion that I'm in a hospital.

A flash of memories floods my mind: the image of Rahil bound to a chair, surrounded by flames, and Rose taking her own life.

I squeeze my eyes shut tightly and clutch my head, hissing in pain.

"Ayezi? Oh my gosh, you're awake?" Laila rushes towards me, tears streaming down her face, and immediately pulls me into a tight hug.

"Are you okay?" she asks, pulling away slightly from the hug.

"I need some water," I say, reaching for my throat, and that's when I notice the IV attached to my hand.

Laila nods. "Okay, I'll get you some water," she quickly makes her way around the bed to the other side.

"Where's Rahil? Is he alright? Is he harmed in anyway?" I swallow, feeling my heart grow restless at the thought of anything happening to him and the scene where he was bound in between the flames, keeps flashing into my mind, making it worse.

"You were unconscious the whole night. Everyone was so worried. Rahil jij stayed by your side the entire time, not resting or sleeping for even a moment. He only left to shower and change his clothes when Addin practically dragged him away. Right now, he's talking with your doctor because he's worried that you didn't wake up."

As Laila hands me the water, I take slow sips from the plastic cup, trying to quench my parched throat.

"I need to see Rahil myself and make sure he's alright." I hand the cup back to her.

In the next moment, I throw the blanket off my body, remove the IV and attempt to step down from the bed, only to stumble forward.

A pair of strong hands firmly grasp my shoulders, preventing me from falling. My hair falls over my face, restricting my view, but I can sense his presence.

His familiar clean masculine scent envelops me, and my heart calms down a bit.

In the blink of an eye, Rahil takes my one hand and wraps it around his neck, his own arm get wounded around my waist and another one below my knees, effortlessly lifting me off my feet.

A startled gasp escapes my lips.

With gentleness, he lays me down back on the bed, tucking me in with the blanket.

As he reattaches the IV to my hand, I can't help but gaze at his face, searching for a glimpse of the warmth and tenderness that usually resides there.

But instead, his expression is distant, almost icy, causing my heart to race with worry.

Just as the silence becomes almost unbearable, Laila clears her throat, breaking the tension in the room.

"I'll be back! Take good rest, Ayezi," she says, her voice filled with concern as she exits the room.

Rahil, still avoiding my gaze, moves around the bed to the other side. He fills a plastic glass with water, his movements mechanical and detached. Without looking into my eyes, he offers me the drink, his usual attentiveness replaced by an unsettling distance.

"I just drank..." I murmur slowly, attempting to sit up. Rahil places the cup to the side and gently helps me rise, adjusting the pillow behind my back for support.

There's something off about his demeanor, something I've never seen before. The coldness emanating from him sends a pang through my heart, leaving me feeling lost and confused.

"Rahil," I whisper.

But he remains silent, his focus on the objects scattered on the bedside table, as he rumbles through them.

"Rahil," I call out again, my voice filled with concern and confusion. But once more, he chooses to ignore me, leaving me in a state of disbelief.

"Rahil, are you okay? Is something wrong?" The words escape my lips, hanging in the air, waiting for a response that never comes.

"I'll bring something for you to eat," he says and attempts to stand up, but before he can, I reach out and firmly grasp his palm, stopping him in his tracks.

Feeling a mix of frustration and worry, I yell slightly.

"I asked you something! What is wrong with you? Why are you behaving this way? Why aren't you listening to me? Why are you ignoring me?"

He finally relents and sits on the bed in front of me.

"Why should I? Did you listen to me when I told you to back off from the fire?" The anger in his voice catches me off guard.

"Tell me, Did you listen when I said to get out of there? No, right?"

"You can't just expect me to leave you there to die," Unable to contain my own frustration, I raise my voice.

"I would've found a way to get out anyhow, Addin was already on his way for our rescue. And for god's sake it was fire, Ayezah! It terrifies you so much! How could you do that?" His voice is cold, filled with anger, frustration and concern.

"I don't care about my fears when it comes to you, Rahil! I was terrified for you more than anything else in that moment."

Rahil's anger starts to soften a little.

"You think I wasn't scared too? My heart was pounding so loudly in my chest when you were trying to reach me. I couldn't bear the thought of you getting hurt. What if you had burned yourself even the slightest? What if you had a panic attack? What if you had collapsed?" His voice trembles with vulnerability.

Tears well up in my eyes, and I quickly turn away.

Rahil's warm palms cradle my cheeks, as he gently makes me turn towards himself.

He presses his forehead against mine softly.

"I'm sorry. I was really so worried. You were unconscious through-out the night. The doctor explained that you experienced severe trauma shock, which kept you from awakening. I was so over-whelmed with fear, with the thought that if you never wake up then what was I going to do? The thought itself didn't let me breathe. I held your hand tightly the whole night, but you remained complete-ly limped, all these made me go absolutely crazy." He murmurs.

I glance into his eyes, mirroring my own glassy gaze, I witness tears welling up, cascading down his face.

The sight tugs at my heart, causing a pang of pain within me.

" I just love you so deeply, Ayezah! I always want to see you safe, fine, breathing and unharmed." his voice is filled with pure sincerity.

I reach out and gently cup his cheeks, feeling the warmth of his skin beneath my palms. He closes his eyes, leans into my touch, pressing his nose against mine, and snuggles even more closer to me.

Tenderly, I brush away his tears with the pad of my thumb.

"I love you just as fiercely, Rahil! The mere thought of you in pain is unbearable to me as well. I couldn't simply leave you in that moment. Please, try to understand," I softly caress his cheeks.

He urgently kisses my damp eyelids, my cheeks, my forehead, and my dry lips, as if his life depends on it.

With each kiss, he softly keeps murmuring, "I love you, I love you, I love you so much."

"I love you!" I exclaim, and eagerly wrap my arms around him, nestling my face in the crook of his neck.

He urgently moves forward in the bed because of the IV connected to my hand and pulls me onto his lap.

I feel an immediate sense of comfort as his strong arms envelop me. He responds with tenderness, pressing a gentle kiss atop my head and resting his cheek against the side of my head.

In that moment, time seems to stand still as I revel in the warmth of his skin against my nose and inhale his intoxicating scent.

After a few precious seconds, I reluctantly pull back, but he remains close, his fingertips delicately fixing my hair behind my ears.

He brushes his knuckles against my dampened cheeks, wiping away the remnants of my tears.

His breathtaking warm smile illuminates his face, causing a slight smile to grace my own lips in response.

My voice trembles slightly as I bring up the topic of the Rose.

"What happened to... Rose?"

"Don't worry, everything is taken care of. It was a suicidal case, and Addin is handling everything," he explains, and I nod.

"I'm sorry," I murmur softly, a tinge of guilt coloring my voice.

"For what, babie?" He leans in, pressing a tender kiss on my forehead.

"For everything."

"For whatever Rose did, somewhere it was all because of me. Also, for being such a coward and-"

Before I can finish my sentence, he interrupts me with a firm peck on my lips.

"Shhh! You aren't a coward."

"You are my tigress, remember? And whatever happened, not a single thing was your fault. You didn't even know anything." His words wash over me, but I can't help but shake my head.

"I'm nothing like a tigress."

"You are, Ayezah. You are my tigress, the strongest woman I know. I've said it before, but I don't think you truly realize just how much I admire you." His voice filled with sincerity.

He takes a moment to gather his thoughts before continuing, his gaze locked with mine.

"If you weren't strong, you would have never risked yourself to save me from that fire. You faced your fear head-on, showing immense bravery. And when Rose threatened you, you weren't being a coward, you were simply protecting me, standing up against any threat that came our way."

His eyes softens. "Your love has always been fierce, evident in every aspect of your being. When you shared the painful truth about what your mom did to you, and yet, you couldn't bring yourself to hate her. The fact that you still wear the pendant she gave you, cherishing only the good memories, speaks volumes about your capacity for forgiveness and compassion."

A warm smile graces his lips. "Being loved by you is an incredible honor, one that I consider myself lucky to experience. You have shown me what it means to be truly cherished and valued."

He reaches out, gently taking my hands in his,"And no matter what, remember that you will always be my fierce tigress. Always, zah."

He bends down a little and presses firm kisses on my knuckles.

His words ignite a wildfire within my chest, causing my heart to race insanely.

I find myself gazing at him, my eyes brimming with tears and my lips curled into a genuine smile.

I reach out and firmly grasp his hand that is still holding mine. Bringing his hand up to my lips, I delicately brush my dry, chapped lips against his fingers.

I then press the backside of his hand against my cheek, closing my eyes and leaning into his touch.

I open my eyes to see him gazing at me with a tender smile, mirroring the love and adoration that fills his eyes, for me.

2 months later :

Rahil's POV:

I was wandering aimlessly, feeling lost in the vast expanse of my own existence. Days passed by without purpose, until one fateful day when she gracefully entered my life.

It wasn't that I was necessarily sad, but a sense of emptiness lingered within me.

In her presence, I discovered the true essence of happiness, a feeling so pure and genuine that it radiated from within.

As I gaze at her now, her laughter fills the air, like music that dances upon the gentle rays of the sun.

She's wearing a lovely, delicate sundress in a soft shade of purple, the dress hugs her curves perfectly, accentuating her graceful fig-ure.

Her shiny black hair, adorned with beautiful chocolate brown highlights, cascades in gentle waves as she tilts her head back and laughs.

The golden glow of the sunlight caresses her already beautiful, radiant skin, accentuating her natural beauty.

Meanwhile, Laila, full of her usual chaotic energy, chases after Adam on the sand, and she laughs at their antics.

We all had actually planned a double date on the beach to watch sunset together.

Her gaze is fixed on them and mine on her.

Now, back to why Laila is chasing Adam. You see, Adam being Adam, proposed Laila for marriage.

His exact words were " Will you be the mummy of my future kids, Laila?"

He is so absolutely foolish, I tell you.

Laila got mad saying how much more of a stupid he can get and exaggerating how toddlers can propose better than him.

Laila delivers a swift kick to Adam's ass, causing him to wince and clutch his bum in an over dramatic way.

Meanwhile, Ayezah, still overcoming with laughter, makes her way towards them, her joyful giggles filling the air. I follow closely behind.

"Okay, guys, let's calm down!" Ayezah interjects, positioning herself between the two, trying to stifle her laughter.

"Move, Ayezi! I'm going to kick his stupid ass out of this planet," Laila exclaims.

"Ayezah! Please save me from this wild cat." Adam hides behind Ayezah, instinctively grabbing onto her shoulders and pleading.

Okay, this is my cue to interfere now.

"Hands off!" I shoot Adam a stern glare and gently pull Ayezah towards me, wrapping a possessive arm around her shoulder, drawing her closer and practically gluing her body with mine.

"Oh, sir, stop being a petty, jealous being."

"Shut up."

" Whatever." He rolls his eyes dismissively.

"Don't you have to propose to Laila?" I raise an eyebrow at him, reminding him of his original intention.

"Oh yeah, yeah!" He quickly drops to his knees in front of Laila, reaching into his pocket to retrieve a ring.

"Laila Siddique, from the very first day I laid my eyes on you, I was total goner. Your beauty surpasses anything I've ever seen before. Being with you has made me realize that—what the hell was I doing with my life before, if not being with you? You bring me immense happiness, and now that I know you so well, I can't imagine my life without you. Will you be my forever, please?" he asks, his voice filled with sincerity.

Laila's eyes well up with tears as she smiles widely.

"No, I won't marry someone as silly as you." She teases and Adam winced.

He then suddenly turns towards Ayezah.

"Okay then! Ayezah Shah, will you marry me?"

The audacity of this little shit—

"What the fuck?" I glare at him, hard.

Laila, swiftly punches his chest and pulls him up and Ayezah bursts into laughter again.

"Do you have a death wish?" Laila asks, pulling him closer by his collar.

He shakes his head, his gaze filled with sincerity as he cups her cheeks.

"No, I have a wish for you to become my wife and be with me forever."

Laila closes her eyes, her forehead gently pressing against his, as a soft smile graces her lips. "Of course, it's a yes, you idiot!"

He pulls back from her, a triumphant smile spreading across his face as he jumps in victory, throwing his fist into the air.

" YAYAYAYA yay!"

"I love you so much, Laila Siddique!" he shouts still jumping, his voice ringing out with pure joy.

Laila's laughter fills the air, her eyes sparkling with happiness. "I love you too, Adam Hussain, always and forever!" she shouts back, jumping with him and he picks her up by her waist and twirls her around, meanwhile she throws her head back and laughs loudly.

Ayezah, unable to contain her excitement, screams 'congratulations guys', her voice filled with genuine happiness.

I can't help but join in and congratulate them, smiling.

They turn towards us, their eyes filled with gratitude, as they thank us for being a part of their special moment.

However, I narrow my eyes at Adam, my tone firm as I address him.

"Also, Adam, she is not Ayezah Shah. She is Ayezah Rahil Ahmed Khan. And next time you do something like this, I'll seriously consider firing you from the job." Adam sulks, while Laila and Ayezah burst into laughter at the exchange.

After few more months :

A y e z a h ' s P O V :

This feels absolutely crazy to me. I can't believe how life has turned this incredibly amazing.

I never thought I would receive the same depth of love that I gave to someone. Someone whom I loved insanely and now he loves me back too.

Right now, my lovely husband is hugging me from behind, on a cool evening as we stand on our room's spacious balcony, overlooking the sparkling pool of the backyard.

We're enjoying the fresh air. The guitar is cradled in my arms, while his arms are wrapped over mine.

He's teaching me how to play the guitar, which has become our everyday routine.

Laila and Adam got married just a month after their chaotic beach proposal, and now we're all planning to go on a honeymoon together in Greece since Rahil and I didn't have the chance before.

Two months ago, Najma gave birth to an adorable babie boy, and just yesterday we found out that Noor is pregnant.

Everyone around us is happy and content. As for me, I couldn't be anymore happier.

After all I have found the most amazing man who makes me feel incredibly special and deeply loved every single second of my life.

It's a feeling I can't capture in mere words. I'm truly blessed. My life with him is nothing short of magical.

"Umm, what's going on in that pretty little head of yours?" he whispers against my ear, his warm breath sending shivers down my spine.

I shake my head, a playful smile tugging at the corners of my lips.

"Just thinking about which song you would like to dedicate to me."

"Umm, let me think! How about a Bollywood song?" he asks, his eyes sparkling with excitement.

I nod eagerly. "Yes! Laila has made me a crazy fan of Bollywood music." A hint of laughter is evident in my voice.

"Okay, I love Bollywood too. But I don't know many songs. However, there's one song I heard that made me think about you. In fact, whenever I listen to any song, it feels like it's all about you." He says, his words melting my heart and making my cheeks blush crimson.

"Okay, so shall I start?" he asks, his fingers effortlessly finding their place on the guitar strings. The air fills with a soft melody as his fingertips dance across the strings.

I'm still in his arms, and the guitar is cradle in mine.

"kisi shaam ki tarah, Tera rang hai khila"

He sings in my ear with his melodic, husky deep voice, and my heart nearly jumps out of my chest.

"Main raat ek tanha Tu chand sa mila"

He nuzzles his nose into my hair and inhales deeply, then presses his cheek against mine and rests his chin on my shoulder blade.

"Haan tujhe dekh ta raha kisi khwaab ki tarah"

His eyes are now fixed intently at me, as he watches my side profile with such intensity that I can feel the heat of his gaze.

"Jo ab saamne hai tuho kaise yakeen bhala"

He pauses, closes his eyes, and sighs in contentment against the curve of neck.

The lyrics flow out of my mouth on its own, before I could even realise it.

" toota jo kabhi tara, sajna ve,tujhe rab se maanga, rabse jo manga. Mileya ve."

I title my head sideways, and smilingly sing along with him.

He jerks his head up from my neck so fast, I doubt that he didn't pull up any muscle.

His eyes are wide open, and he blinks a few times. He recovers quickly and flashes me his breathtakingly gorgeous smile.

"Tu mileya toh jaane na dunga mai "

He then suddenly takes the guitar in his arms and twirls me around. He wears the guitar over his neck, as he holds my palm in his warm and steady grip.

With a mischievous smile, he starts spinning me, his voice carrying through the air like a sweet melody, as he continues to sing, his fingers dance effortlessly across the strings, producing enchanting chords that fill the space around us.

I can't help but burst into laughter, my heart overflowing with joy as we dance together, his music and singing guiding our every step.

After a few precious minutes of dancing and singing together, we sit down on the balcony.

"You sing so well! Your voice is incredibly sweet and melodic, damn!" Rahil exclaims, his words laced with genuine admiration, as we both gulp down the refreshing cold water.

Setting the bottle down, I respond, "Nah, nah! It just flowed out naturally. Laila and I used to have these singing sessions, more like practically screaming shows, during our night outs. Good times, you know?"

"But seriously, you were amazing!"

"And what about you, huh? Your singing voice, with that thick Urdu accent of yours, is downright so hot." I smirk playfully, and he cups the backside of his neck, lowering his head and smiling—an act that he does when he is blushing.

This adorable, adorable man will be the death of me.

"I guess you should speak to me in urdu often." I say.

He looks up at me and frowns.

"You know to speak urdu?"

"Of course, I'm a desi too. So what if I was born and brought up in Australia? My parents are desi, so I know it too," I reply.

"Oh, okay!"

"So, talk to me in Urdu often?"

"Okay, begum jaan. Aur koi hukum?"

I can't help but laugh. We chat for a while, playfully conversing in Urdu.

Then, he brings up a memory.

"Ayezah, do you remember when I first met you at Addin's birthday party, and you asked me if I would like to date you?"

"Of course, how can I ever forget your adorable shocked face, when you choked on your drink."

I recall, and my lips curl up on their own.

"Well, I would like to actually and sincerely answer that now. It's a yes. I would love to date you." he says, and I look at him with utter amusement.

I chuckle, "Well, when I asked you again later you did give me an answer though—" he doesn't let me complete.

" That was because I was a fool, so don't consider it." he says hurriedly.

I shake my head, "We're literally married now." The laughter bubbling in my voice is evident.

"Doesn't matter, I still want to date you. I want to be your boyfriend and spoil you like the other boyfriend's spoils their girlfriends by taking them on numerous dates and shopping and I want to treat you like the most precious gem in the world."

"You can do that while being my husband as well and c'mon you have already spoiled me enough and you already make me feel more than special!"

"The fact that I'm your husband doesn't change, But dating is different."

" You're being so silly right now." I laugh.

"No, I'm serious."

" You've been my first in everything, and that's why I want you to be my first girlfriend as well. I want us to share every little experience together. Even if it's as stupid as it's sounds." I look a little taken aback by his first sentence and he notices it.

" Sure I had a very strong attraction towards someone before, but I can't call it love because the only time I truly felt that intense emotion was with you."

My heart picks up its pace, and thunders loudly into my chest.

I lean forward, cupping his one cheek gently, I tilt my head, and press my lips on his, which he eagerly responds by opening his mouth and sucking on my lower lip.

As our lips move together, I whisper against his mouth, "I love you."

He pulls back slightly, a grin spreading across his face.

"I love you more," his eyes sparkling with pure adoration. I smile back at him.

"Okay then, I'll be your girlfriend."

Rahil's eyes widen like an excited child.

"Really?"

I nod, "Yeah, and since I don't do live-in relationships, I'm going to move to Laila's house until we're dating," I tease, watching his grin drop instantly.

I smirk and stand up moving gracefully towards the room.

I'm in the doorway of the balcony, when I feel a gentle presence behind me, and before I know it, Rahil's strong arm wrap around my waist, scooping me up effortlessly.

A delighted squeal escapes my lips.

" On a second thought, it's so stupid to play this whole dating thingy, when we are literally married. Like you said earlier, we still can go on dates and I can spoil you all i want, while being your husband." I can't help but break into laughter, throwing my head back.

" You are so cute, I wanna kiss you." I say.

"Go ahead, what's stopping you?"

Carrying me gently into our room, Rahil's eyes light up mischievously as he looks into my eyes.

I can't resist the urge to hold his adorable face in my hands and plant sweet kisses on his lips, all while he carries me, sharing my laughter.

Suddenly, Rahil playfully tosses me onto the bed, his body hovering above mine.

"You totally did that on purpose, didn't you? You know very well that I can't go a single day without you, right?" His voice is filled with a mix of adorable accusation

I bite my lip, feigning innocence, but the truth is written all over my face.

I shrug my shoulders playfully and he raises his perfect eyebrow.

In one smooth motion, Rahil flexes his arm backside and removes his t-shirt in one go, revealing his sculpted body.

The sight leaves me breathless, and anticipation fills the air.

"I'm going to devour you alive and make you as obsessed with me as I am with you."

He leans in, his lips finding the crook of my neck, showering it with a cascade of tender kisses.

Laughter bubbles up from within me, unable to contain the joy that radiates through my being.

I gently pull his face away from my neck, meeting his gaze with a loving smile.

" You don't need to make me obsessed. I'm already as obsessed with you as you are with me. I can't bear to be away from you even for a single day as well."

He flashes me his gorgeous widest grin.

I press my lips against his eyelids, cheeks, forehead, chin, and jaw, showering kisses everywhere my lips can find his skin.

"Thank you for loving me back, Rahil." I kiss his jaw again.

"Thank you for accepting me just the way I am." I press my lips on his throat, right on his Adam apple.

A warm smile graces his lips.

"No, thank you for loving me."

"Thank you for never giving up on me. I'm so grateful that you exist, Zah!" He seals his lips with mine in a tender kiss.

After he pulls back from the kiss, with a gentle suck on my lower lip, I swiftly change our position, hovering over him, and trapping his wrists above his head.

"Now, now, husband." I smirk.

" I'm going to devour every inch of you, first."

I lean in, my lips finding their way to his throat, leaving a trail of soft kisses along his neck. I can feel his pulse quicken beneath my touch.

With a playful bite, I elicit a chuckle from him. "Slow down there, my fierce tigress."

Giggling in response, I help him remove my top, from above my head.

I lean back, cupping his cheek with both of my hands and lifting his head a little.

Our eyes meet, forehead pressed against each other and huge smiles light up our faces.

Laughter fills the air, mingling with the sound of our giggles.

Our hearts beat in sync, smile dance upon our lips as we playfully tease each other, and cherish the moment, wrapped in each other's arms, the remaining evening.

And just like that, in the midst of every shattered heart, there exists a gentle mender. Rahil Ahmed khan, with his radiant warmth, became my personal sunbeam, enveloping me in its embrace and whisking me away from the depths of pain.

With him by my side, I find solace in the knowledge that I can bravely face whatever challenges life may throw my way.

Chapter 26

----

5 years later :

A y e z a h ' s   P O V :

"Sarimmmm!!!"

I huff and yell, my voice echoing through the room as I chase after my mischievous and oh-so-naughty four-year-old baby boy.

In my hand, I tightly clutch his uniform shirt, desperately trying to dress him for school.

Sarim Ahmed Khan, our firstborn, is always full of energy and laughter.

His mischievous nature and playful spirit make him the naughtiest child you will ever meet.

His giggles fills the air as he darts around the bed, clad only in a pair of his uniform shorts.

"You can't catch me, Mumma!" he exclaims between fits of laughter, his eyes sparkling with mischief.

I take a moment to catch my breath, pausing and gently placing my hand on my eight-month baby bump.

"Baby, please don't exhaust Mumma."

"Okay mumma, but I don't want to go to school."

With an adorable pout, Sarim looks up at me.

"Sarim!" I say sternly, trying to be strict, but it's nearly impossible with that adorable little creature.

"Mumma!"

He winces out, and then jumps on the bed, starting to hop.

"I don't wanna go to school, I don't wanna go to school." He chants yelling loudly, his soft brown silky hair, which he inherited from his dad, bouncing on his head.

Except for his eye colour which is the only resemblance to mine, he looks exactly like his dad.

It's like I'm staring at a younger version of Rahil, literally.

"Did someone say something about not going to school?"

Just as I'm thinking about Rahil, he appears in the doorway of the room, leaning on the frame with his casual white t-shirt and trousers, looking as handsome as ever.

Time may pass, but Rahil's charm and handsomeness never fade. In fact, I'd say he's getting hotter day by day.

"Papa!" Sarim squeals and hops off the bed to his handsome father.

"Little rockstar."

Rahil picks him up with a gentle swing and plants a kiss on his cheek.

"So you were troubling mumma again?"

"Nah, I just said I didn't want to go to school." Sarim pouts adorably.

Rahil hums and walks towards me with a smile.

He gently places Sarim back on the bed in a standing position and quickly drops a kiss on the top of my head.

"So my little rockstar doesn't want to go to school?" He asks and Sarim eagerly nods his head.

Rahil slowly takes the uniform shirt from my hands.

"Sad! Because I thought I could get you the new video game you've been asking for. I had a special day out planned for just the two of us after school, you know, only papa and little rockstar." Rahil slowly slips the shirt into Sarim's arms, but Sarim's attention is completely captured by Rahil's words.

His eyes widen, and he listens intently.

"Really, papa?" His wide eyes brims with cuteness.

"Of course, but only if you go to school."

Sarim's face lights up with joy.

"I love school."

His grin is infectious, and I burst into laughter, playfully ruffling his hair.

"Mumma, dress me up. I won't trouble you anymore." He turns towards me.

Rahil chuckles, and I meet his gaze with a smile, mouthing a 'thank you' to which he shakes his head and winks at me.

I reach for the tie and gently fasten it around Sarim's neck.

"Don't trouble your mumma again, little rockstar, or else I won't buy you any toys," Rahil warns.

Sarim leans in and plants a kiss on my cheek.

"Of course, papa, I won't. How can I even think of troubling such a sweet mumma like her, again."

He is exactly like his papa. A sly fox.

I laugh, shaking my head.

"Oh my baby! Come here," I open my arms wide, ready to embrace my little boy.

He wraps his small chubby arms around my neck, and I can't help but be overwhelmed by the sweet scent of candies that lingers on his skin. It's a scent that brings me so much joy and comfort.

With a gentle pat on the backside of his head, i close my eyes and sigh in contentment.

He's such a precious bundle of happiness in our lives.

Slowly, he pulls back from the hug, but not completely.

His tiny hand extends towards his papa, beckoning him to join our little hug.

Rahil chuckles, bending down a little and Sarim wraps is another arm around his neck.

Our eyes meet through the tiny space between us, and we share a smile over Sarim's small shoulders.

Sarim pulls back slightly and plants the sweetest kisses on our cheeks, one by one.

" Mumma papa, you both can kiss each other too." He closes his eyes with his tiny palms adorably.

Rahil and I exchange surprise looks, as we are caught off guard.

"Baby, who told you this?" I ask, curious.

"I heard Uncle Adam say to Taha the other day that he should tell Mumma and Papa to kiss each other after he kisses them and close his eyes, good boys do that, he said. Sarim too is a good boy right?" He peeks through the gaps between his tiny fingers.

"Ugh, That annoying creature is seriously unbelievable." Rahil groans under his breath and I can't help but let out a laugh.

"Mumma, papa, are you done?" Sarim asks, still closing his eyes with his small palms.

"Baby-"

Before I can respond, Rahil dips his head down and pecks my lips, causing my eyes to slightly widen.

I hit his chest and glare at him, motioning towards Sarim through my eyes and he just shrugs, mouthing a 'what? his eyes are closed and he demanded this. Will thank Adam-the-idiot later.'

I can't help the wide smile that tugs at my lips.

Rahil and I lock eyes, as he smiles back at me, widely.

Sarim giggles, interrupting our sweet staring contest.

"Mumma papa, I said only one kiss." He presses his small palms on his mouth, giggling.

"Oh yeah? " Rahil scoops up Sarim, his laughter filling the room, as he showers our little baby boy with kisses on his rosy cheeks.

I just stand there, my hand gently resting on my eight-month belly, gazing at my everything, feeling the warmth they bring, seeping into me.

It's in moments like these that I realize just how lucky I am to have these two precious souls in my life, and the one who's soon going to join us.

They bring so much love, joy, and laughter into my world. I feel blessed beyond measure.

"You really didn't have to, you know. I could have gone alone."

The sun begins to set, casting a warm orange glow across the sky as we sit in Rahil's car. He insisted on driving me to my gynecologist because of a slight pain in my lower abdomen.

Rahil was working in the office, when I called him and informed that I'm going to visit my gynaecologist and next moment he was rushing outside while still on the call with me.

"You know I won't let you go alone. The pregnancy is about both of us, not just you, okay?" His lips gently press against my knuckles, our hands intertwined as he skillfully maneuvers the car with one hand, while his other hand draws soothing circles on mine, as if trying to ease my pain.

Rahil has always been the epitome of care and tenderness, the kind of person who goes above and beyond for those he loves.

When I was pregnant with Sarim, as it was my first time, it came with its fair share of challenges.

However, Rahil made it feel effortless. He understood and embraced every mood swing, taking impeccable care of me throughout.

He was and is there for me, always.

Even after Sarim was born, our little onewould trouble us during the nights and Rahil would stay awake soothing him to sleep so that I could rest, despite himself having work the next day.

His dedication and love never cease to amaze me.

I feel my heart swell with love for this incredible man with every passing second.

It's like I fall in love with him all over again, each and every day.

I gently press my lips against the backside of Rahil's hand, a soft smile gracing my lips.

With a contented sigh, I place our entwined hands against my cheek, savoring the warmth of his skin.

As I closed my eyes, I could feel Rahil's gaze upon me, followed by a light chuckle.

We had dropped Sarim to Laila's house so that he could play with Taha, Laila and Adam's adorable baby boy.

Taha was just as old as Sarim, and their playdates were always filled with giggles and mischief.

It was heartwarming to see our little ones grow and bond together.

Adam had been promoted to a higher position in Rahil's office, taking on the role of manager. His dedication and abilities had earned him this well-deserved recognition.

Meanwhile, Laila, my ever-loyal secretary, refuses to take any promotions because she says she loves to stick to me and I too can't have it any other way around.

Life had been kind to us, showering us with endless love and happiness.

Is it possible to murder someone and excuse it as pregnancy mood swings? If yes, then I would definitely kill this receptionist who's been shamelessly flirting with my husband during every visit to my gynecologist without fail.

My once good mood quickly soured, and any slight pain I felt vanished as soon as we entered the hospital.

Right now, we are standing in front of this pretentious woman, who's batting her fake lashes at Rahil and constantly tucking her hair behind her ear in a cringeworthy, cute-girl manner, which is urging me to throw up badly.

Oh, and let's not forget the way she purposefully stretched her neckline down when she spotted Rahil and me approaching.

"It's so nice to see you, Mr. Khan." She smiles sweetly at him, extending her hand for a handshake.

Can't this bitch see me or something?

I tightly wrap my arm around Rahil's bicep, seething with anger. Rahil visibly gulps and politely declines her handshake with a nod.

"We have an appointment." I grit out, and after a couple more seconds of shamelessly gawking at my handsome husband, she reluctantly averts her gaze to me.

Her once smiley expression transforms into a full-on scowl.

HA! The audacity of this bitch I swear to god! She is not even attempting to pretend.

"Yess, ma'am-"

" Mrs. Khan." I assert firmly.

"Huh?"

"It's Mrs. Khan." I say, emphasizing the 'Mrs.' as I purposefully lean in to kiss Rahil's cheek, shooting her a piercing glare. Rahil simply smiles at me.

The receptionist's face contorts with anger, but she quickly masks it, attempting to regain her composure.

"Actually, I personally called Mr. Khan and informed him that you can't have an appointment today." Her voice dripping with false politeness.

"Personally called?" I raise an eyebrow at Rahil, and he blinks back at me.

"But I booked the appointment, and you didn't mention anything at that time." My frustration builds with each passing second.

"That—" she stammers, unable to come up with a valid excuse. I see right through her.

This bitch just wanted an excuse to talk to Rahil and she's crossing every boundary now.

I have this urge to grab her by her extensions and smash her face down. Hard.

"Actually, only for Mr. Khan, I somehow managed to secure the last available appointment." she tucks her hair back, flashing a sweet cringe smile.

My anger reaches its boiling point.

THATS FUCKING ENOUGH.

"Cancel all the upcoming appointments, including this one! I'm changing my gynecologist."

"What? No, you were in pain-" Rahil starts but my glare silences him instantly.

I slam my palm down on the receptionist's desk, my frustration seeping through every word.

"You freaking know that this man right here is mine! My husband and the father of my children. Keep your fucking stupid flirting to yourself, if you want to keep all your pathetic pieces intact."

I snarl angrily, my voice echoing in the room. With that, I storm out of the hospital.

R a h i l ' s P O V :

Silence.

Complete and utter silence enveloped the car as I drove the car to who-knows-where. Ayezah demanded that she doesn't want to go to home right now.

Snowflakes started to gently fall from the darkened sky, creating a serene winter wonderland outside.

Ayezah is wearing a stunning blue long dress made of soft wool which is hugging her eight month belly perfectly, with a white fur coat draped elegantly over her shoulders. Her hair slightly curled at the bottoms, flowing freely.

She always looks so effortlessly gorgeous.

Right now as she seats in the passenger seat with her arms crossed adorably, I could feel the tension in the air growing.

She is mad. Like really mad.

Her anger is palpable.

Her now chubby cheeks are flushed and her nose is tinged a shade of light pink, her plump lips appearing more tempting and all I want to do is kiss all over her adorable face.

I knew this was one of her mood swings, something I had become familiar with during her pregnancy with Sarim. Ayezah had a tendency to become easily angered, even over the smallest things.

I stole glances at this beautiful, adorable and fierce lady beside me, my attention was divided between her and the road ahead.

"Stop the car!"

"What?" I was slightly taken aback.

"Stop the freaking car, Rahil!"

I quickly complied, bringing the car to an abrupt halt, making sure to keep my arm extended across her side.

As soon as the car comes to a halt, she turns towards me with anger blazing in her eyes.

"What exactly did that bitch tell you on the call?"

"Who, the receptionist?"

She shoots me a piercing glare.

Oh this is real bad.

"She called to inform that there were no available appointments, but I pleaded to her and she agreed. She called me just as I was rushing from work back."

I know she's mad and jealous of that stupid woman, and honestly she was getting on my last nerve too but Ayezah doesn't know that I don't give two shits to her, and I was tolerating her all along only for Ayezah's sake.

The gynaecologist is one of the best and renowned in the city, so I didn't wanted to compromise anything when it comes to my wife and child's well being.

"You didn't have to plead." she hisses.

"But you were in pain." I murmur lowly.

" Anyways, let's just forget this and go to some other doctor—"

"No, I told you I'm fine." she huffs, crossing her arms and staring ahead.

I can sense her stubbornness, but I can't help but worry about her.

"But-"

"Get out of the car."

"Excuse me?" I ask, my surprise evident.

"I'm mad at you right now! I don't want you in my sight. Get out."

It's okay Rahil. Pregnancy Mood swings, remember? C'mon, it's Ayezah! She can never willingly be rude to you.

I quietly step out of the car and curse under my breath as the freezing air slams into me. I'm wearing a thin t-shirt, and my coat is abandoned in the backseat.

The snow keeps falling, and I can see the city lights shining.

We have stopped on the bridge covered in snow, people moving and enjoying the beautiful snowflakes falling.

I rub my palms together to generate some heat and blow air into them.

Not more than a few seconds had pass by when I hear the click of the car door opening.

In the next moment, Ayezah steps out, holding my long overcoat in her hands.

She rounds the car and approach me. I silently observe her every movement.

Then, she moves behind me and gently drapes the long brown coat over my shoulders.

I raise my arms, quietly slipping my hands into the long sleeves.

Once in place, she steps in front of me, her hands carefully adjusting the collar.

Standing before me, she seemed to avoid meeting my gaze, her eyes wandering elsewhere.

It was then that I heard it—the soft sound of her sniffles.

I gently curled my forefinger and thumb under her chin, coaxing her to look into my eyes.

My heartbeat accelerated looking at her face.

Her doe-like amber eyes—the most captivating orbs I have ever see— were shimmering with bead of tears and her chin was trembling uncontrollably.

A single tear cascaded down her delicate cheek, causing my heart to stop in response.

"Hey, hey, hey! What's wrong, babie?" I gently cupped her soft pink, and slightly chubby cheeks in the warmth of my palms, her skin feeling cold against mine.

More tears flows down from her beautiful eyes, tugging at my heartstrings.

"Hey, I'm sorry okay?"

I tenderly wipe away her tears with a touch as light as a feather.

" I'm sorry, zah. I'm so sorry for hurting you. I swear I tolerated that receptionist solely because of you. You know the gynaecologist was the best—"

She sobs loudly and next second she throws her arms around my neck, holding onto me tightly.

"Oh, God! Why are you apologizing when it should be me begging for forgiveness for my behaviour earlier towards you?"

She sniffles into the crook of my neck and my arms get wounded around her frame carefully.

"And why are you even explaining yourself? Please, how much nicer can you be? I can't believe you." She slightly hits my shoulder, crying and I chuckle lowly, holding her close.

I breathe in the scent of her hair, deeply filling my lungs with the soothing, flowery fragrance that I love so much. A contented sigh escapes my lips.

My hand tenderly patting her head.

She pulls back slightly from the hug, still in my arms.

"We won't be going back to that gynaecologist ever again. Let's find another doctor." she sniffles, her adorable light pink nose twitching as she rubs it.

I can't help but marvel at how incredibly cute she becomes during her pregnancy. It fills my heart with an overwhelming desire to shower her face with endless kisses.

" Okay, love. Is there anything else?" My fingertips glide across her cheeks and along the side of her forehead, gently wiping away the remnants of her tears and brushing her silky strands back.

"I'm sorry for earlier."

I can't resist pecking her nose.

"Hmmm, It's okay. Anything else? " I lean my forehead on hers, grazing my nose with hers and closing my eyes.

"I'm hungry."

" Okay, as soon as we reach home I'll be cooking your favourite spaghetti."

"Anything else?"

"I love you."

" Okay—" I open my eyes and see her smiling at me widely.

Next second, she leans forward and grazes her lips with mine.

She slightly pulls her head back, I instinctively follow, as if her lips have a magnetic pull of their own.

I tilt my head and capture her lips with mine. The taste of her sweet petals, like a delectable dessert, fills my senses as I savor the moment.

She responds eagerly, our lips hungrily sucking at each other's as if it's our very first kiss.

But that's the thing about Ayezah - every moment with her feels like the first time, no matter how many times it happens.

Every time our lips meet, a delightful tickle runs through me, leaving me yearning for more and more.

With her head slightly pulled back, my own instinctively follows, unwilling to let go. I pepper her lips with gentle pecks, each one making her giggle.

"I love you too! I love you so much." I gaze at her, a wide smile spreading across my face. Our foreheads touching and noses nuzzling against each other.

Her eyes light up with a radiant smile, her gaze roaming over every inch of my face, as if trying to capture every little detail.

Suddenly, her expression changes.

Tears well up in her eyes once again and her chin trembles.

"Oh, Oh, what's the matter now?"

"You are so handsome, so nice, so perfect. It's so overwhelming that it's making me cry." Fat tears roll down her cheeks.

I can't help the laughter bubbling up within me.

"You adorable, adorable woman! You'll kill me one day."

" Come here!" I pull her into the hug and she sobs softly, nuzzling her nose against my neck.

I chuckle lowly, holding her tightly and closing my eyes, cherishing each precious second, surrounded by her presence.

Chapter 27

Laila's POV :

Grateful. Luckiest. Fantastic. Amazing. Unreal.

These are all the emotions that flood through me every single day spent with Adam Hussain. The same person who used to annoy the fuck out of me. The same person whose mere presence I couldn't stand. But now even the thought of living without him is unbearable.

Falling in love with him was so natural, so effortless. He always felt like so easy to love.

As much as cliché it may sound but he truly thought me how to live, not just survive.

Although most of the time he is stupid, but he can be incredibly sensible too, it's astonishing.

Life is easy with him. Life is good with him. Not just good, fantastic, amazing and unreal.

His love for me is like nothing I've ever experienced before, It's deep. And sometimes it aches physically to know that someone could actually love me this much.

He has given me literally everything.

And most importantly, he has given me Taha, our four-year-old baby boy, who is the center of our universe.

"Heyyy princess, where are you lost?" My husband's voice calls out to me as I look up to see him beaming down at me, with Taha perched on his shoulders.

It's a beautiful Sunday, just like all the other Sundays we are on date with our little one.

Adam looks gorgeous as always in his pastel blue long-sleeved t-Shirt paired with jeans. Taha is twining with his dad sporting pastel blue t-shirt and jeans shorts, looking adorable as ever.

As for me, I'm too kinda twinning with them in my straight floor-length floral blue dress.

"Yess, princess mommy, where are you lost?" Taha giggles, revealing his adorable set of tiny teeth.

He's an absolute bundle of fluff, resembling his handsome dad not only in looks but also in his charming and mischievous personality.

He's surely a daddy's boy as he absorbs everything his dad says and even repeats his words, including absolute nonsense that my silly husband tends to come up with.

"Nothing, my loves," I reply, a warm smile spreading across my face.

Adam gently sets Taha down. Our little bundle of energy immediately grabs my hand with one of his tiny ones, giggling with excitement.

" Lesss gooo Mommy, daddy."

With his other hand, he grabs onto Adam's palm, pulling us both towards the entrance of the amusement park with pure excitement.

"Shut it right now. I'm telling you, don't tempt me to give you a good punch right on your nose, right here in front of Taha," I grit out, whispering to the most annoying man standing next to me.

"What? It's true that you are scared of roller coasters." He purposely says it out loud.

I swear to God, this bitch—

"Mommy is scared! Mommy is scared!" Taha jumps up and down excitedly, clapping his hands.

I quickly bend down to his level. "No, baby, I'm not scared. But roller coasters can be scary, especially for little ones like you. I'm just worried about you, my little boy."

"Mommy, I'm a big brave boy now. I'm not scared." Taha grins, showing off his toothy smile, and Adam bursts into laughter.

"See, Mommy? He's not scared. He's a big boy now." Adam teases.

I shoot him a death glare, mouthing 'I'll kill you.' but he simply blows me a flying kiss in response.

THE AUDACITY.

"Mummy, please, let's go! Please, please!" Taha's excitement reaches new heights as he hops up and down more energetically, his soft brown curls bouncing with every motion.

I let out a defeated sigh. "Okay, fine."

"Yayayayya!" the father-son duo exclaims in unison, celebrating their victory with a fist bump.

They always team up against me, but I love them anyway.

My legs are trembling, wobbling like jelly, and my heart is still pounding against my chest like a wild drumbeat.

The roller coaster ride was absolutely terrifying. The only ride which scares the fuck out of me.

But despite my fear, I couldn't help but find a hint of enjoyment, thanks to Taha's infectious laughter and Adam's devilish delight screams.

"Princess, are you okay?" Adam asks, his arm wrapping around my shoulders, genuine concern etched on his face.

I shoot him my best glare and he visibly gulps, quickly averting his gaze.

"Champ, let's go to that little shop." He quickly changes the topic, scooping up Taha in his arms.

It's a charming hair band shop, filled with an array of cute accessories.

Smiling, I gently place a soft bunny hair band on Taha's head, and his face lights up with an adorable grin.

Adam playfully makes me wear a tiger hair band and I can't help but smirk mischievously as I grab a kitten-themed one and place it on his head.

He scowls at me, but wears it anyway.

Take that jerk, huh!

After satisfying our growling stomachs with delicious snacks like churros and Taha's all-time favorite marshmallows dipped in a velvety chocolate fountain, we leisurely stroll through the park.

The air is filled with a mix of laughter, floating of huge bubbles, the tantalizing aroma of cotton candy, and the distant sound of cheerful music.

Suddenly, our eyes are drawn to a vibrant scene unfolding before us.

The circus performers, with their colorful costumes and graceful movements, captivate our attention. Taha's excitement knows no bounds as he tugs at our hands, urging us closer to the show.

Taha watches them with his big, mesmerizing eyes, his giggles hopping around like joyful little butterflies.

Adam and I stand side by side, our gazes fixed on Taha, a small smile tugging at the corners of our lips.

Adam leans in and whispers, his voice a soft caress.

"Enjoying the show, love?"

I raise an eyebrow.

"I don't need to enjoy this circus when I have my very own clown, always clowning around me." I press my lips together, trying to hide a smile, and he scowls at me, groaning.

He then leans impossibly closer, the smell of his clean aftershave envelopes me and his words brush against the shell of my ear, sending shivers down my spine.

"I can be whatever you want me to be, a kitten or a clown, but you and I both know who becomes a little kitten in bed."

My face flushes like a boiled crab, and as I turn my head to look at him, I see his mischievous smirk.

Before I can say anything, he swiftly pecks my lips, leaving me momentarily breathless.

"Let's go to the next ride, champ. C'mon!" he takes Taha's hand in one of his and interlaced his other one with mine as he leads us to another ride.

Clearing my throat and fanning my face with my other free hand, I quietly follow them.

"Ouch!" I hiss in pain, my eyes instinctively shutting as Adam slightly twists my ankle.

"Seriously, why did you run in heels?" Adam glared up at me, concern etched on his face.

We were currently seated on a bench, with me holding onto my throbbing ankle while Adam knelt in front of me, carefully examining it.

We were playing 'catch me if you can' with Taha and In the midst of the chase, I ended up spraining my ankle.

"It's not like it's my first time running in heels. I've done it countless times before. I work as a secretary remember? and secretaries often find themselves needing to rush."

Adam gave me a skeptical look, clearly not convinced.

Taha, who was standing on the bench beside me, asked innocently. "Mommy is hurt?"

His lower lip trembled, and tears welled up in his eyes.

"Oh no, no, baby, I'm okay!" I pulled him closer and gently wiped away the tears from his chubby cheeks. I held him tightly, feeling his little body relax against mine as he sniffled into my neck.

"Really?" Taha asked, pulling away slightly to look at me. I smiled and nodded.

"Don't worry, champy, mommy's just a little hurt in the leg. But guess what? Your strong daddy can carry your princess mommy." Adam smirked at me and I rolled my eyes at him.

Asshole is always so full of himself.

Taha jumped down from the bench, giggling and giving his father a fist bump.

Adam effortlessly scoops me up in his arms, his muscles flexing around his t-shirt.

I can't help but smile, wrapping my arms around his neck.

I gaze into his mesmerizing green eyes, captivated by the depth and intensity of his gaze. His handsome features, chiseled jawline, and perfectly tousled hair never fails to make my heart skip a beat.

Up close, he is even more breathtakingly beautiful.

In that moment, our eyes lock, and I can feel the love and adoration radiating from him. It's as if his eyes hold all the affection in the world, and I can't help but be drawn in by their warmth and sincerity.

Taha's infectious laughter and clapping hands break our trance.

As the evening sets in, we make our way to the car.

Adam gently places me in the passenger seat, and Taha excitedly settles on my lap, his energy still bubbling over. He chatters away, sharing stories about his school and his love for drawing and colouring. Eventually, the excitement wears him out, and he drifts off to sleep, his head resting peacefully on my chest.

Upon arriving at our penthouse, Adam quickly rounds the car and comes to my side.

"I'll first carry my little one inside, then I'll come back and scoop up my other precious bundle." He teases with a mischievous smile on his lips and I shake my head chuckling.

" Stop being so extra, I'm fine, I can walk now."

" Nah-ah princess we need to properly take care of your ankle, just wait here I'll be back really quick."

Before I could say anything, he picks up Taha and carries him inside.

He returns in no time, swiftly carrying me from the passenger seat and just as he carries me out of the car, the rain starts pouring like crazy.

"Oh my gosh!" I quickly put my palms over our heads, but Adam throws his head back and looks up at the sky, enjoying the rain.

I'm totally mesmerized by the way he smiles while looking up.

He has always loved rain.

My lips curves up on their own.

His wet hair covers his forehead, and he looks so handsome with raindrops falling on his face.

"This is so peaceful and perfect, with the rain and you in my arms! Let's not include Taha though, because he catches cold so easily." Adam says, raindrops glistening on his cheeks and I let out a giggle.

"Wanna dance in the rain?"

I give him a confused look. But before I know it, he's spinning us around in the rain, and I can't help but squeal with joy, holding onto him tightly.

Since we're on our private property, the road is pretty empty. Adam keeps moving, dancing to the rhythm of the rain, and I can't stop laughing, throwing my head back in pure delight.

He stops spinning and leans his forehead against mine, Through the glistening rain droplets, I gaze into his eyes, feeling the warmth of his embrace as my arms stay wrapped around his neck.

With a gentle pull on the back of his head, I bring our lips together, and instantly, sparks fly.

He kisses me with desperation and longing, I kiss him back with same intensity, my fingers instinctively entwining in his soft hair.

The rain keeps pouring down. He tugs at my bottom lip and enters his tongue inside, sucking it eagerly like he is sucking air into his lungs.

Breathless, I pull back slightly, my words melting against his lips.

"I love you."

A wide grin spreads across his face, lighting up his eyes with pure joy.

He spins us around, his laughter blending with the sound of the raindrops.

"I love you moreeee." He yells loudly.

"Hey, let's keep it down, silly." I giggle.

"We don't want the whole neighborhood to wake up."

"Alright then, let's quickly go inside and pick up where we left off."

In an instant he leans in and steals another passionate kiss, leaving me breathless and craving more.

Before I can even catch my breath, his rushing towards our home urgently.

"Desperate, are we?" I tease.

"Absolutely." He grins.

We share a laugh, blending with the melody of the raindrops. our love overflowing in the air.

Epilogue

1 6 years later :

Rahil's POV:

My jaw tightens, my fist clenches at my side until they turn as white as paper as I gaze at my 20-year-old son, standing before me in all his glory, his face soaked in crimson blood and bruises.

I take in his entire appearance - a black leather jacket, a black t-shirt, jeans, and black boots.His black guitar hanging on his back, its strap covering his front.

Sarim has grown up to embody Addin.

He is savage, akin to my best friend who used to be as unhinged as him, if not more so.

Perhaps it's our overflowing love—mine and Ayezah's—that has spoiled him to this extent.

My son who was once a sweet kid, has transformed into a built brute.

All he does now is play the guitar and engage in reckless activities, spending his days and nights hanging out on his damn bike like a spoiled brat that he is.

I've lost count of the number of times I've had to visit his college to meet the principal due to his utterly suspencible behaviour.

"What has he done this time?" I grit out, shifting my attention to the background, where Taha—the same age as Sarim and attending the very same university—stands.

Taha is dressed in his usual jeans and white t-shirt, appearing neat and clean, looking nothing like my rugged son.

"ofcourse!" Sarim chuckles mockingly and I notice the faint sight of his bruised knuckles.

We are standing in the living room as the evening begins to settle in.

" I don't know, uncle." Taha murmurs quietly.

As Sarim reminds me of Addin's younger self, Taha reminds me of my younger self. I recall how I used to conceal all the shits of my unruly best friend.

However, Sarim and Taha are anything but friends.

My brat son hates him to core and I have no clue why. They used to get along well back then when they were kids, I don't know what exactly happened to cause their friendship to vanish in thin air.

"Oh, please, golden boy, there's no need to pretend and cover for me as you never have before. You're already in Papa's good graces. So why not now as well tell him." Sarim directs at Taha.

Taha remains composed and silent.

"What's the matter with you, Sarim? How many times must I remind you to shed this attitude and behave? Why do you involve yourself in fights? I continuously clean up after your messes. Just for once, behave and cease this spoiled behavior. I can't tolerate it any longer." I affirm out, struggling to contain my frustration.

"You know nothing, Papa, and I suspect you'll ever wish to understand! As always, you'll believe it's all my fault and that I engage in unnecessary fights. So, you might as well maintain that belief because I'm finished here! Enjoy your little get together, I'm out." He declares and rushes upstairs.

As he ascends the stairs, my wife descends, adorned in a stunning maroon floor-length dress with elegant full sleeves, halting midway.

"Oh my goodness, Sarim! Baby, what happened to your face?" She tenderly cups Sarim's cheeks as they stand together in the center of the staircase.

"It's nothing, Ma! I'm fine. I'm going to my room." He gently lower her hands from his cheeks before dashing upstairs.

I glare at the empty space where my brute of a son vanished.

My wife descends the staircase and approaches me with a look of concern etched on her beautiful face.

"Rahil, what's the matter?"

" Nothing, just the usual—our son acting like the spoiled brat he always is." I sigh.

"Hey, don't label him a brat! Maybe we should have a heart-to-heart with him about what's bothering him. He's acting—"

"Everyone will be arriving soon! It's been ages since we had a gathering, Ayezah! Let's save the discussion about Sarim for later. You know he won't come out even if we knock on his door continuously, and soon he'll be making a racket upstairs with his wild guitar playing."

"But still Rahil, let's talk with him once." She places one of her palms on my chest.

"Okay, I promise to talk to him after the dinner, happy now?" Ayezah nods, smiling slightly.

Today's gathering includes everyone - Adam -Laila, Noor-Addin, Najma-Irfan. And all of their kids.

We planned to have dinner together in the backyard of my penthouse.

" Oh, Taha dear! you are here already? Where's your mom and dad?" Ayezah smiles at Taha and he returns the gesture.

"They'll come soon aunty, until then I'll help you set the table."

"You are such a sweetheart!" Ayezah laughs.

"I'll change and join you both." I say.

I'm still in my formals as I just returned from the work.

I drop a quick kiss on my gorgeous wife's lips and head upstairs.

The backyard is aglow with sparkling lights that dance among the vibrant flowers.

A grand rectangular table stands proudly, adorned with all tasty desi dishes.

I catch sight of Ayezah gracefully moving and setting the plates on table, with Taha next to her, smiling and helping her out.

Donned in a crisp blue shirt and dress pants, I approach them with a smile, ready to help in setting the table.

Just then, my beautiful 16-year-old daughter Zeya makes her entrance into the backyard, clad in a simple yet elegant white top and black jeans.

Her brown hair is pulled up high, in a sleek ponytail, not a strand out of place.

In her hand, she carries her small sketch pad —which she carries almost everywhere as she loves sketching—her ponytail swaying gracefully as she moves. Her steps are confident.

Zeya bears a striking resemblance to Ayezah, inheriting her mother's soft beautiful features. Only her eyes are exactly like mine. The colour and all.

"Papa!" Zeya greets me with a sweet side hug, prompting a smile as I plant a tender kiss on the top of her head.

"Mumma!" She then turns to her mother, embracing her as Ayezah showers her with noisy kisses on the cheeks.

I don't fail to notice how Zeya's smile wavers upon seeing Taha, though she swiftly conceals it behind a composed facade and absolutely ignores his existence.

In my preperical vision, I see how Taha's smile has vanished, and now he's full-on staring at my daughter. The look in his eyes, I don't like that look for some reason, but I could be mistaken, right?

"How was school, baby?" Ayezah asks.

"As usual, Ma! Anyway, where's everyone? Hasn't arrived yet?" Zeya's gaze keeps flicking to Taha.

Why do I feel like there's something wrong between them too? I guess both my kids have some serious problems with Taha.

"Laila aunty!!!" Zeya squeals suddenly when Laila and Adam enter the backyard. She quickly hurries to Laila, hugs her, and Laila laughs, hugging her back, cupping her cheeks and placing kisses on them as they engross themselves in their talks.

Laila and Zeya's bond is something very different. Laila is like Zeya's godmother; when she was young, Zeya would often go to their home and play with Laila, so she's grown more fond of her. Ayezah joins them too, and they're kind of like a trio, as Zeya likes to say.

Adam approaches me and Taha where we are standing.

"You little rascal! Why didn't you come home? Rahil, I'm telling you, just adopt this punk and give me your sweet daughter, he likes to live here more than his own home."

"C'mon, dad, stop being so dramatic always. I directly came here from college with Sarim." Taha rolls his eyes and approaches his dad to greet him in a side hug.

Later on, everyone arrives.

Najma and her husband with their son Ibrahim, the eldest of all. Ibrahim is a reserved kid, often lost in his own thoughts.

Noor and Addin make their entrance, with Addin holding Noor close by her waist.

Amal and Ayat are the mischievous twins, known for their unstoppable energy and short tempers just like their father. They are like a dynamic duo.

Rizwan, Addin's younger son, is an absolute troublemaker and so he gets along with my son quite well.

Upon not finding Sarim around, he quickly leaves, probably to join my son in whatever chaos he's up to in his room with that damn guitar.

It's a wonder how Noor manages to keep up with all of them.

Then there's the fourth daughter, Amaya, a calm yet energetic soul. She is same age as Zeya but a few months younger.

She warmly greets everyone and heads straight to Zeya, eager to share some 'girl gossip' as they say.

The dinner table is alive with chatter.

Adam and Laila are bickering on something as usual.

Addin is grunting groaning like always, eager to go home with his wife. I swear the man doesn't even pretend to like it here.

Najma, Noor and Ayezah are talking and laughing together, while the other younger ladies on table—Amal, Ayat, Zeya and Amaya—are too engrossed in their own talks.

I'm having conversation with my sharp-minded nephew- Ibrahim, who tells me about his newfound passion for business post-college.

Taha is sitting next to Ibrahim and quietly eating his food.

The dinner goes by smoothly, and later we all just sit in the backyard and talk about old times, sharing stories and laughter.

The evening feels happy, homely and family.

I sit on the edge of the bed in our room, a heavy sigh escaping my lips.

I had planned to talk to Sarim after dinner, just like I promised Ayezah. But that punk is nowhere to be found in his room, and when I tried calling him, he didn't pick up.

So, I rang Rizwan, knowing they probably went out together to find some trouble. He informed me they're out partying somewhere for the night. And then my wife tells me not to call him a spoiled brat.

Just when I'm thinking about Ayezah, sheappears, stepping out of the bathroom, dressed in a stunning black satin night robe that molds around her tits and clings to her every curve perfectly.

Her damp hair cascades down, glistening as it sticks to the skin of her cheeks and neck.

I wonder does this woman age backwards because she just keeps getting more gorgeous day by day.

Upon seeing me, a radiant smile forms on her lips as she moves gracefully to the dressing table.

Her fresh flowery scent fills the air, making me inhale deeply.

I couldn't look away, enchanted by her every move, like always.

After drying her hair and applying her night cream, she comes over to me.

"It was so much fun today, wasn't it? It's been ages since we all gathered like this, perhaps a year since our last get-together at Addin-Noor's place." Standing before me, she flashes me her beautiful smile.

I return the smile wearily and nod.

"Hey, what's troubling you?" She gently grabs my cheeks in her palms.

I close my eyes, leaning into the warmth of her skin.

I pull her by waist and hug her tightly, resting my head on her stomach. Her fingers tenderly stroke my hair.

"Is Sarim not in his room?" she softly questions.

"Nope, once again out partying." I hear her sigh.

"It's alright, Rahil, we'll figure out whatever is troubling our baby! You know your little rockstar, right? Sarim is our boy Rahil and there's definitely something bothering him, that he's behaving this way. I'm sure, don't you think?"

I pull back with a heavy sigh and nod.

"For now, my husband seems utterly exhausted, so let me just ease some of his tension." she teases with a smirk.

She climbs on top of me, tossing me onto the bed, and I land on my back with a soft plop.

In the next instant, she straddles my waist, and I prop myself up on my elbow as she skillfully unbuttons my shirt, letting it fall to the floor.

With a graceful motion, she sheds her thin satin robe, revealing her long-black thin strap inner

My gaze roams on the enticing contours of her body, and fixes on her cleavage.

Her nipples hardens under my intense gaze and my mouth waters to suck, bite and feast on them.

"This is the perfect way to ease the tension."

I remark with a sly grin, before swiftly shifting our positions, now hovering over her. She lets out a delighted squeal as I pepper kisses all over her neck, jaw, collarbones and cleavage.

She grabs my face up and presses her soft luscious lips to mine, kissing me fiercely and I don't waste a beat to return the kiss with same insanity.

In Life, not every thread is spun from roses or painted with rainbows and sunshine. We each bear our burdens of troubles and hurdles along the way.

Yet, I hold the unwavering belief that as long as I have my woman by my side, I can overcome any challenge, for she is not just my wife; she is the very essence of my home.

My forever.